CHASING FIRE

BRANDT LEGG

By Brandt Legg

Chase Malone Thriller

Chasing Rain
Chasing Fire
Chasing Wind
Chasing Dirt
Chasing Life
Chasing Kill
Chasing Risk
Chasing Mind
Chasing Time
Chasing Lies
Chasing Fear
Chasing Lost

*As always, this book is dedicated to
Teakki and Ro*

Vinci Books

vinci-books.com

Published by Vinci Books Ltd in 2025

1

Copyright © Brandt Legg 2019

The author has asserted their moral right to be identified as the author of this work in accordance with the Copyright, Designs and Patents Act 1988. This work is a work of fiction. Names, characters, places and incidents are the product of the author's imagination or are used fictitiously. Any resemblance to actual persons, living or dead, places and incidents is entirely coincidental.

All rights reserved. No part of this publication may be copied, reproduced, distributed, stored in any retrieval system, or transmitted in any form or by any means, including photocopying, recording, or other electronic or mechanical methods, nor used as a source for any form of machine learning including AI datasets, without the prior written permission of the publisher.

The publisher and the author have made every effort to obtain permissions for any third party material used in this book and to comply with copyright law. Any queries in this respect should be brought to the attention of the publisher and any omissions will be corrected in future editions.

A CIP catalogue record for this book is available from the British Library.

Paperback ISBN: 9781036705213

Printed and bound in Great Britain by Clays Ltd, Elcograf S.p.A.

Chapter One

Proud of the massive destruction he was about to unleash, Powder took a moment to honor the Founding Fathers as Fourth of July fireworks filled the air across the Potomac River in Washington, DC. The revelry, easily visible from his rooftop vantage point in Crystal City, Virginia, reminded him of the Star Spangled Banner.

> *And the rockets' red glare, the bombs bursting in air,*
> *Gave proof through the night that our flag was still there;*
> *O say does that star-spangled banner yet wave,*
> *O'er the land of the free and the home of the brave?*

As millions celebrated the anniversary of the signing of the Declaration of Independence, few could have guessed that a second American revolution had just begun. A powerful militia group had taken upon themselves the role of *nuevo* "minute men," with the goal not of starting a new country, but rather of saving the old one. Their odds of success seemed just as unlikely as those patriots who'd met in Philadelphia more than two centuries earlier.

> *And where is that band who so vauntingly swore*
> *That the havoc of war and the battle's confusion,*

Powder, one of the rogue band who'd sworn to do whatever necessary to stop the unraveling of 'the greatest nation on earth,' wired fuses and set a detonator. He often told people, *"I've been an American and a soldier since before I was born."* In fact, he was seventh generation military. Since childhood, he'd kept his coal-black hair high and tight—clipping it himself. Tradition had made him a patriot, the army had forged him into an explosives expert, but Gunner, his leader, the head of the militia, had transformed Powder into a would-be hero, one of the revolutionaries who would save the Republic.

> *A home and a country, should leave us no more?*
> *Their blood has washed out their foul footsteps' pollution.*

Gunner had chosen the date for more than just symbolism. Although appreciating the irony of the first bomb exploding on July 4th, a tight timetable lay ahead. *Each target gets more difficult than the one before,* he reminded himself. *But, if everything goes well, all my bombings will be complete in July.* He took a deep breath. *August is when the real action will happen—when the treasure is used—and by Labor day the country of today will be a thing of the past. Hell of a summer.*

The national anthem continued in his head.

> *O thus be it ever, when freemen shall stand,*
> *Between their loved homes and the war's desolation.*

Blest with vict'ry and peace, may the Heav'n rescued land,
Praise the Power that hath made and preserved us a nation!

Hearing the rumbling of loud reports as the fireworks increased dramatically in successive builds, Powder paused again to watch the dazzling display of red, silver, and blue whirling showers cascade into thousands and thousands of shattering sparks, illuminating the silhouetted Washington Monument. *I love this country!* As the colored smoke trailed off and a skyward parade of shimmering purple waterfalls tumbled down into yellow and green bursting flowers, he turned back to his work, resuming the countdown.

Everything is on schedule. We're about to put them on notice.
We're taking it back.

Wen Sung, a slender yet lethal twenty-eight-year old former Chinese intelligence agent, looked at her boyfriend while walking down the beach. "Happy Fourth of July," she said, smiling.

"Is it the fourth?" Chase Malone, a brilliant tech billionaire, only a year older, replied, returning her smile. "I guess it is, back in the States."

"In the Philippines, too," Wen said, dancing around him as he walked. "They also celebrate gaining their freedom and independence on the fourth."

"From what country?" Chase asked, curious, pulling her playfully into the surf.

"From the United States of America," Wen replied gleefully, as she ran ahead.

The two of them had fled civilization a few months earlier, living as recluses on the remote south Pacific island of Nuku Hiva, a three-hour flight from Tahiti. Even in the thrill of being with Wen, as they made their way barefoot down the shore, Chase couldn't help but steal a glance at the steep, verdant cliffs in search of an invasion, always listening for the sounds of an approaching helicopter.

"Miss it?" she asked, familiar with his behavior of checking. There were several reasons they'd given up on their old existence—the Chinese secret police could still be looking for Wen, a dangerous corporate security force, led by a man who'd sworn to kill Chase, remained active, and the couple's status with the CIA remained unclear. However, they had decided to leave for an even more urgent reason: balance. They felt the world teetering and believed they could help.

Chase stopped, looked out at the turquoise water, felt the soft sand beneath his feet, and motioned to the palm trees moving in the warm breeze. He stared into Wen's eyes. "Surrounded by this much beauty, how could I miss anything?"

His words, though true, sounded hollow because the dream felt shaky. No one could hide forever. They both felt the world was at a place where even a small stumble could create a disastrous chain reaction. Chase knew the power of technology, how it could be utilized to improve lives and, ultimately, the world—or the opposite. It being used to the advantage of only a few, resulting in the end of humanity's fragile society.

"We'll have to go back some day," Wen said, walking again. Her first-hand knowledge of the toll government corruption had taken constantly waged an internal battle against bitterness. Before her defection from China, she'd been involved with a group known as "WOLF," or simply "The Cause," a scattering of like-minded people across the globe bent on reversing the startling and growing inequality between the wealthy elites and everyone else. Several had died so that she and Chase could live.

"I know." Chase had already had one of his representatives use a shell company to discreetly purchase a three-million-dollar penthouse overlooking one of the one-hundred-sixty-three canals in Amsterdam, a city that served as the unofficial headquarters of WOLF. "But not for a few more months," he added.

She nodded her agreement, acknowledging they both needed to recharge after everything they'd been through. They were damned lucky not to be in prison, luckier still to even be alive. Yet, as the salty breeze carried a fresh floral scent she'd come to love, Wen knew that the tranquility couldn't last much longer. They could run to the edge of the earth, but the past would always be close behind.

Chapter Two

Powder finished the final wiring, synced the detonator, then checked his watch. The celebration on the National Mall still had almost thirty minutes before the fireworks' grand finale. He planned on adding some big booms to that patriotic finish. Walking to the edge of the eleven-story building, as if heading to the bar to order another beer, he looked down at the entrance, spotting the expected fire engine as it approached from the west, right on time.

"Perfect," he said to himself. "We are underway," he texted to the man who'd declared this war that Powder stood ready to ignite.

He stowed the rest of his gear into a black duffel and slung it over his shoulder. As the fire engine rolled to a stop in front of the building, Powder crossed to the rear side of the roof and stepped backwards off the ledge. Extending his legs and leaning back, he repelled quickly, silently, with military-trained-expertise. Powder's feet hit the ground in less than fifty seconds.

By the time he walked the block and a half to his car,

the six phony firemen had the premises evacuated. Even on a regular night there would have been less than a dozen people inside, but on a holiday, just six essential personnel were present. As planned, those workers and the helpful "firemen" were already at a safe distance when Powder pressed the button.

A nanosecond later, the Tri-Knight Avionics building erupted.

The magical clouds of sparkling colors, filling the sky over the Washington Monument, were not enough to mask the fury of what Powder had unleashed across the river in Crystal City. A series of explosions boomed, shaking the structure as if an internal blitzkrieg had been initiated from the depths of hell. Glass showered the sidewalks as jets of smoke and flames burst from all directions. When fire engulfed the middle floors, the "firemen" were nowhere to be found, having already abandoned their truck and uniforms. The phony crew, now in an unmarked passenger van traveling on US-1, heading south to Reagan National Airport, would be on four different flights before the authorities could even begin to piece things together.

Meanwhile, Powder drove the speed limit on his way to Dulles International Airport. He'd be cutting it close to make his boarding time for a flight to Seattle, but that was part of the plan—be gone before they started checking the airports. This one had been easy, but each attack would grow progressively more difficult as the authorities threw resources at the crisis and investigators discovered the patterns. A speculating media and mounting public pressure were predictable. The world's attention would be riveted on when the next attack would happen, but by Labor Day, they'd know the truth—that it was far worse.

A war had begun.

In a cheap Philadelphia basement rental under an unmaintained low-rise (leftover from more prosperous times in the early part of the last century), Bull alternated between voice commands and two different keyboards as her eyes blurred across six computer monitors arranged in an inverted pyramid. An ashtray overflowed with cigarette butts, a trail of smoke still climbing into the stale air from one she'd forgotten. Instead, she reached for a slender blue silver and red energy drink. Bull's love of the caffeine infused beverage had earned her the nickname. Everybody in her line of work had one.

She was a hacker, one of the best in the west, a shadowy profession that had grown so dangerous it had unofficially surpassed logging for the highest job-related fatality rate.

Her hand knocked over eight or nine empties that she'd consumed in the last twenty-four hours. "Damn it," the skinny twenty-year old muttered, her fingers shaking.

Lenny Nenganowski, her business partner who'd dropped out of law school the day he'd met Bull at a funeral, had only an average knowledge of computers, and was amazed by her ability to crack open the web. Lenny also worshiped Bull, never missing a chance to attempt to impress her or plead his case that they should be a thing, even though he was seven years older. "What's wrong?" he asked, watching every move she made. Her blonde buzz cut, baggy fatigues, and combat boots gave her the impression of an army recruit recently AWOL from basic training. *A very hot army recruit*, Lenny thought.

"I've got something," she said, sounding more worried than excited.

"Something to make us some money?" Lenny asked.

Their regular routine had Bull extracting useful—meaning *valuable*—data from some distant server and Lenny then selling it to a shady customer. Occasionally they did contract work, but mostly their income came from freelance gigs where Bull went scavenging around until she came up with "gold"—consumer information, passwords, accounts, social security numbers, banking and credit card reports. Lately they'd mined dating sites and email accounts to blackmail cheating husbands. They didn't really care what they got, as long as they could make some cash. Each had their own reasons for the scams, but both knew that Bull was world class and playing well beneath her skill set. She could have been employed at NSA, CIA, Google, Apple, or a hundred other places, making much more money and not worrying about getting busted or angering the wrong party, but Bull had no interest in going legit.

"What do you have?" Lenny asked again, watching her light a smoke like a movie star, wishing he could be the end of the cigarette. "Something good?"

"No." Bull shook her head, inhaled a full drag, never taking her eyes from the screens, then exhaled. "Something that's going to get us killed."

Chapter Three

Three weeks after the July 4th bombing at Tri-Knight Avionics, outside Washington DC, the world had indeed figured out that an incredible string of attacks had begun—they just didn't know *why*. No group had issued any demands or even claimed responsibility. Law enforcement could not yet confirm the—now seven—terror strikes were connected. There appeared to be only two common threads: each bombing had targeted a different tech company, and, in every case, the terrorists had gone to great lengths to avoid any loss of human life. The bombs always hit at night after last-minute phoned warnings or fake police or firefighters evacuated just prior to the explosions. The media had dubbed the terrorist the "Fire Bomber," or "Fire Bombers," as no one knew if it was a single person or a group, which led to constant debating after each strike.

The FBI were the lead investigators on all the cases, but really in charge, even if no one knew, was Tess Federgreen, a dynamic woman, tougher than she looked, and head of the CIA's most secret division. *"The world isn't run by govern-*

ments anymore, and intelligence is our last advantage," she often said.

Tess studied the list of attack locations for the hundredth time since her first cup of coffee at three-twelve AM. She had stopped keeping track of how much—or rather how little—sleep she'd gotten. Last night it had been maybe four hours, just not all at once. The list taunted her.

- Crystal City, Virginia
- Seattle, Washington
- Austin, Texas
- Cincinnati, Ohio
- Albuquerque, New Mexico
- Chapel Hill, North Carolina
- Huntsville, Alabama
- San Jose, California
- San Francisco, California

Six of the sites were some kind of tech companies, two were in aerospace, and one made auto parts. She'd read transcripts of FBI interviews with each of the companies' CEOs. None of them could figure a connection to more than one or two of the others. Government databases and bureau computers had also failed to find a definitive link among the list. "It's as if the bombers are phantoms," the FBI agent in charge had told his supervisor during the last briefing.

The FBI had units coordinating with CIA and NSA and two dozen other agencies, exploring theories ranging from Chinese sabotage to economic terrorism and scores of other far-fetched ideas. The form of explosives used was new and highly advanced. Prior to the first attacks, the US Military had believed they were the only ones with knowledge of, or access to, it. It presented one of the many desperate questions which stole her sleep:

1. How are they destroying buildings with a relatively small amount of explosives?
2. How are they choosing their targets?
3. What do they want? What are they trying to achieve?
4. Who are they?
5. How do we stop them?

For three weeks, Bull and Lenny had been arguing about how to handle "the find," as they called it. Each passing day had made it more valuable, and exponentially more dangerous.

"We've got to sell it," Lenny said, trying not to shout, as he found Bull in front of her computers with a video window open to a news report of the latest bombing in Huntsville. "We're running out of time."

"How the hell do *you* know?" she snapped back. He could tell she hadn't slept. Whenever Bull pulled an all-nighter, her face scrunched into a permanent squint and her voice took on an edgy-whiney pitch instead of her normal lilt.

"They're gonna figure it out," he responded tensely. "And then we've got nothing . . . except maybe some trouble."

"F that! It's up to me. You forget, you make the deals, but *I* make the product."

He thought she sounded like a drug kingpin. However, this was by far the most serious game he'd ever played in, and that was saying something. He and Bull had dealt with the mob, blackmailed a state senator, sold banking info to hack houses, even done a contract job with the Russians once, but this—*the find*—made all that look like shoplifting at the local convenience store. This meant millions, or the morgue.

"We gotta move this," he tried again.

Bull stared at the screens for a long time—numb, oblivious, concentrating, lost . . . Lenny didn't know what. Finally, she spoke. "Call that dude, the one you know, the convict."

"Why him?"

"Cause I'm too young to die."

The beeping noise gave Chase an instant headache. He and Wen had just returned from a naked swim in a waterfall, and the piercing din emanating from his pack in the corner of their bedroom felt like an assault on his bliss.

"Are you going to answer it?" Wen asked, combing her wet hair.

Chase retrieved the offending device, looked at the scrambled satellite-phone as if it were an armed intruder, then glanced back at Wen, still nude. "It's not a scheduled call. It can't be good news."

She nodded, pulled on a loose tee-shirt, and instinctively looked at the day pack she'd taken to the waterfall that now lay on the bed, containing a QSZ-92 semi-automatic pistol. Her preferred Glock 19 was under the pillow. She blew him a playful kiss, but her eyes showed concern. Guns made Chase nervous, ever since his best friend accidentally shot himself in elementary school.

"Yeah?" Chase said into the phone after seeing it was

Flint Jones, his security chief. Flint, a fifty-six-year-old former CIA agent, was one of only a handful of people who knew how to reach them. Chase's brother, Boone, his business partner, Dez, a convict at Lompoc Federal Prison—a man called Mars—who also happened to be Chase's oldest friend, and a mysterious math savant known as "the Astronaut," were the others.

Flint was the last one of those insiders that Chase ever wanted to hear from.

"We have a problem," Flint said.

"Tell me something I don't already know." Although billionaire status did nothing to his ego, Chase's life was not what it used to be. He'd been forced to hide his funds around the globe and live like a fugitive with a price on his head, all because he wanted to make the world a better place. Even in his snarky reply, he wondered which pursuer was onto them. He looked back at Wen, a woman he'd nearly died to save, knowing he wouldn't hesitate to do it again. But Chase realized she'd be the one more likely to be saving him, as he recalled watching her kill two men on a runway not that long ago when they were actively trying to save the world. "Who's coming?"

"You are," Flint said. "You've got to come home immediately."

Chapter Four

After their quiet existence on the island, the hectic bustle of the 1.5 million-square-foot Jeppesen Terminal at Denver airport left Chase feeling disoriented. The fact that, at Wen's insistence, he also had a handgun concealed in his waistband under his shirt furthered his uneasiness. If Chase had known that several people were intently watching his every move, he would have already been running.

Wen and Chase had taken a small plane from Nuku Hiva to Tahiti, where they boarded Chase's new $74 million Bombardier-8000 private jet. He'd reluctantly had to liquidate his beloved customized Gulfstream since it could be traced to him—the new plane was registered to a foreign shell company. He didn't like the Bombardier as much. It lacked his personal touches, but it had excellent range, and they were able to fly directly to Denver from Tahiti. Their luggage was safely stored on the plane, except for a backpack Wen wore, which held their most valuable possession.

Wen didn't like airports, and had repeatedly told Chase,

"It's an insane idea, too public, too much exposure." As usual, Wen carried two weapons, but she knew that in these types of surroundings, it would be her MSS training and field experience that would be more important to their survival. She kept looking behind them, but with thousands of travelers moving in every direction, it was impossible to tell if they were being followed.

Flint claimed the CIA had requested their presence. "Not really a request, though," he'd said. "A command performance."

A man wearing casual business attire but looking like a battle-hardened military vet walked far enough back to go undetected. He struggled to keep Chase and Wen in sight. "I have them," he said, speaking into a bluetooth headset. "We are in the terminal, level five."

They had left Nuku Hiva immediately after the call with Flint, and had been constantly on the move for more than sixteen hours. For most of that time, Wen had cautioned against attending the meeting at all. "Testing Flint's loyalty is not smart," she'd said. "If he fails the test, we'll be in prison, or dead."

Chase agreed, but also believed being on the wrong side of the CIA would mean running forever. *And how far will we get?* he thought again, as they wove in and out of the pushing crowds.

Adding to his stress, as they got off the plane, Wen had confided that travel fatigue could cost her the edge needed to handle whatever might come.

"It's impossible to defend in a busy airport."

"Nothing is going to happen," Chase said. "Flint is okay. Mars vouched for him."

There was no one in the world Chase trusted more than Mars, a man he'd known since childhood. Although now serving a long prison term, he had a network that wielded stunning power and influence in both the criminal and noncriminal worlds. Mars often claimed, *"Everything and everyone is connected to the underworld whether they know it or not. Everyone is a criminal, at least by association."* Mars had used that knowledge and those connections to make a fortune for himself and, more recently, to aid Chase in his bid to disappear.

"I wish I could see Mars on this trip," Chase said to Wen as they scanned the throngs of travelers, looking for Flint.

"Too risky," Wen said tersely. They'd already had that conversation twice during the long flight.

"There's Flint," Chase said, resisting the urge to point at his security chief who stood next to a large bronze statue of aviation pioneer, Elrey Jeppesen.

A man in a leather jacket, leaning against the wall twenty yards away, saw Flint, too. He stuck a piece of gum in his mouth as he watched Chase and Wen approach the statue.

Chase introduced Wen to Flint. Wen, normally a quick judge of character, couldn't decide if she liked him or not. That fact kept her on more of an edge than usual.

"Where's Tess?" Chase asked, still annoyed to be meeting the head of the CIA's most secret division, Corporate Intelligence Security Section—CISS—which had been formed four years earlier. The division, a joint operation of the CIA, NSA, and FBI, had a mandate to prevent war between corporations. The Department of Homeland Security created CISS, reacting to a World Economic Forum report showing that only thirty-one of the top one hundred global economic entities were countries, with the other sixty-nine being corporations. The shocking trend, expected to continue, meant that in the next fifteen years, ninety-five conglomerates would dominate the list with only five countries remaining. A secret government study concluded that a shift from nation states to corporate states made the likelihood of major conflicts—or "wars"—erupting between corporations and countries highly probable as the world entered a new phase of decentralized power. CISS's mandate was to keep the peace, or, at least, make sure the "right" side won.

"Tess will be along any minute," Flint said, motioning them to begin walking. "And remember, be nice."

"Me?" Chase said. "I hope you've told *her* the same thing." The last time he'd seen Tess, she'd had him detained and interrogated on an airport runway. He was not a fan. Still, Flint had convinced Chase that he owed his continued freedom, at least in part, to Tess. Wen saw things differently, believing Tess was working to protect the interests of various corporate powers that wanted Chase out of the way.

The bluetooth man continued to follow. However, the man chewing gum headed in the opposite direction, toward the up escalator.

"We are walking into a trap," Wen said to Chase. "Whether Flint knows it or not."

Flint ignored the comment. "Unfortunately, this little reunion will have to be a bit shorter than we'd planned," Flint said, ushering them around the back of a long escalator. "Just before you arrived, she texted me. An emergency requires her to return to Washington right away. We'll only be able to speak with her for a few minutes."

"We just flew halfway around the world for a meeting that we should have been able to do over the phone, and now you're telling me we're not even going to have that meeting."

"You had to come back anyway," Flint said as they passed a gift shop. None of them had noticed the two people following them, or the third man now watching them from behind a rack of the latest paperbacks.

Chapter Five

Chase, suddenly more worried, grabbed Flint's shoulder to stop him. "What happened? Why did we need to come back?"

"Because you can't do what you have to do from some little speck of land in the middle of the ocean," Flint said, carefully scanning the crowd behind them instead of looking at Chase. "Have you heard about the Fire Bomber?"

"What's a Fire Bomber?" Chase asked.

"You don't see any news in paradise?" Flint asked, astonished, as they started walking again.

"That's by design," Wen said. "We dropped out. Or at least we were *trying* to, until you called."

"The Fire Bomber," Flint began, as they dodged a family of six, each of whom pulled their own luggage, "is a person, or persons, some sort of terrorist group, we don't really know. They've bombed seven corporate targets in the United States over the past three weeks. No one knows why."

"Which companies?" Chase asked.

"What's this have to do with us?" Wen asked at the same time. "We're not wanted for those crimes, too, are we?"

"Tess will explain," Flint said, nodding toward a woman with long auburn hair.

Chase followed Flint's gaze and immediately recognized Tess, certain her hair had been a different color last time he saw her—maybe blonde. The woman whose personality, in spite of her jeans and faded gray leather jacket, did not match her attractive and laid-back appearance. *She's more like her snakeskin cowboy boots*, Chase thought, recalling what he'd learned since their first meeting. Tess Federgreen had risen through the ranks of the NSA with an impressive list of Washington contacts, and knew more than her share of secrets. She ran the CISS in the way J. Edgar Hoover had run the FBI—as if accountable to no one and willing to do whatever necessary to achieve the desired results.

The bluetooth man slowed down. The gift shop man, who'd moved into the terminal, also stopped, as if checking his boarding pass.

Tess and a towering African American man greeted them. For a moment, it looked as if Tess might hug Flint, but it passed in a hurried awkwardness most people would have missed, but Wen would ask Chase about it later.

"Thanks for coming," Tess said to Chase. "Sorry, but we need to have this conversation while walking."

The man with Tess extended his hand to Chase. "Travis Watts. I'm very glad to finally meet you." Travis smiled. "I'm Director of Field Operations for CISS."

Chase shook his hand and stared into his eyes. "You're the Yang."

Travis raised an eyebrow. "Seems our friend here has been doing some homework." Tess and Travis were co-directors of CISS, and many of their colleagues referred to the pair as "Yin and Yang."

"Yes, I have," Chase said. "You're thirty-six, born in Atlanta, the eldest son of Nigerian immigrants. University of North Carolina. Officer Training School. Army Major. CIA recruited you. Officially, you began your career as an analyst, since you're fluent in four languages, but unofficially you were a member of the agency's dark ops."

"*Classified* research, even," Travis said, impressed, as they kept walking, trying to outpace the seemingly endless flow of people.

"I'm not going to ask what you found out about me," Tess said, her eyes—the color of wet jade—flashing in anger.

"Good idea," Chase shot back.

"We're all on the same side here," Flint said as they went under a bank of Departures monitors.

"Are we?" Wen asked.

"We'd better be," Tess said, checking the time, then picking up her stride. "Which brings me to the reason we're here. I need your help, Chase."

Her words surprised him. Up until then, he'd believed he might be in more trouble. "Last time you said that I almost died. In fact, I would have died if it wasn't for Wen." Flint shot him a *just-shut-up-and-listen-for-one-minute* look. "Okay, I'm listening."

The bluetooth man was now only fifteen feet behind them.

"You are, no doubt, aware of the Fire Bombers," Tess said.

"More than one?" Chase asked, as if he'd been following the story from the beginning.

"Have to be. Nine sites in three weeks, no casualties, no

witnesses. No single person could . . . Anyway, I want you and Wen to find out who's behind this."

"Why do you need *us*?" Chase asked, astonished. "Isn't the FBI investigating?"

"Of course."

"And what about CISS, or the rest of the CIA?"

"Yes, we're working on it, too," Tess said. "But I'd prefer you find out who it is before the FBI does."

"Why?" Wen asked, just as a loudspeaker called a passenger back to a gate area.

"I have my reasons," Tess said. They were passing a busy cafe and the rich aroma of fresh-ground coffee mixed with a cocktail of cologne from the nearby duty-free shop made Chase squint his exasperated eyes and look at Wen.

The gift shop man, thirty feet behind and struggling to push through the rush of travelers, looked to the upper walkways, as if expecting someone, or something to happen.

Chapter Six

Wen continued searching the airport crowds for threats. The more she heard from Tess, the more she believed they shouldn't be there. It seemed beyond crazy that this powerful woman from the CIA would be asking for their help—an engineer and a former Chinese agent. It could only be a trap. They were walking so fast, it was difficult for Wen to sweep the entire area, but her training told her the most important places to look—ahead and above

"What *we* do that the CIA or FBI can't?" Chase asked, his tone incredulous.

"We have certain limitations," Tess said. "And you have none."

Chase scoffed. "Now you're really insulting my intelligence. That's *ridiculous!*"

"What's in your pack, Wen?" Tess asked, tapping Wen's backpack. "Something you aren't supposed to have?" Her mouth showed a smile. Her eyes did not.

Wen considered taking Tess down and then running.

"Something she shouldn't even *know* about?" Travis added.

Wen ignored them. Her eyes continuing to roam.

"She does have quite a past," Tess said as the group momentarily got caught in an overflowing line at a car rental kiosk. "We need someone objective. And you—"

"What if we say no?" Chase interrupted. They returned to their brisk pace through the terminal.

"Now, why would you say no?" Tess asked. "Don't you want to help your country? Stop violence? Save lives?"

"I thought no one has been injured yet."

"How long do you think that will last?" Tess asked, clearly irritated.

"What's the connection between the sites?"

"I'm hoping you'll be able to tell me that."

"You're way overestimating me," he said.

She stopped and turned to face Chase. "You *owe* me."

He glared back at her. "Why?"

Flint stepped between them. "Chase, you're not in jail. You're *alive*. Tess is the reason."

Chase shook his head, appalled, recalling the many deaths that had occurred around him months earlier. Ultimately, none were his fault, yet he wore the responsibility around his neck like a noose.

"Vancouver, Edmonton, San Francisco, Seattle," Tess listed. "Do you want to try to explain all that?"

"Do *you*?" Chase asked. People had died in those cities —some trying to protect Chase, some trying to kill him. "You've got more invested than me. You and your screwed up secret CIA—"

"Careful, Chase, you wouldn't want to offend me." Tess began walking again.

"I seriously doubt you *can* be offended," Chase said,

rubbing the stubble on his chin. "You had a chance to stop at least some of those deaths, but you chose corporate greed over common good."

"You don't know what you're talking about," Tess said, sounding as if she were addressing an errant pupil. "The world is more complex than a tropical island."

She knew where we were, Wen thought.

"I'm not interested in helping you do whatever you're trying to do."

"I'm *trying* to save lives," Tess said sharply. "And you will help, because you're a very bright man, and I'm certain that once you've had a calm moment to consider the situation, you'll change your mind." She paused, her dark green eyes connecting with his. "And I'm sure you don't want me bringing up your girlfriend to our friends in the MSS."

"Friends?" Wen asked.

"These are strange times," Tess said. "We do what we have to do."

Flint gave Chase a pleading look, and a slight nod.

"I'll give you three hours to say yes," she said, smoothing her jeans. "But by the time I land in Washington, you need to be on the team."

Before Chase could respond, Tess stopped again, this time in front of a door marked: *Authorized Personnel Only*.

"I'm not saying yes, but if I did," Chase began, "where would I even start?"

Travis entered a code into the keypad above the handle and the door opened.

The bluetooth man, now close enough to hear, fidgeted with a device in his pocket and looked around as if lost. No one noticed him.

"Try your friend, the Astronaut," Tess said, turning abruptly and entering the door. Before disappearing into the corridor, she announced one final warning. "Three hours, Chase. I'm not a patient woman."

The door closed, and she was gone.

Wen, standing amidst the rushing crowd, looked at Chase as if he was out of his mind to even be considering cooperating. A man bumped into Chase. Wen yanked her weapon out, but quickly hid it again as the person kept going.

"Let's get out of here," Chase said.

"Where to?" Flint asked.

Chase eyed Flint suspiciously. "Maybe I should ask you."

The bluetooth man suddenly rushed toward Chase, raising his gun.

Being a weapons expert, Wen involuntarily identified it as a Sig Sauer P226 pistol with a suppressor. In the instant blur of the confrontation, she pulled her Glock 19 and launched into a spinning round kick. But before she could fire her gun or reach the assailant, a shot rang out.

Chapter Seven

Lenny couldn't just ring up "the convict dude," as Bull called his contact. "Guy's in the joint," Lenny told her. "He ain't got an iPhone."

"You make the deals," she reminded him for the sixth time. "Find a way."

So he did. As good as Bull was at extracting valuable bits and pixels from the net, he was equally talented at working contacts. Lenny knew people. Lots of them—the good, the bad, and mostly the ugly.

Sixteen hours after Bull gave him the green light, Lenny had the convict on the phone. Turned out the guy *did* have a hidden iPhone.

"Don't tell him what we got," Bull had warned.

"Then what am I going to say?"

"Tell him without telling him. Damn, what do I need you for?"

"I got this. Don't worry." As soon as he'd uttered the words, he'd regretted them. She did worry. That's all she did, and him telling her not to meant she would only worry more.

Bull hadn't responded, only killed him a few times with a glance that instead of insulting him as she'd intended, had actually turned him on. Maybe if they got this deal done, if they got some large cash, she'd relax long enough to realize he was the king to her queen, he was worthy of her. Maybe if . . . maybe if they lived long enough, survived the damned drama, *actually pulled off* the deal of a lifetime, they could get a place in Spain. She'd always wanted to go to Barcelona.

"I'm short on time," the convict said, then, realizing the irony, added, "For the call, not my sentence. What do you have, or need?"

Lenny had only dealt with him once before, when Bull had dredged up reams of security questions from a major California Internet firm. A friend of a friend of a friend connected him to the convict—said he knew everyone on both sides of the law. It seemed true. The convict arranged for the company to outbid another scam-organization to buy back their own data before they had to make an embarrassing public disclosure. Neat and tidy.

But then the whole thing went bad. FBI came in as part of some larger embezzlement investigation and traced the security questions sale back to the convict. Instead of giving up Lenny, he'd sat firm. He could've gotten time off his sentence if he'd rolled on Lenny and Bull. Instead, he took a new charge and got more time. And he'd never mentioned it, never asked for anything in return. That, and the depth of his connections, as well as her own desperation, was why Bull had decided to go to him.

Lenny, while walking down a seedy street in Atlantic

City, New Jersey, continuously looked over his shoulder as he explained the product in loose and hypothetical terms.

The convict, an expert at reading between the lines, with a special understanding of threats and profits, caught on quickly.

"You're in a world of danger."

"Yeah, we sort of know that," Lenny said weakly.

"Sort of?" He laughed. "You don't have a clue. If we talk another few minutes, I might actually still be on the line while they kill you."

Lenny jumped as a homeless man stumbled from the shadows of an alley. "Can you help us move it?"

"Are you joking? Why are you bringing this to *me*?"

"We trust you."

"Stupid mistake number three for you. You want my help? Leave it alone. Bury it and then disappear. Get far away. Not Mexico or anywhere easy. I'm talking Pakistan, Somalia, or some place where civilized people aren't likely to go. If you're alive in a week, you've won the lottery. If you make it a month, then you must have found God. Still breathing in a year, you might be able to come home . . . "

"We can't go," Lenny said.

"Why the hell not?"

"They know."

"What?" the convict asked.

"That we have it."

"They can't possibly know."

"Why not?"

"I'm not a dammed psychic! I don't talk to the deceased. And if *they* know, then you're already dead."

Chapter Eight

Screams filled the air as the echo of a gunshot rippled across Denver's busy Jeppesen Terminal. Panicking people fled in every direction.

Less than three feet from Chase, the bluetooth man fell dead. His Sig Sauer pistol clattered to the floor. Blood instantly pooled.

Flint grabbed Chase. "We gotta get you out of here!"

"What happened?" Chase asked as Flint and Wen pushed him into the fleeing rush. "Who was that?"

Wen searched for more threats while Flint navigated their escape route through the frantically stampeding crowds.

Chase, realizing that either the bullet that had killed the man on the floor, or one from the dead man's pistol, was meant for *him*, broke loose from Flint's grip and stopped. The flow of travelers plowed into him. If Wen hadn't shoved him toward the wall, he would have been knocked down.

"What are you *doing*?" Flint shouted, fighting back

through the surge to reach Chase. "It's too dangerous to stay here!"

"Who *was* that?" Chase repeated angrily. "How did he know I'd be here?"

"I don't know," Flint said, looking around nervously. "But I know we're not safe. We need to keep moving."

"Are there more?"

"Exactly why we need to go!" Flint urged. "We'll figure it out later."

"Who killed the shooter?" Wen asked. "The man had communications on, a Sig Sauer P226 ready to take out Chase—"

"My guy," Flint said, clearly frustrated. "My guy hit him, okay?"

"*Your* guy?" Chase asked.

"Did you really think I'd bring you two into a busy airport without backup?"

"But how did the dead man know?" Chase asked again. "Only you and Tess knew I'd be here."

"Why do you want to do this now?" Flint asked, making eye contact for a second before continuing to scan the area. "Are you trying to get killed? Whoever that guy worked for is still out there. The pros know that it's the second shooter who's most dangerous."

"He's right," Wen said. "We can argue and accuse later. We need to move and get to the plane."

"How are we even going to get out of here?" Chase questioned, motioning to the chaotic scene.

Flint worked his cell phone. "We've got a powerful friend," he said as they all began moving again. Flint explained their plight to the person on the other end of the phone, who could only have been Tess. "Back the way we came," he announced, abruptly halting. "They're locking the airport down. We have to get back to the secure door where we left Tess and Travis.

As they pushed through against the desperate travelers, Wen spotted an armed man on the level above them and pulled her Glock.

A passing woman saw Wen's weapon and screamed, "She's got a gun!"

The crowd parted away from them in a fresh wave of terror. The armed man above them used the pandemonium to vanish, and Wen lost her shot.

"Is this a good idea?" Chase asked Wen as they jogged. "Walking back into Tess' web?"

"If you want to question my relationships," Flint shouted back from ahead of them, "perhaps you should start with my relationship with Mars."

"You have to admit this looks bad," Chase said breathlessly.

Flint turned and forced Chase into the wall. Wen pointed her Glock at him, but in a fluid move only possible with years of training and experience, Flint pinned Chase to the wall with one arm and held his gun toward Wen with the other. "Don't do anything stupid!" Flint said to Wen.

"What, like you just did?" Wen said, moving closer.

"You need me to get you out of here alive."

"We wouldn't even be here if it wasn't for you."

"Think about it, Chase. If I wanted you dead, you'd be dead."

Wen, ignoring the shouts of passers-by, now had her Glock inches from Flint's, which she'd identified as a Beretta Model 96D Brigadier pistol. He had at least an eight inch height advantage on her. "Back off!" she barked.

"Put the guns away!" Chase said.

"We're all history if you two don't start trusting me," Flint said.

"I don't normally trust people who point guns at me," Wen replied.

Flint stared into her eyes, relaxed his grip on the Beretta so it spun back on his finger with the barrel pointing up, and handed it to her.

Wen cautiously reached forward and took it by the barrel.

"Follow me or not," Flint said. "I'm just trying to do my damned job and keep you alive."

He released Chase and resumed his attempt to jog back to the secure door.

Wen, now holding three handguns, looked at Chase, then stuffed one in her pack. "We need to get to the plane."

Chase nodded and ran after Flint, noticing the crowd had thinned considerably.

Suddenly they were back at the bluetooth man's body. Security officials had only just arrived. Five Colorado State Police officers appeared behind Wen and quickly surrounded them.

"Drop your weapons!" one of the officers demanded as all five pointed revolvers at them.

Chase slowly pulled the pistol out from his waistband, imagining they would shoot him as soon as they saw it. He carefully placed it on the floor, immediately raising his hands as he'd seen in countless movies.

Wen, being the only one of the three now holding, scanned the area, not wanting to relinquish control. More officers approached. There would be no escape.

"Now!" the man repeated. "Do it now!" He glared, a bloody body behind him on the floor, an airport brimming with tension and fear. Wen had no doubt the man was about to pull the trigger.

Chapter Nine

Wen, facing overwhelming odds, stole one last glance around the upper reaches of Jeppesen Terminal for additional threats, took a deep breath, knowing she would be deported to China, and slowly let the Glock and her QSZ-92 semi-automatic pistol fall to the ground. Instantly, someone shoved her to the ground, and rough hands were patting her down. She struggled to see Chase, face down just a few feet from her and receiving the same treatment.

Other than Chase, all she cared about was the Antimatter Machine in her pack, where they'd also discover Flint's Beretta. Wen knew that three guns in the hands of a former MSS agent, at the site of an airport killing, all spelled terrorist. She'd be going to some secret CIA prison forever.

A few minutes later, they were in handcuffs, being ushered into the bowels of the airport. Wen continued to calculate the odds, looking for any angle. There were eight, maybe nine cops escorting them. They were likely not trained beyond straight academy tactics. Even cuffed, she and Flint could take them. But would he act? Two uniforms had him in front, two more flanked Chase, then there were three on her, and one or two taking up the rear. Wen looked for a choke point where she could do a backflip off a wall, come crashing round, grab a weapon, and tear through a few, but then, unless Flint joined in, the cops would regain control, and probably kill her in the process.

They turned a corner. To Wen's disappointment, the corridor opened wider, and up ahead more officers headed toward them—three in uniform, four plain clothes. The odds had collapsed, but facing deportation and certain death in China, Wen looked for any advantage while scheming another plan.

If it was just me, she thought, *these three would already be on the floor and I'd have a weapon.*

But Wen couldn't risk Chase getting killed in the crossfire.

I can't count on Flint since there's no way to be sure if he's on our side, is loyal to Tess and the CIA, or working for someone else.

The approaching men reached them and everyone stopped. An officer who'd been behind Wen made his way to the front of the group. "We need to release these three," one of the plain clothes said.

"On whose order?"

Plain-clothes held up a computer tablet for the officer to read.

Wen held her breath, unsure how this could be possible, alert for another trap.

"But they were right there," the officer protested after finishing with the tablet. "They were in possession of *four* handguns!"

"The attack was directed at them. He was the target."

Plain-clothes pointed to Chase. "We've got seven different camera angles backing that up."

"Even if that's true," the exasperated officer began, "we need to question them."

"Not today. You read the order. That comes from way above our pay grade."

Wen guessed Tess had pulled the strings. *Amazing she has the clout to get us released when we're in the middle of an event like this.*

"But this is *our* jurisdiction," the officer argued.

Plain-clothes shook his head. "Let them go . . . right now."

The officer let out a moaning expletive. "You do it. I've got a homicide to investigate and a shooter still on the loose." He grabbed two other officers and headed back the way they'd come.

"You'll be in my report!" Plain-clothes, shouted at the officer.

The officer waved him off without bothering to turn around.

Plain-clothes motioned to one of the men he'd come with. "Release them, return their weapons, and make sure they get safely to their plane."

"But all flights are grounded," another cop said.

"Not theirs," Plain-clothes said.

One of the officers removed the cuffs from Flint, Chase, and finally Wen. Someone gave their weapons and Wen's pack containing the Antimatter Machine to Plain-clothes, who handed them to Flint.

At the same time, in a nondescript aircraft hangar at a Virginia military base, an elite group of highly trained 'secret agents' readied themselves to launch a massive covert operation. On any given day, every day, in as many as seventy countries around the globe, US Dark Ops commandos routinely took part in an undeclared global war, a fact ignored by the mainstream media and unknown by the American public.

However, this team was different. They were not SEALs, Green Berets, Rangers, Night Stalkers, or any of the other special units regularly deployed by the Pentagon. These one-hundred and eighty-four highly trained men and women belonged to the NSA, and while they were armed with HK MP5N 9mm submachine guns and HK Mk 23 SOCOM .45 ACP pistols, they rarely used them. Their preferred tools were the highest tech the US intelligence community had in its arsenal. These IT-Squads had one purpose—obtaining and disseminating the most powerful and dangerous weapon of all: information.

Six IT-Squads, each having nine operatives, were loaded onto six specially outfitted Cessna Citation X jets. Each plane would head to a different destination. Their goal was to find the Fire Bomber before any other US government Agency. IT-Squads worked by different rules than other services—rather, they followed no rules. Loyalty to the mission ranked above country.

Whatever it took to get the job done.

Less than fifteen minutes after being released, Chase and Wen were back on the Bombardier-8000, cleared for takeoff.

"You were right," Chase admitted as the plane taxied. "We never should have come."

"Maybe," Wen replied, staring out the window. "But we can't hide. Whoever wanted to kill you isn't going away." She turned back to Chase. "We have to find them."

"And the Fire Bomber?"

"It's all connected. The Fire Bomber is the reason we're here."

Chase nodded as the plane picked up speed. "Maybe we should have let Flint come with us."

"He needs to stay in Denver and clean up his mess. If Flint really wasn't involved, then he can be a bigger help tracking down who was. And besides," she added as the jet lifted into the air, "he can't come where we're going."

Chapter Ten

Cane Westfield sat behind his large desk, reportedly made from WWII aircraft carrier steel, getting an update on the latest problem. A determined and disgusted expression creased his face, already hardened by decades of dealing with such problems and having to make difficult decisions.

This one might be a little different, he thought. *Every damned year the pressures compound, and the world gets more complex.*

At sixty-four, his lean, hard build had seen a lot of change, and more than his share of life and death issues. His wife still expected him to retire next year, and he'd like to have more time to spend with his four grandchildren, but that was never going to happen. Westfield would keep working until the moment he died, and if he could get past this latest firestorm, he hoped his funeral would still be a long way off.

"People as mean as me live forever," he would sometimes say. "That's one of God's cruel jokes—the good die young, and old snakes like me go on and on."

Considered an important man, Westfield, always well

appointed, though with a permanent look of disdain, was kept well-paid, comfortable, and left alone to do the kind of work that not many wanted to do, and even fewer could handle. His budget had almost no ceiling; he could easily spend tens of millions on a "project", and, if needed, more. Whatever his current focus, all he had to do was ask.

Westfield enjoyed and exerted nearly unlimited power.

He touched a button. A female voice responded, "Yes, sir?"

"Send them in," he said in a thick, gravelly voice, which he attempted to clear with black coffee as he went back to reading one of the screens on his desk. Even after weeks of reviewing the data and consulting with colleagues, he was still trying to decide the best course of action. Westfield always responded to a crisis with ruthless intent.

Some of his co-workers, the few who knew him at all, speculated that it was power that fueled his drive, but they were wrong. His secretary, the woman who'd responded on the intercom, believed the challenge and thrill of the chase kept Westfield going, but she wasn't right either. Westfield did what he did every day because he believed he was making the world a better place for his grandchildren, and was absolutely sure that no one else could do it but him.

The two men who walked into the sparse, elegant office, could have been younger versions of himself. It was one of the reasons they were his top go-to team. Like him, they'd both been raised in small, rural American towns, played high school football, attended church, and believed in the same version of right and wrong: that some people were better than others and they needed to protect the weak from the weak.

"Ryker," Westfield said coolly, looking at the taller of the two and wondering again why a man who was only thirty-two would shave his head completely bald. "Damon," Westfield said, nodding to the other man, a few inches shorter than Ryker, but still a solid six-foot frame. Unlike his partner, he had a full head of brown hair. Damon also clearly spent more time in the gym; his biceps appeared to be waging an angry battle to escape his sports jacket.

"Sir," both men said in unison.

"Sit." Westfield swept his hand impatiently. "I've got a real train wreck for you this time."

"Aren't they all?" Ryker asked proudly, knowing he and Damon were the A-Team, meaning they always drew the tough assignments.

"Yes," Westfield said, appearing as if he'd eaten something disagreeable. "But I suspect this one could be your greatest challenge."

Damon stole a quick glance at Ryker, who'd kept his eyes glued on Westfield and recalled their last job—a nothing little village in the Middle East . . . they'd barely gotten out alive—wondering what the hell was in store for them now.

"Are you familiar with Chase Malone?" Westfield asked.

"The billionaire?" Ryker replied. "Invented some kind of artificial intelligence something or another."

"That's right," Westfield said, not surprised they knew of the target since Chase had been in the news when he sold his RAI program a while back. "I need you to find him, have a talk."

"That's it?" Damon asked, surprised, pulling out a cinnamon toothpick and clenching on it like an old cowboy curling his lip around chew. "That shouldn't be too difficult. Recognizable guy like that."

Ryker, already figuring the security a man like that would employ and the resources he'd have at his disposal, asked the obvious question. "What are we talking to him about?"

"A short talk. A *very* short one." Westfield glared, as if strangling Ryker with his eyes. Both men understood the instruction—kill Chase Malone.

"Where is he?" Damon asked.

"Malone's gone dark," Westfield said. "Completely off-grid."

"Not easy to do."

"Unless you have a billion dollars," Ryker said.

"And some help," Westfield said. "Professional help."

"*Our* kind of professional?" Ryker asked.

"Unfortunately." Westfield handed them each a computer tablet loaded with the case files and full details of the mission.

Ryker took one look at the screen on his tablet and understood why Westfield said it would be their most challenging job.

"Timeline?" Ryker asked.

Westfield shook his head. "There isn't one. Should've been in his grave yesterday."

Chapter Eleven

Tess and Travis were met by a car and driver upon landing at Dulles International Airport in the Washington DC suburbs of Virginia. Typically hot and muggy summer conditions hit them like a steam bath. Tess couldn't stand the nation's capital weather, and August, the worst month for unbearably swampy conditions, was less than a week away. The thought reminded her how much time had gone past since the Fire Bomber's assaults had begun.

"Chase is our best chance at finding these terrorists," Tess said as the car sped toward the secret CISS headquarters in Vienna, Virginia.

"You were right about Chase. I'm still surprised he agreed to take the assignment."

"I wasn't so sure, after talking to him. And Wen Sung is definitely going to give me plenty of headaches, but you can't deny she's fearless."

"Dangerous."

"Maybe. Even so, I'm not certain Chase would've gone

along with us if someone hadn't tried to kill him at the airport."

"Doesn't that worry you?" Travis asked as they drove along Lawyers Road.

"I don't care why he agreed, so long as he did." She moved uncomfortably in her seat, tapping nervously on the turquoise bracelet she always wore as if it might respond to her.

"No, I mean aren't you concerned that somebody knew he'd be there and is taking shots at him?"

"All billionaires have enemies," she said, continuing to sound distracted. "Chase Malone has even more than his fair share. But that's Flint's problem to deal with."

"Chase can't find the terrorists if he's dead." Travis had been against bringing Chase into the mix, believing his CISS field operatives and IT-Squads could handle the situation, but with each passing bomb attack, even he had to admit something more was needed.

"As Chase proved again today," Tess said, "he's not an easy target, and should not be underestimated."

"Particularly with his MSS agent girlfriend."

"*Former* MSS agent," Tess corrected.

"Do we know that for sure?" Travis asked, adjusting his silver and lilac tie. After his army fatigues and special ops mud and wet "uniforms," Travis preferred dark tailored suits. Tess often joked that he probably slept in a pinstripe suit.

Tess gave him a disapproving look. Then she seemed to reconsider her position. "Okay. Find out who took those shots at the airport."

They continued to volley possibilities and consequences of the latest situation waiting for them at the CISS crisis center, known as "Mission Control." The Fire Bomber had struck again, surprisingly in India, but this time they had a suspect.

Chase's Bombardier-8000 began its decent into the Redding Municipal Airport in northern California. "Are we making a mistake?" Wen asked. "Why does Tess want us to start with the Astronaut?"

There were eleven known brilliant savants called "Astronauts" who were sought after by the major intelligence services. These super-intelligent individuals were nearly impossible to locate, and extremely difficult to work with. In the days before advancements in artificial intelligence, their off-the-charts brain power in certain areas made them critical weapons as each country vied for advantage in arms/space/tech races.

"Because she knows what the Astronaut is capable of," Chase said. "Maybe she wants us to lead them to him."

"When I was with the MSS, we kept lists about these specific astronauts and were continually adding known data on them. They are constantly afraid that one side will eliminate them."

"Why haven't they?" Chase asked as the wheels touched the runway.

"There have been rumors of attempts, but they are too important. Even AI can't reason like them."

"So the astronauts use those same smarts to hide?"

"There are three who are above the others—substantially brighter. Those are the most sought after ones, and they can almost never be found," Wen said as the plane slowed, then, adding quietly, "And those three are the most dangerous ones."

"Is our astronaut one of the three?"

"Yes," Wen said, recalling how their astronaut, Nash Graham, had saved her twice.

"He sold you the Antimatter Machine," Chase said. "Tess knew you had it with you. Why didn't she just take it?"

The Antimatter Machine, a customized, portable "super-computer," built by the Astronaut, that allegedly couldn't be traced, took its name from actual antimatter, which could not be seen. It used an atom transistor and included many powerful features, one of Wen's favorites being an icon which would put her in immediate touch with the Astronaut. Wen shivered involuntarily as she recalled his warning when he'd given it to her.

"Always remember what happens when matter and antimatter meet . . . they are both annihilated."

"I think Tess let us keep it," Wen began. "Because we're going to need it in order to find the Fire Bombers."

Chase used a false identity to pick up a rental car. He was pleased they had a Ford Mustang GT convertible. He always loved to drive fast. As they began the seventy minute drive to their destination on the outskirts of the tiny mountain town of Mt. Shasta, they continued to discuss why Tess really needed them, and if it was actually possible they could do something that the CIA, NSA, and FBI could not.

"Flint suggested those agencies are too big, too bureaucratic," Chase said as he passed a UPS tandem trailer. "When he gave us the flash drive, he said that this situation needs something more nimble." The drive contained all data and reports thus far on the Fire Bomber.

"Or," Wen began, pulling out the Antimatter Machine, "Tess is just using the Fire Bomber as a way to trap us or trick us into revealing something."

"What could that possibly be?" Chase asked, not sure he wanted the answer, almost wishing they could simply enjoy the scenery.

Wen hit a few keys on the Antimatter Machine. "That's exactly what we need to find out."

Chapter Twelve

Gunner Easton, a hard man with a deceptively friendly face, emerged from the woods at a bend in the river wearing olive drab military fatigues covered in mud and dust. He stood near the edge of a three-thousand-acre swath of wilderness known as the "Training Fields," looking up at the sky, judging the wind by the movement of the clouds and concentrating on the sound of distant machine gun fire.

Another man, clad in heavy camo, jogged over. "The next order is sent."

Gunner nodded approvingly, checking his watch while starting to jog. "And he got word?"

"Yes, sir," the man replied, a salute in his voice.

Gunner would have smiled, if he remembered how. Ever since he'd begun "the machine wars" a grave seriousness had overtaken his normally jovial manner. "Do you know why we're doing this?" Gunner asked rhetorically, continuing to run at a quicker pace.

The man kept up with his boss. "Yes, sir."

"A man is not a man unless he's fought the fight." Gunner stopped to listen for the sounds of battle. "America is under siege. We once thought it would be from the outside—the communists, Islamic extremists, but the greatest threat to our country, our way of life, is from the inside. From the titans of technology." He picked up a jog again, looking around since an ambush could happen at any moment.

"Yes, sir," the man said again, ducking at a branch Gunner had pushed away and snapped back. He'd heard the sermon many times before, believed it, believed in Gunner, and had decided to do his part to take the country back and save his children, and their children, from the kind of hellish future that Hollywood had shown in glittery prophecies.

"We're being careful," Gunner added, reaching for his binoculars and scouring the area. "Even so, people don't always know what they're running from. Most of the time those needing to be liberated don't understand. Damn, those damned—look out!"

Both men hit the ground.

"Thing is, they'll be coming for me," Gunner whispered, looking up at the sky again as if it might now be filled with black gunships ready to descend on his expansive compound. He knew they could see him, knew they would find him. "Even now, they're using their technology to search for patterns, motives, connections, suspects . . . crosschecking and digging into the archives of every recorded phone call, text message, and email ever sent." He stood up and looked back at his subordinate as if just remembering he'd been talking to someone other than himself. "Not too long from now, they'll come here."

"And we'll fight, sir."

"And we'll lose," Gunner said, as if the taste of the words might have stolen his courage for a split second.

"The battle, but not the war."

Gunner nodded. Another smile fought its way to his face, but died well before seeing the light. "Yes, we will win the war . . . we must."

Wen made another pitch to Chase about WOLF, an acronym for "World of Liberty and Freedom," which she sometimes also simply referred to as "The Cause."

"I think we have enough troubles," Chase said as they merged onto I-5 North toward Mt. Shasta, California.

"Our ideas and goals are similar to The Cause," Wen said, checking the rearview mirror. "That means our problems are also the same."

"Did someone try to kill the leader of WOLF this morning?" Chase asked. "Because someone tried to kill *me*."

"WOLF stays hidden, working in the background. No one knows what they do, who they are." She cut an apple for the two of them.

He bit into a slice. "I know. My point is we're not facing the same issues."

"They, like us, want to see the world in balance. You should meet with them, and you will understand. For many years, they have been working to try to correct the inequality." She pointed the apple at him, then took a bite seductively.

"And for all that time, it has been getting worse."

"It is a big problem. The corruption is overwhelming, but now with technology, there is a chance to finally make progress. Want another slice?"

On that point, Chase agreed with her. The world was at a tipping point. Technology—specifically machine learning and artificial intelligence—was ushering a revolutionary change. Afterwards, either the super-rich would forever be an elite ruling class, or the majority of the population would finally have a chance to prosper.

"The odds are against the masses—the ninety-five percent of the world's population who share less than a quarter of global wealth." Chase waved an arm toward the vast and wild landscape. "Look at this beautiful country. Mt. Shasta is supposedly dormant, but it appears as if it could go at any moment."

"That's why they need The Cause . . . *and* us. And more of this incredibly beautiful scenery!"

"The odds are against us, too."

"Then why do we try? Hey, watch that semi, it's pulling over."

Chase switched into the next lane, then back, and noticed a cop behind him. "Because such odds make stubborn people like me want to prove something wrong."

"Then you'll meet with WOLF? The speed limit is seventy here, by the way"

"I didn't say that. I know, that cop's following me."

"Don't worry about him, he's just—oh, there, he's passing."

"For all I know, your subversive friends at The Cause have simply decided to blow up the tech companies they don't agree with."

Ryker and Damon boarded a flight to California, their mission clear: stop Chase Malone from finding the truth.

There were others already moving—sixteen other mercenaries looking for the secretive billionaire—but Ryker and Damon had the "license to kill." They were the only ones that Westfield had met with personally.

"What do you think?" Damon asked as they buckled up in first class seats.

Ryker adjusted the air control. He hated cold blowing across his bald head. "Parents. That's our ace."

Damon didn't really like the plan, thought family ought to be off limits, but this mission had a stratospheric priority level, so he'd do what had to be done. Westfield had assured them full authority and total protection. It meant, if need be, that they could "exterminate anyone who'd ever known the guy." One way or another, Chase Malone was going to die in the next forty-eight hours. The only question remaining was how many people would go down with him.

"Parents are good bait," Damon said quietly. "I just hope they'll still be around to attend their son's funeral."

Chapter Thirteen

With Wen now driving, as they neared their destination, Chase placed a call to his parents.

His mother, Daisy, a classic car mechanic, had owned an auto repair shop since before he was born. Her grandfather had also been a mechanic in World War II, whose knowledge was passed onto his granddaughter. She, in turn, had taught her sons, Chase and Boone. They could all repair anything from Tanks to Toyotas, and because Daisy's father had owned a plumbing and electrical contracting business, they could pretty much handle anything along those lines as well. They were a close family, and Chase's recent troubles had been difficult for all of them.

"Daisy's," his mother said, answering the phone. He was surprised she picked up. From the sounds he could tell she was in the funky old brick building, long ago transformed into a two door garage, located in the lazy, hip town of Cotati, California, where he'd been raised, about forty-five miles north of San Francisco. Although the shop specialized in classic cars from the fifties and sixties, she could fix anything, and the town of around eight thousand kept her constantly busy. His father, Zack, a CPA, ran the business end of things, and kept books for other small businesses on the side.

"Mom, I need—"

"Convoy! Are you back in the country? Are you coming home?" his mother asked, using the nickname she'd called him by since he was a baby.

Wen took the Mt. Shasta exit.

"Yeah, I'm in the States, but I can't come by. There's more trouble."

"What kind of trouble?"

His dad picked up an extension. "Chase, are you and Wen okay?"

"We're fine, but I'm afraid you two are in danger."

"We'll be fine," his mother said. Daisy was fearless. Both his parents were skydivers, scuba divers, and all-around adventure nuts. Even though Chase and his older brother had inherited their parents' zest for life, Chase's form of it exceeded the others. Boone had started a window-washing business and grown it to the point where he now did most of the major buildings in San Francisco, clearing seven figures annually.

"I need you to take a vacation. My treat."

"Last time you asked us to do that we were followed to Mexico. It was a close call," his dad said.

Chase, talking through the car's speaker, looked over at Wen, as if she might be able to convince them even though they'd only met briefly a few months earlier. Wen shrugged and checked the speedometer to make certain she was keeping it within the speed limit.

"We learned from that experience. No credit cards. I'll have someone bring you some cash. You can stay in the country—Maine, the Florida keys, Montana. Just for a couple of weeks?"

"We're here," Wen said, checking the rearview mirror as they turned onto a small dirt road into the woods.

"Mom, Dad, I've got to go, but I'm serious. I don't know who's after me, but there's a strong chance they'll use you to try to get to me. *Please* go."

"We'll talk about it, Convoy, but you know I'm not one to up and run."

"It's a good time to take a vacation," Chase said. "Talk to Mars, see what he says. I'll call you later."

Mars, fifteen years older than Chase, had worked at Daisy's throughout Chase's entire childhood. During most of that time he'd done law school part time, finally earning a degree and passing the bar almost a decade ago. A few years later, after a deal with the wrong businessman turned politician, Mars wound up in Lompoc Federal Prison. He still had the better part of "a dime"—ten years—remaining on his sentence. Chase considered him a second brother, and was confident he would persuade his parents to leave town.

"Are you sure this is the place?" Chase asked Wen after the call ended. "It looks like no one's been here for years." An overgrown dump filled with the kind of exotic weeds that only California could claim—spindly cactus-looking things, prickly straw colored organisms, wild vegetation that belonged in a Dr. Seuss book.

"There," Wen said, pointing to a rusty sheet metal Quonset hut that seemed in jeopardy of being consumed by the man-eating plants.

She steered their vehicle into what turned out to be an old workshop, open on both ends and filled with broken and useless tools that matched the rusty structure. There was also a 1990s pickup truck, and three people standing next to it. One of them was the Astronaut, and although he smiled at the sight of Wen as their car came to a stop, his eyes were filled with concern. He waved his arm frantically, rushing them in.

"Get out of the car, now!" he shouted.

Chapter Fourteen

Tess and Travis hunkered down inside CISS Mission Control, a room located in the basement of the CISS building filled with wall-sized monitors and computer terminals, making it look like a futuristic version of NASA's Mission Control—thus the name. They watched a direct feed of "the world's most wanted man" being apprehended. Twenty minutes earlier he'd been responsible for the firebombing of Aadyah Action & Air, a leading aerospace company in Bangalore, India.

"They got the Fire Bomber!" Tess said, celebrating as police placed restraints on the man and led him toward a van. "How close do we have a team who can take custody?"

Travis looked away from the large monitor showing the live satellite images of the capture and over at one of the technicians, who was busy searching for an answer.

"We can have someone there in thirty-five or forty minutes," the tech said.

"Do it," Travis said.

"What the hell?" Tess shouted.

Travis turned back to the screen in time to see the suspect burst into flames. He didn't just catch fire but, for an instant, actually looked like a human comet. The police escorting him dove away, collapsing and reeling in pain from instant burns, two of them also catching fire themselves before dropping and rolling to extinguish their clothes.

"How did that happen?" Tess yelled, as if by witnessing something horrific so close she might also burn. "He's been completely consumed by the flames!" Usually a cold woman, this caught her by such surprise her eyes teared for a moment before she caught herself.

"A fitting end to the Fire Bomber," Travis said, stunned by the graphic sight of a human melting.

"Maybe it wasn't him," Tess said, sounding desperate. "This was the first attack in India. He could have been a copycat."

"Call from the Pentagon," an assistant said to Tess.

"I'll take it in the Secure," Tess said, heading to a small conference room at the other end of Mission Control.

"Tess, what the hell is going on?" the Deputy Assistant Secretary of Defense asked. "India? Is this *our* Fire Bomber?"

"I hope so," she said. "Because he's dead."

"Excellent. Then maybe this is done?"

"You know better than that. We still have no idea who the Bomber was working for." Although she'd never believed there was only one bomber, the official theory had not changed.

"When the hell are we going to know?"

She thought of Chase, and the Astronaut he was headed to see. "Hopefully, before the next attack."

"It had better be. I've talked to the President, and I

don't have to tell you he is extremely concerned that the FBI —or, God help us, the media—finds out about our project."

"We don't know for sure this has anything to do with horUS," Tess replied tersely.

"India makes five out of the ten companies. Five companies form *the* list. Starting to look like a very big coincidence."

"But it could be just that."

"Come on, Tess, there's no such thing as coincidence!"

"The odds just shifted, but it's a big list, and the Bomber obviously doesn't like tech companies."

"Regardless of *why*, we still don't know *who*!"

"I understand the importance of stopping the Bomber," Tess said impatiently, rubbing a bit of dry dirt off her cowboy boot. "We've sent IT Squads to every attack site, and another ten Squads are canvassing potential targets prior to possible strikes. But, need I remind you, it isn't just CISS who has come up empty—your Defense Intelligence Agency, a dozen other intel services, local law enforcement, *and* the FBI have also failed." The momentary lapse earlier had been replaced with her typical expertise and decisiveness.

"Good God, we'll be dead if someone finds out who the Bombers are before us!" the Deputy Assistant Secretary of Defense managed to shout without raising his voice. "There are only a few of us who know what's at stake here. And this is at the heart of CISS's mission. I'm counting on you, Tess. Keep horUS safe."

The project, "horUS," was so far above any official classified level that only nine people in the country were privy to the full scope of it. In spite of her years in the intelligence world and all the time spent on horUS, every time she heard the word, which rhymed with "chorus," it actually startled her—almost scared her. Still, she wasn't convinced the Fire Bomber was targeting horUS, but it was possible . .

She thought of Chase again. In spite of all the specialized personnel CISS had out there trying to crack the case and find out who was conducting this war, Tess believed Chase had the best chance. But during sleepless nights, one gnawing question haunted her: *How could the bombers know about horUS?*

Tess ended her call with a defiant pledge she had to believe. "We. Will. Find. Them."

Inside the rusted metal Quonset hut, Chase and Wen did as the Astronaut commanded and quickly jumped out of the car. Wen held her Glock ready, eyes taking in the area, unsure of the danger. Without introductions, the other two people who'd been waiting immediately climbed in the front seat of Chase and Wen's vehicle.

"Nash, what's going on?" Wen asked the Astronaut, staring intently into his own Antimatter Machine.

The Astronaut shook his head without answering as he quickly passed an electronic wand up and down their bodies. It beeped only when he reached her backpack. A few seconds later, the Astronaut pulled a tiny chip about the size of a US nickel out of her pack.

"GPS tracking devise," the Astronaut said, handing the chip to the woman in the driver's seat. "Go!"

Before Chase or Wen could protest, the unidentified couple pulled away in Chase's rental car and disappeared out the other end of the shed.

"What the . . . ?" Chase said.

"I assume the chip wasn't yours," the Astronaut said, smiling, but at the same time his face held a serious and worried expression. He looked back into the monitor of his machine.

"No," Wen answered. "It wasn't. Tess must have put it on when she patted my pack."

"Or the police did it while they had all our stuff," Chase said.

"How did you know?" Wen asked the Astronaut.

"The question is, how did *you* miss it?" He stared at her a moment, a teacher disappointed in a pupil. "No matter, now. If all goes well, they will continue to track your car all the way to Seattle."

"Who was that couple?" Wen asked.

"Friends," the Astronaut said.

"Thank you," Chase said, holding out his hand. "And nice to finally meet you in person."

"No offense," the Astronaut said, not taking his hand, "physical contact is not easy for me."

"Okay, none taken."

Wen wrapped her arms around the old man, who closed his eyes.

Chase smiled. Even a man who could not bear to be touched couldn't resist Wen.

"Chase, I've admired your work for quite a while," the Astronaut said, once Wen released him.

"RAI?" Chase said, referring to the artificial intelligence program he'd created that had amassed most of his fortune.

"No," the Astronaut said, looking directly into Chase's eyes. "SEER."

Chase could not mask his shock. SEER, an acronym for Search Entire Existence Result, had been secretly developed by Chase and his business partner, Dez. It employed advanced photonic quantum information processors and utilized deep learning, AI, quantum algorithms, and virtually every data point in digital existence to predict the future with stunning accuracy. Chase believed it could be used to do incredible good, to solve society's greatest problems, to liberate humans from complex burdens. He also knew that it would be extremely dangerous for the invention to become public. His imagination constantly created hundreds of possible ways SEER could be misused. He'd only entrusted the information to the five people closest to him.

"How did you learn of SEER?" Chase asked suspiciously.

The Astronaut, who'd been gazing intently into the monitor, looked at Chase as if he were a naïve child. "We must leave immediately," he said, folding up his Antimatter Machine. "Follow me. I'll explain on the way."

Chapter Fifteen

The normally hectic flow of the summer travel season at Philadelphia International Airport, like all major transportation hubs, had become even more crazy due to the fire bombings and the search for the Fire Bomber.

"So is he helping us or not?" Bull asked Lenny as they snaked through a gaggle of travelers between airline ticket counters.

"Yes. I mean, sort of," Lenny replied, agitated. "I told you what he said already." Then Lenny tripped over a toddler sitting on a suitcase.

Bull shook her head in exasperation and gave him a hand up. "Yeah, you did, and it doesn't make sense. Telling us to get out of town doesn't seem like much help."

"It is."

"I still don't even agree."

"They know," Lenny said, stopping to make eye contact. A man with two suitcases plowed into him.

"Idiot!" the man said as he untangled himself and continued rushing toward his gate.

"They know what you found," Lenny repeated. "You know they do. And they're looking for us right now."

"We're not easy to find," she said, looking around as if not believing what she'd just said.

"We can't just sit and wait for them." He started moving again.

"We're safer hiding in the city we know," she said, following him. "How do you know that the convict hasn't already sold us out?"

"He doesn't *do* that. That's why we went to him in the first place. Trust. He's working on it."

"Trust nothing!"

"He'll help us, but he can't do anything if we're *dead*."

Bull checked behind them again. Crowds of people coming and going, everybody seemed to be watching her. An assassin in the angry mob. She clenched her fist to stop her hands from shaking. Bull told herself she needed caffeine, but that wasn't really the cause of the shakes this time. Pure anxiety. What she knew had been creeping up on her ever since she'd first found it.

We're either about to be very rich, or I'm finally going to find out if there really is life after death, she thought, checking her pocket for the boarding pass for their flight to Los Angeles. *To live or die in LA.*

Chase and Wen followed the Astronaut through the woods, weaving past sugar pines, scrub oaks, juniper, and madrone, providing a thick canopy and making the three of them momentarily invisible from aerial surveillance. They oscillated between a tiny trail and picking their way through the underbrush.

"So CISS wants you to help find out who's behind the fire bombings," the Astronaut said, panting as they climbed a slight rise. "As you know, I'm an extremely logical person. And things that are not logical agitate me. Their request bothers me a great deal."

"Because it doesn't make sense that we could solve something that they could not?" Wen asked.

"No, because it means you're in serious danger, and we must figure out how this all connects."

"The question is how are all the targets linked?" Chase said, stumbling over an exposed root.

"One of the many questions," the Astronaut replied as they entered a denser section of Douglas fir, maples, and larger oaks. "Could your company, Balance Engineering, be a target of the Fire Bomber?"

"I don't see how," Chase said. "As you know, after I sold my artificial intelligence program, RAI, I reduced the number of employees dramatically, and even more once I became a fugitive. BE has less than forty employees now, and I have little to do with the day-to-day operations."

"But your work is important."

"These other companies all have thousands or tens of thousands, even hundreds of thousands of employees. BE has dropped completely off the radar in the tech world."

"But SEER—"

"It's such a secret project that most of our employees don't even know about it."

"Dez and Adya are running your company?"

Chase and his partner, Desmond "Dez" Jefferson, a brilliant African American engineer, had met at Stanford's renowned AI Lab, known as "SAIL." They'd founded Balance Engineering, then created Rapid Artificial Intelligence, "RAI," the most advanced form of AI ever devised.

It'd made them famous in the tech world, and also wealthy. After selling their invention for billions, they'd plowed the windfall into their next project, SEER. However, this one they kept secret. Only six people knew it existed.

"How do you know this stuff?" Chase suddenly asked, trying to sound calm.

"You can't contact them," the Astronaut said, ignoring his question.

"Why not?" Chase asked, incensed.

"Because if you analyze all the data, consider every angle, you will find that your company is indeed a target."

"And you've done all that just since we contacted you?"

"I've done it all just since you arrived." The Astronaut led them off the trail again to avoid an opening in the canopy which would have left them visible to the sky. "I expect Balance Engineering's headquarters will be hit by the Fire Bomber sometime within the next three days."

Chapter Sixteen

Still in Mission Control, Tess and Travis finally received the report answering the second most important question of the investigation: How were the bombers able to totally destroy buildings with apparently such limited effort and minimal amounts of explosives?

She read the summary while the technical adviser who'd delivered it waited. Travis, still on the phone, would read it later.

Tess wanted to clarify several points, even though the underlying conclusion left little doubt that the Fire Bomber had penetrated US intelligence at the highest levels, but she already knew that. The alarming part, that had her as close to panicking as Tess could ever be, was that the Bombers, or the people controlling them, also had a level of sophistication only possessed by the top three militaries in the world. And, even worse, the Fire Bomber understood how to stop the very thing she was charged with protecting.

She wanted to pace, she wanted to scream, she wanted to smash something—*anything*. "So they're using Doomsday," Tess said calmly, referring to the ARMA2020 Poly Explosive which the few with clearances high enough to be privy to its existence called "Doomsday" rather than by "the APE Bomb" acronym that the manufacturers had hoped it would be known. "But they've enhanced it beyond . . . "

"Yes, ma'am," the adviser began. "As you know, Doomsday, made by SkyNok, is a third-generation material created with a patented and classified manufacturing technique, and combined with tactically engineered components. The result is a lightweight and pliable material, packing ninety-two times more force than any prior forms of compound-explosives. However, that wouldn't be enough to bring these buildings down."

"Then how?"

"We don't know yet. There are forensic teams still scouring every bomb site and labs analyzing debris around the clock, but they aren't getting anything conclusive on other explosives yet."

"But there has to be another explosive, right?" Tess asked, keeping her voice level while walking to a monitor with a view of the outside.

"Yes. All the experts agree you can't cause this kind of destruction without something significant paired with Doomsday.

"What if they found a way to increase the Doomsday's potency, for lack of a better word?" Travis asked. "Have we talked to APE's manufacturer?"

"Is that possible? Tess asked.

The advisor nodded. "I guess so, but it's hard to imagine that they could push the yield on Doomsday to the point of that kind of destruction." He motioned to photos of the leveled buildings.

"What if the Fire Bombers are bringing more

Doomsday into the building than we think?" Travis suggested.

"But all the evidence points to there being one bomber at each location," Tess said. "It could be the same person, logistically speaking."

"I think we should look at that," the advisor said. "They could be using cloaking methods to get into the building undetected. Nothing more than shadows has been picked up on monitors, and satellites are getting nothing."

"Either way, ten people, or just one person, walking into any building in the world and dropping some Doomsday . . . However they're doing it, that kind of power, to bring down a building . . . Piece by piece they could destroy a city, the entire economy . . ."

"Yes," the adviser said, looking distraught. "Doomsday might have been the right name after all."

Powder checked his watch: two-thirty AM. *Time to move,* he thought while doing one final review on the plans. *I wish they would tell me why we're doing this one.* He didn't like being in New York City under normal circumstances—too many people—but getting ready to blow up a building there particularly bothered him. *This target has nothing to do with the mission, and that puts everything in jeopardy.*

Typically, Powder received his orders less than twenty-four hours before a scheduled strike, then operated using someone else's reconnaissance. Although that's how they'd done it during his time in special forces—relying on intel being fed to him during an ongoing operation—it made him crazy. *If someone gets killed, I don't mind taking the fall,* he thought, double-checking the equipment and his full-tocapacity hundred-pound pack. *I'm on the right side of history. I believe in this . . . this war.*

His smile disappeared as he chewed on beef jerky. He started moving toward the building. At this hour, it was unlikely he'd encounter anyone, but being in the city that never sleeps, Powder took precautions. His short black hair, disarming smile, and swimming pool-blue eyes made him look like the most trustworthy guy in the world—anything but a terrorist. He also wore a security uniform to further the honest image.

His mind raced back to the resentment. *But* this *has nothing to do with our war. This strike is a vendetta, and something that I shouldn't be involved with.*

He had considered refusing the order, or going up the chain of command and demanding an explanation as to why this strike was necessary. He'd even rehearsed telling them that he was cool with the risks of the other jobs because he understood the purpose—it all made sense. Powder was not a stupid man, and for the better part of the last twenty-four hours he'd been trying to figure out how this job fit.

But, in the end, he had decided to follow orders, for no other reason than he was a good soldier, and being that was more important to him than almost anything else.

Twenty-two minutes later, he was unpacking Doomsday and setting up the sacrificial laptop that would control the mayhem about to be unleashed on an unsuspecting and unrelated target. These people, unlike all the others, had done nothing wrong.

War is hell.

Chapter Seventeen

It was nearly midnight in Mt. Shasta, California, when Chase and Wen finally got ready to sleep. The Astronaut had taught them so much in the hours they'd been together that their minds felt numb.

"I keep replaying the surveillance footage over in my mind," Chase said as they lay in the darkness of a small, one-room cabin, referring to the video feeds the Astronaut had tapped into from Denver International Airport. They'd identified the bluetooth man and the gift shop man as following them. The Astronaut was able to use facial recognition programs to ID them as former US military—dropouts with no record since discharge. But the shooter who'd taken out the bluetooth man, the one Flint had claimed worked for him, was not identifiable.

Chase needed to know for sure that he was one of Flint's people. There was something in the footage that bothered him, but he couldn't figure out what. They'd watched it seven or eight times; it had been like seeing an action movie—a dozen angles, from different cameras, skillfully edited by the Astronaut—one in which Chase had the starring role, a hero about to be killed by enemy agents, only to be saved . . . by *whom*?

"Do you think he was with Flint?" Chase asked, reaching out to touch Wen softly.

"Yes."

"But was Flint's man trying to shoot me?" The troubling theory had been eating at him even before they saw the footage, and the surveillance video had not proved conclusive either way.

"He hit the bluetooth man at a distance of more than one thousand feet, from an impossible angle, with a kill shot. If he was aiming for you, you'd be dead on that terminal floor instead of the bluetooth man. Flint's man saved your life."

Chase wanted so much to believe her.

They fell into each other's arms kissing, caressing. The adrenaline of the day finally easing, and although exhausted, they made love. In the uncertainty of their situation, they found truth in each other.

Bull and Lenny were already exhausted when their flight landed at LAX. Sleep had been spotty ever since "the discovery," and stress had been constant. They'd switched planes twice for the cheaper fare, and there'd been a screaming baby in the row in front of them who hadn't stopped wailing for the entire three hour flight.

A fellow hacker called Skrunch met them and helped load their carry-on luggage into her 1984 VW Rabbit GTI. Bull told Lenny that Skrunch had gotten the moniker because after staring at a computer monitor 24/7 in a dark room, her face had kind of permanently scrunched up. Lenny stared at her, and had to agree it fit her.

Skrunch navigated relatively light traffic as they headed to Chesterfield Square, a seedy section of South LA. Her "apartment" was in a half-abandoned building. Homeless, drug dealers, junkies, squatters, and a few other hackers occupied the bulk of the dilapidated parts while a few struggling families tried to maintain some level of normalcy in the units still remaining in fairly livable condition.

Lenny didn't like the place, didn't care for Skrunch, and thought south Florida—where he had relatives—would have been a better place to hide than South LA. But Bull was in charge, and he didn't want to upset her—or, for that matter, endanger his family. The more Bull showed him about what she'd found, the more he understood that the people who owned the secrets would murder all his relatives and everyone in their neighborhood.

While Skrunch asked too many questions that Bull artfully blew off or steered back to inquiries about Skrunch's own exploits, Lenny sat lost in paranoid thoughts. He recalled a hacker they knew, a twenty-six-year-old "kid" who'd made a decent living doing identity theft and then selling security back to the victims to prevent identity theft. In his off-time, the kid spent way too much time gaming and watching vintage sci-fi flicks. All went well in his small life until, one night while fishing, he somehow became entangled in a series of blind communication websites and discovered that a gas explosion which had taken out a row of homes in California had actually been a professional hit, a hit that linked into some kind of deep government cover-up. They'd killed eight and injured thirteen "just to be sure." The kid didn't know what to do with the information —how to cash in—and asked a few people for advice. Less than twenty-four hours after he made the find, the kid's body was found floating in the Ohio River.

Lenny shivered.

"What's your problem?" Bull asked, noticing his discomfort.

"Nothing," Lenny replied defensively, realizing they were suddenly alone for the moment.

"You're putting too much negative into this. We're gonna make big. Stop worrying so much."

"Okay."

She regarded him skeptically. "Okay, like hell. You're thinking about the kid and the gas explosion, aren't you?"

"No." He didn't look at her when he answered. Lenny raked his greasy hair with shaky fingers. He needed a long, hot shower and a cold Coke.

"You are." She laughed in that way people do sometimes when they know they're right and someone is lying to them. "Well stop thinking about it. The kid was an idiot, blabbed like a baby, and anyway, no one knows where we are."

"Skrunch."

"I told you, don't be worrying about Skrunch. She's one of us. And besides, she doesn't even know what we got."

"She knows enough to know we're in trouble. She knows it's big—big spelled with a capital "B" and an "F-U.""

"We're here for one night. Time enough to sleep. We need to sleep, you know."

Lenny nodded. *Gone in the morning*, he thought. *And then the little threat from Skrunch would look like a tea party . . . Gone in the morning.*

Chapter Eighteen

The Astronaut showed up with the sunrise. Chase would've liked three more hours of sleep, but Wen appeared as if she'd just returned from a relaxing vacation, now ready to tackle anything.

"There's been another bombing, a few hours ago," the Astronaut said as Chase pulled on a shirt and found his shoes. "AutoSun, a vehicle software firm in New York."

"Any injuries?" he asked, unsure why the Astronaut was still helping them. He'd sold Wen the Antimatter Machine and never should have seen her again, but he was an extraordinarily odd man, and had apparently taken a liking to Wen. At least that's what her theory was.

It didn't matter, they *needed* him. "*The man is a super-IQ-hero!*" Wen liked to say in a cheerleading tone of voice.

"No injuries," the Astronaut said in his mechanical voice. "Same as the others. Middle of the night. Warning, phony evacuation." He handed them each an apple, a couple of muffins, and protein bars.

"Have you checked to see if it helps identify the

pattern?" Chase asked, nodding his head in thanks for the food.

The prior evening, during their long conversations, the Astronaut had put forth a theory that the bombings were no act of terror, but rather an orchestrated attack on something specific. "Because all the targets, thus far, have been tech companies," he'd explained, "all we need to do is find a common denominator between what each company does. Then a pattern will become clear and the motive should unlock. That will enable us to narrow down the list of suspects."

Chase and Wen had been thinking along the same lines, as had the FBI and everyone else going after the answer, but the Astronaut had a special gift for patterns—he could see details in data that even computers missed.

"When I plugged AutoSun into the system," the Astronaut said, "it actually scattered our previous build."

"That's crazy," Chase said, chewing on a muffin. "Inputting another incident, with all the pertinent details, should *narrow* the results. You're telling me it *broadened* them?"

"It's as if they bombed AutoSun just to confuse us."

"That's an awful lot of trouble," Wen said, pulling her pack on.

Chase looked puzzled and impatient. "We might have to just throw out the new results and leave AutoSun out of all future queries—"

"That will invalidate the findings," the Astronaut said. "You can't just choose which data set to employ."

"No offense, but SEER might have better luck correlating the facts and patterns than whatever you're using," Chase countered.

"I've told you, SEER is too risky to use right now," the

Astronaut said firmly. "Remember, SEER is likely a target." He motioned them toward the door.

"You told us you believed Balance was a target, not SEER. No one knows about SEER."

"These people know about everything," the Astronaut said, as if Chase was a fool not to understand this.

"Then it may be too dangerous *not* to use SEER," Chase shot back.

Wen gave him a disapproving look.

"I've told you my reservations," the Astronaut said, maintaining his patience. "But, of course, it's up to you." The Astronaut turned to Wen, took both her hands in his, looked into her eyes, then quickly turned away and blinked several times. He squeezed her fingers tightly, and whispered, "Don't let him. Please don't let him."

Chase heard the savant's words, but ignored them. He had no doubt the Astronaut was a wizard with math and computers, but Chase wasn't sure the brilliance carried over to simpler things.

The Astronaut allowed a hug from Wen, then waved to Chase. He'd arranged for them to use an old Nissan 4X4 pickup, and although it didn't look roadworthy, the Astronaut had given the engine a complete inspection and his stamp of approval.

"I'll see you in Heaven," were his final words to them, referring to the ultra-classified intelligence computer/satellite network. As they drove out of the trees, Chase took on the Astronaut's paranoia and suddenly felt as if all his enemies could see them again.

Chapter Nineteen

Flint Jones used the cab ride from New York's LaGuardia Airport to the AutoSun blast site as a chance to study the treacherous puzzle threatening the US economy and Chase's life.

The pieces don't fit, he thought. *Too few clues. They should have this guy by now . . .*

In order to keep up with the Fire Bomber, Balance Engineering had leased him a jet and pilot; nothing as fancy as Chase's Bombardier-8000, but it got the security chief where he needed to go. The trail of destruction left in the Fire Bomber's wake had stunned the normally jaded Flint. That such a weapon existed at all was scary enough, but that it had fallen into the hands of radical economic terrorists terrified him.

He pursued the Bomber because his job of protecting Chase required it. That Tess desperately needed to know the identity of the people behind the bombings, added to his urgency.

The assassination attempt at the Denver airport demonstrated the danger Chase faced. He should have been sent to a safe-house, but it wasn't Flint's call. Chase, being the boss, had even refused shadowing from Flint. Flint didn't even know Chase's current location—he hadn't been willing to share that information either. Fortunately, Tess had CISS resources keeping tabs on the tech billionaire.

Why would a man with so much to lose, risk his life unnecessarily?

Tess had also been feeding Flint a steady stream of data about the bombings, including the most recent of AutoSun, an advanced-stage start-up that made "brains" for vehicles —a system that monitored and computed everything from fuel usage, mileage, tire wear, battery life, and virtually every engine part to increase efficiency and avoid breakdowns.

Why would anyone want to destroy this company? Flint wondered. *How are these lunatics choosing their targets?* Flint knew they weren't really crazy, that the people blowing up these buildings were more dangerous than he wanted to think about, but he did anyway. *What if they turn their attention onto government buildings? What about universities, shopping malls, elementary schools? What if they decide they want to start killing people?* He knew why Tess was concerned—the Fire Bomber could turn order into chaos in a matter of days. And the government didn't have a clue as to who they were.

The media, with few concrete facts, had, in recent days, begun to speculate that perhaps the Chinese were behind the attacks—the motive being to take out all competition, particularly in military technology. Tense relations between the world's two biggest economies were already straining further. The Aadyah Action & Air bombing in India only fueled the theory more.

If this doesn't stop soon, he thought as he stepped out of the cab and approached the police line with credentials courtesy of Tess, *we're going to find out why they're doing this, and by then it'll be too late—either the economy will have collapsed, we'll be at war with China, or they will have manipulated us into some other unimaginable, apocalyptic scenario.*

The AutoSun building, like the others before it, could no longer be called anything other than a disaster area, a blasted-out urban war zone. In all his years with the CIA, working just about every third world coup and trouble spot, he'd never seen anything like the damage that the Fire Bomber inflicted—precise, total, and fast. As Flint surveyed the scene, a foreboding sense of disbelief overtook him as he tried to come to grips with the incredible destructive force of whatever super-weapon the Fire Bomber had unleashed. He talked to police officials, the fire chief, and representatives from the mayor's office.

"All people present and accounted for, no injuries or deaths." Astonishing.

While Flint stared at the cratered, burning wreckage of a once thriving business, he wondered the same thing everyone else had been asking since the 4th of July.

How do they choose their targets? What are they trying to accomplish? Why are they so careful not to kill anyone? Who's next? And, most desperately important, who the hell are they?

Flint's phone rang. Caller ID showed "unavailable." It could have been any number of people, but based on the fact that he was standing in the smoldering wreckage of the Fire Bomber's latest attack, he guessed Tess. As Flint accepted the call, an app on the phone immediately lit green, indicating the conversation would be encrypted.

"Hello?"

"Chase went and saw the Astronaut last night," Tess said without returning his greeting.

"Are you happy now that you've picked up the Astronaut?"

"No," Tess said. "I'm not happy at all. We didn't get the Astronaut, and we've temporarily lost Chase."

"How long ago did you lose him?" Normally, Flint might have been amused by an Astronaut yet again thwarting an intelligence agency, but he'd been counting on them to keep Chase safe while he tried to find out who was trying to kill him.

"Chase and Wen disappeared late yesterday. That's how we know he found the Astronaut. Without help, he never could have given us the slip."

"Where?"

"Southern Oregon, but they probably escaped miles before that."

"Escaped?" Flint echoed, questioning her word choice.

"Don't worry," Travis said, his voice startling Flint. "We'll find them."

Flint had no doubt that they would. CISS's resources exceeded even those of the NSA. If there was a more important government agency or a more powerful intelligence division, he didn't know about it.

Chapter Twenty

Tess turned to Travis after the call with Flint Jones, a worried look on her face. "What are they doing?" she asked as they left Mission Control and headed from the basement up to the helipad.

"Which they?"

"The Fire Bombers," she replied impatiently. "AutoSun isn't on the list. That company has nothing to do with horUS."

"Unless the Bomber knows something we don't," Travis said, checking notes on his computer tablet.

"Hell, they know a hundred things we don't—how they acquired the tech to bring a building down with a single bomb, where they got the information to choose the targets, what order they're going in—I could go on and on, but the most important thing they know is how they got the list. *Nine* people know about the list. *Nine* people understand horUS. How did the Bomber get the damned list?"

"Are you suggesting one of the nine leaked or sold the list?" Travis asked, trying to keep up as Tess nearly sprinted down the corridor toward the waiting chopper. He couldn't believe she was questioning that one of the nine high-level officials, who'd conceived and were overseeing horUS, could have been compromised.

"Of course not," Tess said as she juggled two tablets and touched commands on the screen of one of them. "The caliber of the horUS inner circle is unequaled—the President, the Director of National Intelligence, the Secretary of Defense, the CIA Director, the NSA Director, you, me . . ."

"Then someone got into the system—hacked?"

"Isn't that supposed to be impossible?" She looked at her tablets as if they might suddenly give them a contagious disease.

"No system is completely safe."

"Of course not, but we've been searching for a breach since the third bomb and nothing."

"Not *yet*."

"What if someone was really smart? Someone inside one of the companies, a person working on horUS without actually knowing they were—it's completely compartmentalized." She stormed around a corner, almost plowing into a startled group of analysts on their way to a meeting. "But this mystery employee . . . *saw* something. A pattern that told them that a section, or grouping, wasn't quite right, so he put some more pieces together, and then went searching, and boom, finds what he was looking for at every other company he checked. And just like that, by accident, he figured the whole damned thing out."

"These firms do have some of the smartest people working for them," Travis said, exploring her theory. "But then you've got a mighty big coincidence."

She stopped and turned to Travis. "What's that?"

"This mystery employee who stumbles into the most classified secret since the Manhattan Project puts together all the complex aspects of horUS in such a way—the precise and only possible way—to have it make sense, to be able to understand what it is, and then—and this is the *really* big leap—they are so troubled by what they discovered that they decide to stop it. They take it upon themselves to blow up every company linked to horUS."

"I'll admit that it's a little far-fetched, but so was nineteen Muslims bringing down the twin towers," she said, walking again.

Travis nodded. The thirty-seven-year-old rubbed his short goatee. The son of Nigerian immigrants, Travis, who spoke four languages fluently, a few more with passing form, had the experience to lead CISS alone, but the sub-agency had been given so much power that the President and Director of National Intelligence wanted it as a joint assignment. As a vet going from the army to CIA dark ops, Travis had navigated missions in dozens of hot spots earlier in his career, and had been given oversight of CISS's massive field operations, including the IT-Squad program, while Tess handled the admin side and case strategy. Travis, accomplished and tough, and having worked with Tess for years, thought she might be winging it. As good as she was, the Bombers were proving better. They were beating everyone.

Up until the Fire Bomber case, Tess and Travis had operated in perfect balance with each other, sharing duties and decisions as co-equals. They were often amused knowing that subordinates referred them as Yin and Yang. However, they were both feeling the strain on this one.

"Then we have a similar issue," Travis said, returning to his theory. "This mystery employee also just happens to not only be an expert in bombs, but is able to create and deploy what is possibly the most advanced explosive device ever conceived. One even we still don't understand, and by "we" I mean every weapons engineer and the complete intelligence apparatus of the most powerful military in the history of the world."

"Yes," Tess said, a look of sudden recognition on her face that quickly changed to one of horror. "It is possible that employee was, or is, working at the behest of a foreign power?" she whispered.

Travis's expression also contoured into a grimace. "Oh no . . . That would explain a lot. We need to profile every employee at every company on the list."

Tess nodded. "We need to do it today."

"It could take weeks to be thorough."

"We don't have weeks. Bring in NSA teams. Start with the companies that haven't been hit yet."

"Why?"

"Because the employee wouldn't want to decimate his source of information until near the end. If his building gets destroyed, so does his ability to siphon more data." She climbed into the waiting helicopter. "The Bomber is in one of those remaining tech corporations. Let's find the bastard!"

Chapter Twenty-One

While Flint combed through the debris for clues he would never find, Powder drove past a building in Austin, Texas that would not be standing in eighteen hours. He'd slept some on the flight, but not enough. Fortunately, his time in the military and a troubled childhood had taught him to rest when not fighting and sleep whenever a moment could be found.

All the details of the job had been sent via the normal encrypted method—a self-erasing site on the darknet which required three alphanumeric passwords to access and a double code key to read. He wondered how long it would take for the authorities, or someone else, to anticipate where he'd be next.

Surely the tech titans or intel kings can devise a way to use prior bomb sites to predict future ones. Surely those lying, manipulating snakes at the Pentagon and CIA have a list—the same list that my superiors possess. Surely they know why this is happening, and surely they could have people waiting at each remaining location, waiting to stop me and our righteous revolution, waiting to kill me. He bit down on an herbal cough drop. *So why don't they?*

Staring over a line of men shooting at targets, Gunner contemplated the success of the bombings thus far. The sound of gunfire, like a lullaby to him, fostered deep thinking. He needed to strategize. Their stealth operations had been flawless—other than India, though, losing a man was an acceptable loss. AAA was a critical piece in the path to victory.

He absently traced the scar on his cheek, something nagging at him. The government had been slower than he'd anticipated. He wondered if one of the secret alphabet agencies might be setting up to use the bombings as a false flag.

Another excuse to take more of our freedoms, a reason to arrest and clamp down on innocent and legitimate opposition groups and outspoken individuals. The idiots on social media don't realize that Uncle Sam keeps tabs on everything they say on their clumsy newsfeed, reads all their emails, records their calls, tracks them through their cell phones . . . He kicked the dirt with steel-toed combat boots. His double layer canvas pants and drab-green tee-shirt, hugging his muscled frame, were splattered with mud.

Another man dressed in fatigues jogged over to Gunner, interrupting his thoughts.

"We've just received word that Chase Malone is involved."

The news came as no surprise to Gunner. However, the militia leader did not welcome it. He knew Chase as the inventor of RAI, a super enhanced artificial intelligence program that accelerated the dangerous race that could only end in humanity losing out to the supremacy of machines.

"Malone's off grid," Gunner said, recalling an intelligence report he'd seen. The militia had people tracking thirty-seven tech titans that Gunner considered the most dangerous. Chase Malone might be the top of that list because of RAI, the rumors of a secret project even more advanced, and the fact that he had apparently decided to disappear. People only do that for two reasons—they want to do something bad, or bad people are after them. He didn't know which one it was with Malone, but even if it was the latter, that was yet another sign of trouble.

"Apparently not anymore."

Gunner turned to his subordinate. "If Malone has come out of hiding and is looking for me, I've got no choice but to issue a K-order on him."

The man looked at him, concerned. "Should we wait for the next report?"

Gunner encouraged debate among his people, so the question didn't bother him, but he didn't want to waste time. "He's already on the track list. Do you know what that means?"

"That he's the enemy," the man responded without hesitation.

"Exactly," Gunner said, pulling a ball cap over his thick, sandy-blond hair after realizing his forehead and nose were getting sunburned. "He is dangerous. A threat to us and to the way of life we are trying to save. Chase Malone is not just an enemy to you and me, he is an enemy to all humanity."

"Yes, sir."

His dark eyes raged. "So I'm certainly not going to wait until he learns the truth."

"But with the bombings at a critical point, it doesn't seem to be the best time to take such drastic action."

"Because of the bombings, it's precisely the right time." He looked toward the east horizon.

"Yes, sir," the man said, still looking concerned. "I'll get the order out right away. Is this something we should make Powder aware of?"

"No. He needs no distractions," Gunner said, reaching for the binoculars hanging at his belt. "If Malone is working with the CIA, they'll soon be able to identify the targets before we get there. That means Powder's job is getting more difficult every minute."

Lenny, ripped from a fitful sleep, heard the Russian accent just before a hand slapped his face and another clutched his upper arm so tightly he cried out in pain.

"Get up stupid!" a man barked as he lifted Lenny from the mattress and shoved him against the wall.

"What, who?" Lenny managed to say before getting slapped again.

"You owe me money, you stolen dog!"

"Who?" Lenny repeated. He heard Bull screaming and tried to get past the large Russian who smelled like wet cement and over-used restaurant grease.

"Your pretty girlfriend owes us money, too," the brute said, laughing. "She can pay in another way. Spread your legs baby!"

Lenny swung at the man, kicking at the same time. His fist connected, but the retaliation came hard, and the excruciating pounding against his head felt for a split second as if his skull had opened. Then everything went black.

Chapter Twenty-Two

Westfield relayed the report to Ryker. "We've located them."

"How far from us?" Ryker asked. His black knit clothes didn't hide his beer gut, yet everything else was sculpted.

Westfield checked the large screen across from his desk. "You're about sixty-five minutes out. We should have them by then. Cox and his team are ready to strike."

"They have a visual?"

"Eyes on." Westfield pressed a series of keys. "I just sent you their coordinates."

"Got 'em. We're on our way," Ryker said, signing off.

Damon checked the new GPS coordinates, then turned to his partner. "We've got to turn around. Get off at the next exit."

"So, are you happy?" Ryker asked. "We don't have to visit Malone's parents after all."

Damon continued scanning reports. "I'll be happy when we actually get Chase."

"Cox could still screw this up," Ryker said, steering the

car onto the exit. "But how hard is it to put a bullet in a man's head?"

As Chase drove the old pickup south down Interstate 5, he and Wen had another debate about WOLF.

"They may be able to help us," Wen said. "They're plugged into just about every alternative group around—subversives, resistance, militias, rebels, misfits, whatever."

"Hey, if you think The Cause might have a lead, by all means call them. But that doesn't mean I'm joining."

Wen nodded and let it rest. Her silence brought Chase's hand to hers.

"What are you thinking?"

"I was recruited into MSS as a child because my dad served with them. They like kids of parents who were incredibly good and clever. My dad always said one thing: '*Never betray yourself*.' I think it was his way of saying *don't let the State control you*." She looked into the distance. "I don't like war. I don't like fighting." She turned and stared at him, hard. "But I like to win, and it's all I really know."

"I know," Chase said, squeezing her hand. "I thought I was going to disappear into the Tibetan mountains and meditate to find my path, but it really wasn't in my cards. What about your mother? You don't mention her much."

"I miss her very much, but I'm much more like my father. I think my mother found much of their lives overwhelming. But she did say to me, at least one thousand times, what translates into English as, '*Rise to the occasion*.' Perhaps it was her own personal mantra, but I often hear her at unexpected times, saying those four words to me . . . and I try my best."

"I wish I could have known her," Chase said quietly.

For the next few miles Wen checked out the Antimatter Machine.

"Can you notice a difference with it?" Chase asked, referring to the changes the Astronaut had made to her special computer.

"It's faster. There are a few more icons. He told me this one is a direct link to Heaven and that it's cloaked."

"Meaning the NSA can't see when you're connected?"

"Right, and it gives us three more minutes before they can track our login."

"So twelve minutes twenty-nine seconds? Not twenty-eight, or thirty-two?"

"Those seconds can add up, believe me. I'd be dead a few times without shaving seconds from a situation."

"I'm sure. I'm just saying, it's pretty precise."

"The Astronaut is precise."

"Strange dude."

"Wonderfully so."

"Reminds me of Rain Man."

"Who?"

"Dustin Hoffman, Tom Cruise, the movie Rain Man . . ."

She looked at him blankly.

"Never mind," Chase said. "What about that icon?"

"This one gives us the string to access CISS."

"*All* of CISS?"

"Just their Fire Bomber files."

"But they're giving us those anyway."

"Not everything," she said as an unusually strong gust of wind hit the car. "This lets us see what they decided not to share with us—such as their agents, list of suspects, forensics from the scenes, and more."

"Are you in there now?" Chase asked, checking the time.

"No, I don't want to risk it yet."

"I thought it was cloaked for twelve-twenty-nine and thirty-eight point-five milliseconds," Chase said, gripping the wheel tighter as powerful winds rocked a semi just ahead of them.

"The Astronaut warned that nothing is ever certain," she answered, ignoring his usual sarcastic attempt at humor.

"That's an understatement."

"Where's all that smoke coming from?" Wen asked. Traffic slowed as all the other drivers caught sight of the massive columns of smoke.

"Must be a forest fire."

"Or a bomb," Wen said, shifting in her seat. "That's a *big* fire." She began searching for information on the Antimatter Machine.

The smoke dominated the southern sky, going thick and black on the horizon to hazy brown, and then dense billowy white monsters that looked as if they could produce a catastrophic thunderstorm.

"The wind must really be fanning the flames," Chase said as he passed a semi traveling with its hazards on up the steep grade. "It's completely filling in."

"Here's some information," Wen said, reading from her screen. "The fire is believed to have started before sunrise. The first reports came in at six-eighteen PM last evening, near Gold Hills subdivision outside of Redding. But it exploded overnight."

"Redding? Is the airport still open?" Chase asked. "Is our plane safe?"

"The unusually low humidity, and winds exceeding fifty miles per hour, combined to form perfect conditions for a mega-fire," Wen said, reading from a news site. "Oh, and it says here that authorities are using the airport as an evacuation center and shelter."

"Already?" he asked as they came down the next rise, where the extent of the fire became more clear.

Smoke descended, filling the area like a heavy fog. The smell of burning trees invaded even through the truck's air conditioning. As they drove around the next bend, it appeared as if a giant bomb had been dropped. The smoke lifted momentarily, revealing lines of high flames in the near distance.

"We'd better turn back," he said. "It's not all bad. We can stop at that diner back in Fisher. The Astronaut said they have really great fries."

Wen's response was lost as the back window of the pickup suddenly shattered.

Chapter Twenty-Three

Crystals of glass exploded into the pickup's interior, showering them with the jagged pieces, cutting into their exposed skin, and hitting the windshield. Wen undid her seatbelt, spun around, and aimed her Glock 19 simultaneously while Chase swerved and then righted the truck.

"Was that a gun shot?"

"Yes, and it's about to be another one!" Wen shouted, firing her gun at a silver Toyota ForeRunner. "Get us out of here!"

Chase cut over to the shoulder, sped up, and raced past the slowing line of vehicles before driving back onto the highway about a quarter of a mile ahead.

"There it is again!" Wen yelled as the ForeRunner pulled out from around a semi and came up fast. "It's that silver ForeRunner back there."

Chase checked the rearview mirror. "We've got to get off the interstate," he said, stomping on the accelerator.

"That's going to happen anyway," Wen said, glancing at

the Antimatter Machine. "About eight miles ahead, they've closed I-5 in both directions and they're going to detour us."

"Is there an exit before that?"

"Yes."

"Then that's the one we're taking. I don't want to be trapped in a line of cars crawling along at ten miles an hour on some secondary road while Mr. ForeRunner takes shots at us." Chase continued to weave through the thickening traffic at an increasing speed.

"They've got a better engine than us," Wen said as the speedometer passed ninety. The silver ForeRunner continued to close in on them.

"Everyone has a better engine than this Tonka Toy, but they don't have a better driver!" Chase laughed like an evil wizard, then winked at Wen as he switched back to the shoulder about a mile and a half before the exit. In his heart, he had always thought of himself as a race car driver.

"The ForeRunner just got cut off," Wen said.

Chase checked his mirrors and saw several other cars were now driving on the shoulder between them. "That's the break we needed." He pushed the truck to its limit, spraying gravel and fighting the wheel to maintain control. They flew down the exit ramp and only slowed to sixty to take the turn at the stop sign, then hit the gas pedal again, heading in the direction of the smoke.

"Is this a good idea?" Wen asked, motioning to the darkening sky.

Chase glanced into the rearview mirror in time to see the ForeRunner come off the ramp less than a thousand yards behind them. "At least we're still moving."

"But for how long?" Wen asked. "We're driving straight into the fire." She slid an extra clip into her gun and another into her pocket, readying for the inevitable shootout. The road was empty—no one else was this crazy.

"Look up ahead, the smoke is killing visibility. It's like fog," Chase said above the roar of the engine. "Soon we won't be able to see ten feet ahead of us." The wind and smoke created a storm of blowing leaves and ash. "If we can just find a place to pull in . . . "

"Hopefully the ForeRunner will sail right past," Wen said, catching on. "If they don't, then we'll be waiting for them."

"Right," Chase said, starting to cough.

"Okay." Wen slapped a clip in a third gun. "We don't know what they've got in that ForeRunner. You're gonna have to shoot, too."

Chase nodded. Wen knew he didn't like guns, but she also knew he liked dying even less. She touched his thigh. They smiled quickly at each other, both knowing they could be done for, both knowing the feelings for each other strengthened their luck, or was it—

"Ah, hell," Chase said, squeezing her hand. "How the hell did we get into this!"

"I always thought Nuku Hiva was boring," Wen said, smiling, and also starting to cough. "How many days can you really spend on a sunny beach in paradise?"

"Speak for yourself. I wish we were there now!"

As predicted, the smoke enveloped them as he drove faster into the blind.

"Damn it," he barked. "I didn't count on the smoke also making it impossible for us to see a place to hide. We're going to have to pull to the side somewhere and hope."

"They'll see us for sure," Wen said, looking back into the gray smoke.

"We'll just have to be ready."

They jumped out of the truck, forced their way into the underbrush, and pointed their guns back to the road. Chase wasn't sure who was getting ambushed—the men in the ForeRunner, or themselves.

Chapter Twenty-Four

The ForeRunner passed Chase and Wen's truck faster than visibility would normally allow—at least forty miles per hour.

"Did they see us?" Wen asked, instinctively whispering.

"I can't tell," Chase said, his hand sweaty on the gun. "Let's get back in the truck and drive the other direction—away from them *and* the fire—before they figure it out."

Chase handed the gun back to Wen.

"Keep it," she said. "You need to get used to carrying one." She winked at him, giving her most seductive smile.

"O-kay," Chase said hesitantly, trying not to inhale more smoke. He thought about stuffing it in the daypack slung over his shoulder, but there wouldn't be time to retrieve it if he needed it. The other option would be putting it in his waistband, but he worried he might accidentally shoot off something important, so he just held it in his left hand and headed back toward the truck.

Before he reached the driver's door handle, the smoky

silence gave way to the rumble of an approaching vehicle from the wrong direction.

"I'm sure that's them!" Wen whispered loudly, pointing her Glock toward the sound.

"We won't know until it's too late."

"They'll expect us to be near the truck. Let's surprise them from over there instead." She pointed to a drop-off on the other side of the road under a solid stand of trees. "We might even get a chance to see how many there are."

Chase wasn't sure about giving up the cover and only means of escape in the truck, but Wen knew a lot more about these things than he did.

Visibility, now less than twenty feet, was both a help and a hindrance. They couldn't easily be seen, but nor could they see their pursuers.

The silver ForeRunner slowly crawled out of the thick smoke like a serpent ready to strike. It slowed at the side of their pickup truck, idling for a long, evil moment. Two men jumped out of the back, fanning machine guns, looking for targets. With a sudden lurch, the ForeRunner swung in behind their truck and stopped. The driver and another man quickly climbed out and inspected the pickup.

"Should we attack?" Chase whispered.

"Four guys with HK MP7 submachine guns? No. Not until we have to. Nothing personal, but it's really four against one."

A sound must have caught the men's attention, as suddenly they sprayed machine-gun fire in the direction they'd just driven from. In those few seconds, Wen and Chase made a dash for the ForeRunner, diving into the open driver's side door.

Even as they untangled themselves, Chase pushed the

ignition button, hoping one of the men was close enough to make it work. The engine came to life. Chase shifted into reverse and pressed on the gas pedal with both feet.

The pickup truck blocked the wall of bullets that the men unloaded in their direction. Chase couldn't see more than a few feet beyond the end of the hood, but never eased up on the accelerator. They sailed into the smoke, using the scraping branches and loose, crumbling edge of the road to keep them on the graded surface.

"We should be okay to slow down," Chase said, concerned they might plow into a tree or an oncoming vehicle.

"What's to stop them from coming after us in our truck?"

"I've got the keys in my pocket."

"That'll only slow them down for a minute," she said. "But the smoke should be clearing as we get back to the interstate." Wen held up an extra key fob with a car rental company tag she found sitting in the console. "I guess this is how it started."

"Lucky for us they always give you two."

"They'll be behind us any second," Wen said as the smoke thinned. "And the Interstate is closed." She pulled the Antimatter machine out and began searching the maps while Chase compulsively checked the rearview mirror. "There's a network of logging roads all through here. Let's find one."

A few minutes later, the Antimatter Machine lost signal.

"There's one," Wen said, pointing. "Take it." She glanced behind to make sure the truck wasn't in sight.

"It's more like a trail," Chase said, but turned anyway.

The winding "trail" turned out to be a Forest Service

road and was in decent shape. They put some distance between them and the main highway until the smoke shifted again. As the ForeRunner climbed to the top of a steep turn, flames raced in from the South.

"I don't think we should attend this party," Chase said, in his best English accent.

Sparks and cinders swirled with ash through the air, creating a sweeping barrier.

"Turn around and get us back to the main road," Wen said.

"Behind us!" he shouted.

Wen spun around in her seat and saw a wall of flames chasing them. "We're totally boxed in!"

"We've still got road ahead of us."

"But we don't even know where it goes!" she yelled, still unable to get satellite imaging of the area, or even a cell signal. They guessed the fire and smoke had cut off all forms of communication. Wen tried the astronaut's icon, which failed to do anything other than frustrate her.

"It's gotta go *somewhere*," Chase yelled.

"Yeah, deeper into the fire."

Chase pushed the forerunner, desperately testing its four-wheel-drive abilities as they bounced along the now rutted dirt road.

"Look!" Wen shouted, pointing.

Chase followed her arm and saw the terrifying sight. The fire had jumped the road and was now about to overtake them on the north side. "If it gets ahead of us, we're done!" Chase yelled, giving the accelerator everything, fighting to maintain control as the ForeRunner careened across holes, rocks, and knobby roots. Flying cinders and debris landed on the hood, burning like a campfire across the windshield. Through the sunroof, they could see sparks caught in the luggage rack as fire and flame rained around them. Both were coughing and choking on the suffocating heat and smoke.

"We're going to burn up!" Wen screamed.

Chapter Twenty-Five

Halfway to the Pentagon for a briefing on horUS and the bomber, Tess and Travis received an urgent message and ordered the pilot to return to CISS headquarters. Twenty minutes later, they were in Mission Control, watching north central California burn.

"He's *in* that?" Tess asked the analyst who'd been briefing them. She pointed at the massive monitor filled with close-up satellite images of what was being called the Redding Complex Fire.

"Yes, ma'am. That's our best guess."

"Can we get him out of there?"

"Two IT-Squads en route."

"ETA?"

"First Squad will drop in twenty-two minutes."

"Unbelievable!" Travis cut in. "When's the second Squad getting there, tomorrow?"

Tess ignored his usual sarcasm, knowing he probably felt partially to blame since he was in charge of field operations and they should have had Squads closer. "Are there any local officials who can get in faster?"

"They're kind of busy evacuating and fighting the fire. You can see it's a monster," the analyst said. "Even if we could persuade anyone to lend us people, we don't know where to send them yet."

"We're reviewing the satellite feeds," another analyst said. "Matching data and the computer—"

"When will you have something?" Travis interrupted. "Tell me it will be before my Squad gets there," he checked the timer on one of the monitors, "in nineteen minutes."

"That's possible."

"Make it happen," Tess said, but they all knew it might not. There was a ton of data and they still hadn't isolated Chase and Wen's exact location since they'd lost them at the Astronaut's shed. A team had stopped and questioned the couple heading north on I-5 who had the tracking chip, but they knew nothing and were released.

The computers were narrowing the real location by going in backwards—the programs could tell them everywhere Chase wasn't, but there were still quite a few places open.

"Communications are down, and our closest satellites are having trouble seeing through the smoke."

Travis shook his head. "Even nineteen minutes won't do it. The IT-Squad could drop miles from wherever Chase is. It's a damned inferno. They could be bar-b-cued by the time we get to them!"

Tess looked back at the screen. "They could already be barbecued."

Lenny woke dizzily in an alley, head throbbing like a drummer from a heavy-metal band had taken up residence in his brain. He tried to stand, but his wobbly legs wouldn't allow it. Taking deep breaths, he slowly attempted to put it back together.

Los Angeles, I'm in LA, Skrunch, the Russian thug . . . Bull— where is Bull!

He scanned the area—a homeless man sleeping on discarded newspapers, a big, unidentifiable rusting piece of machinery, a haphazardly stacked assortment of too many empty beer boxes, and two overfilled dumpsters.

"Oh no!" he yelled, forcing himself to his feet and stumbling to the first dumpster. He twisted and pulled, trying get high enough to see inside, hoping her body wasn't . . . but he fell back to the ground and threw up, his head protesting the efforts by inflicting more blinding pain and louder drumming. He absently realized his ribs were making it hard to breathe. He wiped his mouth.

A ringing startled him. He didn't recognize the tone, but it seemed to be coming from his pants. Hoping it was a call from Bull, Lenny fished the phone from his pocket.

"Hey, mangy dog, you are awake," the Russian said.

"Where's Bull, you son of—"

"What a silly name for a pretty girl," the Russian said. "We think she should be called something nicer, like rose petal or play-thing, or—"

"*Where is she?*"

"Listen to me, dirt-for-brains, you do not ask the questions. You want to see your girlfriend again, then sell your score and bring me the money."

"What score? I don't—"

"Shut up! You have forty-eight hours. Do not lose this phone."

"Wait!"

Nothing.

"Damn it," Lenny said, about to throw the phone against the wall before realizing it was his only lifeline to Bull.

I don't have the score. Bull didn't...

But then he remembered.

There is a way.

"Lenny," a familiar voice echoed down the alley—a voice he hated, a voice he would like to hear wheezing for her last breath: Skrunch.

He turned, summoning draining strength, searching for a brick, a pipe, anything that could inflict pain. She had to suffer like he and Bull were suffering—but her appearance halted his rage.

Skrunch looked awful, torn clothes, a bruise on her face, and her eyes were scared. Then he noticed the blood.

"Lenny," she called out again. Their eyes met and suddenly her expression turned to pure fear.

His anger shifted to panic as he felt the world begin to spin. His legs went rubbery, and he crumpled to the ground. The last thing he heard was Skrunch yelling his name one more time.

Chapter Twenty-Six

Towering, raging flames closed in on the ForeRunner as Chase and Wen continued to choke on the heat and increasing smoke.

"There's no way out!" Wen yelled above the roar of the fire.

Chase cut the wheel hard to the right—the direction the flames had last filled—and floored it, driving straight into the blaze. The ForeRunner bounced over small fallen trees and burst through burning foliage. The sizzling heat seared a warning into their minds that time was running out. They couldn't see anything but fire.

"I don't know if we're still going the right way!" Chase yelled.

"There *is* no right way!"

Chase, hoping they could reach somewhere that the fire had already burned through before the ForeRunner became engulfed, kept his foot pressed all the way down. The ForeRunner hit a rise, caught air, and went soaring into the torturous abyss. It felt as if they were flying over the canyons of hell, and that an evil, glowing claw might snatch them at any second.

This isn't going to end well, Chase thought, envisioning them dropping into a volcanic cauldron.

They didn't see the tree—a towering Ponderosa Pine—until the front of the ForeRunner buckled like an aluminum can as it rocketed into its mighty trunk. Airbags hit Chase and Wen as the SUV held—partially wrapped around the broad trunk—suspended in midair among the burning branches for a mere moment, before plummeting to the charred ground. A stand of young cedars in full flame broke their fall as the vehicle hit the blackened earth on the two driver's side tires, rolling twice before its continuing momentum pushed it sliding down an open slope. When the ForeRunner met one more tree, a cottonwood, gliding almost slow motion into the trunk under still-green leaves, they were both conscious and gasping, gulping in fresh air like a free-diver coming up from the depths.

"Are you okay?" Chase asked, surprised at the sound of his own voice as the battered—nearly unrecognizable—silver SUV stopped, upright and flame-free.

"Alive. You?"

"Good enough. Let's get out of this thing before it blows up or something."

"That only happens in the movies."

"Isn't this a movie? Sure feels like 007 should be showing up any second," he said, untangling from the airbag and pulling off the seatbelt that had just saved his life.

"You are 007," Wen said, unsuccessfully trying to get her belt off. "I'm stuck, something must have jammed the thing."

Chase pulled out his Leatherman-Wave multi-tool and quickly cut her belt.

"See, you really are James Bond," she said, freeing herself and grabbing her pack.

Her door was mashed into the cottonwood and his wouldn't open, so they both slid out the driver's side window. The metal of the door was still hot to the touch, and the ground was smoking.

They scrambled to get away from the fire, the flames flicking just feet away from the mangled ForeRunner and the miraculously saved cottonwood tree, then they saw the only thing that could save them.

"Water!" Wen yelled.

"It must be Shasta Lake," Chase said as they ran through a break in the fire and down the hill. "I remember seeing it on the way up."

"Look at all that water," Wen said, reaching the bank. "And you were right—this must be a movie. Look!"

Chase followed her gaze and saw a faded old canoe, with two oars and a cooler sitting in it. Chase checked the cooler, hoping for a cold beer, a wet anything. "Empty."

"Let's go!"

Minutes later, they were forty feet from shore and rowing into the middle of the largest reservoir in California. Wen and Chase could see the fire had expanded to both sides of the lake, but forty-seven square miles of water now protected them.

"We're safe," Chase said.

Wen looked to the open sky as the wind carried the smoke to the north. "We're never safe."

"Tess, we got 'em," Travis said, calling her away from a phone call in a corner of Mission Control.

She went to the giant monitor. A technician shifted the view.

"Zoom in," she demanded. A second later, they were watching Chase and Wen rowing across Shasta Lake. "If it wasn't for the ring of fire surrounding them, they could be lovers on a romantic picnic," she mused.

"Well, they're about to have some uninvited guests," Travis said. "The first IT-Squad will be splashing in on them in about seven minutes."

Chapter Twenty-Seven

Chase and Wen paddled out to the middle of the reservoir. It seemed as if they were trapped in a volcano, with flames racing to the shore all around them. The winds, gusting over fifty miles per hour, tossed their little boat in the choppy water as if it were a toy in a bath.

"Our crazy movie has turned into an Armageddon sequel," Chase said, brushing glowing embers from his hair as burning debris and ash continued to pelt them. He scooped handfuls of water on his head. "Get your hair as wet as possible. There's fire everywhere!"

"Not there," Wen said, pointing to the dam. "If we can make it to the dam, maybe there's a vehicle we can 'borrow,' or at least a working land line."

Chase pushed the oar faster to match Wen's stride. The smoke-filled air made the exertion difficult.

"Chase!" Wen shouted.

He turned quickly to see a small fire burning right behind him. Wen splashed up some lake water and doused the flames the wind had sent.

"Your shirt!"

Chase patted several sparks off his shirt. "I thought we'd be safe in the water."

"Would you rather be where we were?" Wen pointed back to the shore they'd come from, which was now a wall of fire.

Chase shook his head. A few harrowing minutes later, they saw a sign:

WARNING DAM AHEAD - RESTRICTED AREA - DANGER
DO NOT GO PAST THIS POINT

"We can't turn back now," Chase said, resuming his paddling.

The suction of the dam suddenly pulled them fast through the water. The smoky winds swirled.

"This is crazy!" Chase said as the canoe became unstable. "We're going to capsize."

"Would James Bond say that?" Wen asked.

"In this case, I think he might."

Their boat slammed into the concrete wall, the force of the water rocking and battering the boat.

"We've got to get out," Wen said as the boat was pulled away from the wall and then slammed back again.

Chase, who'd spent a summer climbing skyscrapers for his brother's window washing business, spotted a handhold —a pipe or conduit just out of reach. "If we can get to that, we might make it to the catwalk!"

Wen looked up as the canoe smashed into the wall again. There was a walkway hanging on the backside of the dam next to the spillway intakes. She wasn't sure the leap was doable, but knew Chase could make it. "Go!" she yelled.

Timing the rocking motion, Chase thrust the blade of the oar into the tiny space behind the pipe. It didn't hold, but he used the momentum to swing himself up and clutched at the pipe, which was bigger than he thought. While kicking at the wall, his hands somehow gained purchase and held. "Do the same thing!" he yelled back while climbing higher.

Wen's oar broke as it struck the concrete, but she was already flying through the air. Chase saw she wasn't going to make it and slid down the pipe, swinging his legs out in a desperate attempt for her to have something to grab.

Her left hand caught his right foot as she expelled a silent scream from the pain of her body slamming the hard slab. Wen's strength and concentration, honed by years of training in the Chinese elite MSS, came forth, and she pulled her body up until they were both holding onto the pipe. A minute later, they climbed onto the catwalk.

"Well, that was fun," Chase said, grabbing her for a quick, celebratory kiss. "You okay?"

"Good enough. You think that was exciting, we still have to get through *that*," she said, holding her side while pointing to the towering flames and smoke consuming trees at an incredible rate.

"Maybe we can get the Antimatter Machine up and call in some help," Chase said as they rushed onto the deserted dam.

Tess took the call from the Deputy Assistant Secretary of Defense. Many joked that he'd been a permanent fixture in

Washington since the days of Abraham Lincoln, but Tess knew there was nothing funny about the Under Secretary. The two of them, more than anyone else, had been responsible for developing and protecting horUS, the most secret government project in the more than seven decades of the CIA's existence. They both knew that as much good as the horUS project could do, its exposure would be the biggest scandal in all of American history.

"They'll riot in the streets," the Under Secretary said.

"We still don't know that this is about horUS," Tess said as a driver opened her door. She got out and walked briskly across the hot tarmac. "New York is not on the list."

"You're smarter than that, Tess. The Bombers may have multiple agendas, but they clearly know about horUS."

"I disagree," she said, climbing the stairs of a waiting plane. "There are a lot of tech firms on the list. So far less than half of the Fire Bomber's targets are horUS companies."

"That's a load of guff! You need to get Squads at every horUS company and catch these bastards."

"Even if I had the manpower, how would I explain that to the media? Why those companies and not Apple, or Oracle—"

"They're big enough to take care of themselves."

"Really? What about Texas Instruments, Emerson, Qualtech—"

"Who?"

"Exactly. There are too many companies that fit the target profile."

"I don't care. We can make the media do the story the way it needs to be."

"This story is too big. Sure, we can control all the larger outlets, but the internet is filled with fifty, a hundred, even more so-called news sites that will pick us apart."

"We can't let them do any more. If you won't do it, then I'll send troops."

"Oh, the media will love that. Troops surrounding every business in America affiliated with technology."

"The media *will* love it if we spin it the right way. They sure as hell don't like the Fire Bomber crapping all over us like this."

"Are you trying to prevent them from stopping horUS, or exposing it?"

"Both!" the Under Secretary barked. "And I'm trying to win World War III—or hadn't you noticed it's started?"

Chapter Twenty-Eight

Wen and Chase stood atop Shasta Dam, looking at the fire running up to the lake on three sides.

"Incredibly, we made it," Chase said.

"It's still a long walk," Wen replied.

"Look at that." Chase pointed to a sign. "When Shasta Dam was completed, it was considered one of the greatest engineering feats in history, and was the second-tallest dam in the United States. Only Hoover dam was taller. It's six hundred and two-feet straight down to the Sacramento river."

"Great," Wen said. "Forgive me if I'm not in the mood for sightseeing."

"I'm an engineer . . . it's cool . . . "

"Cell service is still out, but we might be able to get a satellite link from here." She started to pull her pack off to retrieve the Antimatter Machine when four armed men appeared at the north end of the dam.

"Who are those guys?" Chase asked, exasperated, thinking he recognized some of them as the original crew from the ForeRunner. "How are they finding us? What kind of surveillance are they using?"

"I don't know, but they must be fireproof," Wen said, motioning toward the acres of forest burning behind the men. "Here they come!"

The four started running at them, guns pointed. Wen and Chase ran in the opposite direction until they spotted a large SUV squealing to a stop on the south end of the dam. Five more heavily armed men jumped out.

"Makes you kind of miss the fire," Chase said as they stopped running.

"We'd rather not do this here, Malone!" a husky man in black fatigues yelled from the north end. "Surrender now, make it easy on yourselves."

Chase had no idea how the men had found them, or how they'd even gotten through the apocalyptic fire with a vehicle and managed to surround them. But he knew that even with Wen's skills and all three of their guns, it was unlikely they were going to live through a shootout against nine machine guns.

"We could go at the four," Wen said, indicating the man on the north end. "No vehicle, one less shooter. We get them shooting, maybe we get lucky and one or two of their guys go down in the crossfire."

Chase scoffed. "*We're* the ones most likely to go down."

"I'm giving you three seconds Malone!" the man shouted as all nine adversaries inched closer to them.

Chase wondered where "Dam Security" was, if there was such a thing, or any personnel at all, but assumed they were all busy elsewhere with the fire. Still, he clung to the hope that the cavalry would show up at the last second. These goons weren't even trying to conceal their weapons as they marched closer. Chase fumbled with his pistol. Wen had both her guns out, waving them at the two groups as if she were some sort of cowboy in the middle of a showdown—it still felt like a movie to him, but he didn't like the way it was going to end. Chase had been close to death before, however, this time there appeared to be no escape.

"Put the guns *down*," the man said loudly, now less than twenty feet away. "No need to commit suicide by getting yourself shot. We're just gonna take you two for a nice ride. Get you out of all this smoke."

Wen pointed the gun at him. "Not another step!"

The man halted. They all did. He smiled. "Why don't you just let us take you to someplace safe?"

"We're good here," Chase yelled, pointing his gun at another one.

The man laughed hard. "I'm sure you are, but just the same, why don't you come with us? We'll all get a beer. You're probably hungry after rowing that boat clear across this big, ginormous lake."

"No thanks, we had a nice breakfast."

Wen kept fanning her guns between the groups. Then she suddenly heard a noise that told her what to do.

"Look at you," the man said loudly. "You're all black and dirty."

"Shut up!" Wen shouted. She knew he was talking for two reasons—one, so she couldn't think, and two, so they could get close enough to shoot them without any trouble.

"Okay darling," the man said, taking half a step toward them. "No need to get all riled up. Hey, I'm trying to be real social, and you—"

Wen shot him. A chunk of his face blew off as he dropped straight to the pavement. She instantly aimed her guns at two other men. Remarkably, for an instant, everyone froze. Chase couldn't believe they hadn't been shot instantly;

surely they were in range now, but the men hadn't returned fire at all.

"Do you trust me, Chase?" Wen whispered loudly.

"Completely," he replied in the same tone, surprised she would even need to ask such a question.

"Then follow me, and don't stop."

"Okay."

She made brief eye contact with him. "I mean it. No matter what. Don't. Stop."

The men, shaking their momentary shock, began advancing again, all their guns aimed.

"Ready?" Wen said under her breath. "As soon as I'm done talking, shoot somebody on the north end."

"Wait, shoot who, what?"

"Then follow me, *and don't stop*."

Wen shot the two men she'd been aiming at. Chase fired toward the other one, and immediately bolted after Wen, toward the western edge of the dam. Bullets whizzed all around them.

A van screeched to a stop behind the SUV on the south end. Five more armed men got out and started running onto the dam.

Wen kept firing her guns as she closed the distance to the edge of the dam. Chase, right behind her, only realized Wen's intention as they leapt onto the round guardrail. In that instant, he understood where she was going, and knew it was too late to turn back.

"Go!" she yelled, dropping a gun, grabbing his hand, then jumping off the dam.

"Noooo!" Chase screamed, gulping air as his feet found nothing.

Chapter Twenty-Nine

Lenny woke up again, feeling as if he'd been run over by a truck. His legs were tangled and cramped against a car door. Worn and split upholstery and the smell of stale cigarettes were fairly good clues as to his whereabouts. As he pulled himself up, it took a moment for him to quiet the knocking vibrations in his head.

"He's alive," Skrunch said in an eerie, horror movie voice.

"What the hell am I doing back in your garbage car?" Lenny asked, looking out the window, trying to get a sense of where they were.

"I rescued you. You're welcome."

"Rescued? You really are a crazy freak, you know that? My head may be a mess, but the way I remember it, you sold us out, almost got me killed, and . . . where the hell is Bull?"

"Those guys are Russian mafia. *I* didn't call them. I would *never* call those monsters. They were watching me—I had no idea."

"You're a liar."

"Then why did I rescue you?"

"Stop saying you rescued me. Are you taking me to the hospital?"

"No. We're going to a doctor who owes me a favor. I hacked all his records and sold them back to him."

"Why is that a favor?"

"He doesn't know I hacked them. He just thinks I got them from another hacker and, out of the goodness of my heart, decided not to destroy his practice."

"And you want *me* to trust you?"

"I don't care one way or the other. But you and I want the same thing—to save Bull."

"And, by coincidence, you know where they have her?" Lenny asked sarcastically.

"I wish. But I have a phone number, and as soon as we have the money, I'll call them and set up the trade."

"What money?"

"We're going to sell the data you and Bull found. I sure hope it's worth half a million dollars because that's what they're asking to give Bull back."

"But I don't even have access to it," Lenny said.

"You'd better figure out a way to get it." Skrunch pulled into a fancy campus of medical buildings. "Otherwise, they'll kill Bull, then come looking for us."

Chase was certain these were the last precious seconds of his life. The thundering roar of water plummeting hundreds of feet to the newly deep and churning river below made it impossible to hear his own screams. His legs continued running, as if in a cartoon, unaware there was no longer solid ground beneath them. With his left arm flailing wildly, it took a moment to realize that Wen still had a hold of his right hand and was pulling it hard. Chase looked over at her, surprised by her calm and concentrating expression, while sure his own was of pure panic.

Her mouth moved. It seemed like she was saying, "Water," which seemed ridiculous, since they were both about to be smashed to bits and buried by a force of liquid angrier than he'd ever witnessed. Wen pointed at the openings on the sloped face of the dam from which the pent-up, raging flow was being released.

Chase knew from his time working with his brother on the skyscrapers around San Francisco that a human body in free-fall accelerates at thirty-two feet per second squared while plummeting to the earth. Meaning, that the velocity increases by an *additional* thirty-two feet per second *every* second! Somehow, in what he was sure would be the final fleeting moment of his life, his brilliant mind crunched another calculation, estimating that they would smash down in less than five seconds.

Wen pulled hard again. And continued to point at the jetting water.

He suddenly got it. The angle of the dam—it meant that they were about to land on those jets. They weren't going to fall all the way. And what would those jets do? Could they actually ride those currents of propulsion down to the river?

Before an answer came, they dropped into the jets. It was as if someone had opened a thousand fire hoses on them. It felt as if the powerful streams of water cut him in half, and he was no longer sure if he was upside down, heading sideways, or falling at all anymore. For an instant, Chase thought he might already be in the river below, swirling in the rapids, whirlpools, and eddies caused by the massive waterfalls coming from the dam.

The rolling water suddenly slammed them into the dam, his knees taking the brunt of the impact, but he didn't care about that. He needed air. The millions of gallons and incalculable weight of the water was drowning him in a force he could not fight.

Wen's idea had been good, but I'm going to die anyway. Where is Wen? Is she already at the bottom? How many seconds have passed? Am I already dead?

Chapter Thirty

The first IT-Squad began dropping on the dam mere seconds after Chase and Wen went over. The gusting winds and heavy smoke made maneuvering challenging. Two Sikorsky Black Hawk choppers accompanied by a modified Bell AH-1Z Viper attack helicopter hovered above the dam. Normally the Viper would have sent a couple Hellfire missiles to vaporize the armed men who were mostly looking over the edge of the dam, trying to figure out if there was any way Chase and Wen could live through their insane jump. However, there would be no way to avoid catastrophic structural damage to the dam, and the area didn't need a second major disaster in one day.

The IT-Squad leader had just gotten through to Tess at Mission Control, and didn't know how long the connection would hold. "No sign of targets," he began. "More than a dozen hostiles. Should we engage?"

"Are there casualties?" Tess asked from on board a military plane.

"Looks like three down."

"Are you certain they are not our targets?"

"Negative," the leader said. "Targets are not present, repeat not present."

"We need to know who the hell those hostiles are."

"We are under fire, and are now engaging the hostiles."

Travis muted the mic and spoke firmly to Tess. "I don't like the fact that we're now in the middle of a firefight with an unknown force, in *broad daylight*, atop a critical-strategic dam, on US soil."

"Neither do I, but we stumbled into this storm. We can't just pretend they aren't there *shooting* at us."

"I don't want to get dragged before the Senate Select Committee," Travis said as the second IT-Squad arrived.

"You know this is beyond the Committee's reach." Tess turned back to the screen and watched as the IT-Squads cleared the dam in short order. "There, now this is nothing more than another mess to clean up."

"Not that easy. With the fire, I don't think we can safely get a scrub crew in there."

"Then the IT-Squads will have to handle it."

"Wouldn't you rather have them trying to locate Chase and Wen?"

"Dammit, Travis, split them up. These are the best-trained and experienced operatives in the world—they can do it all. I am confident of that."

Travis nodded and gave the command to the Squad leader. "Scour the area for Chase and Wen and remove all trace of hostiles."

Immediately, the leader had one of the Black Hawks begin to ferry dead bodies to a secure location while the Viper and other Black Hawk continued the search. The two IT-Squads, totaling nineteen operatives, diverged on each side of the dam.

With horrible visibility from the smoke storm and raging fire even before the IT-Squads arrived, the reconnaissance had never been solid. Now, with conditions deteriorating further, they were not aware of the fact that one of the hostiles had escaped, undetected, back into the smoldering forest.

Westfield took the call like an alcoholic takes a drink. "Cox, what the hell took you so long?" His gaze was on his fraternity ring as he turned it slowly on his finger.

"This isn't Cox," the man said. "Cox is dead."

"Good God! Then who in the hell is this, and who killed Cox?" He focused on a picture hanging on the wall opposite his desk of a younger version of himself standing with Dick Cheney.

"I'm Tarsoni, one of Cox's men. I don't know who killed him. We had just lost Chase Malone and—"

"Wait, you *lost* Malone?" Westfield wanted to reach through his phone and shake this guy to death.

"After he and the girl took our SUV, we—"

"*What?* You mean they escaped in *your* vehicle?" Westfield looked at his phone as if it had suddenly changed into one of those crying baby dolls. *This can't be happening.*

"There's this massive fire, the whole damned forest is burning, smoke everywhere . . . "

"Where did Malone *go*?" Westfield said slowly.

"He and the girl jumped off the dam. They couldn't have survived. I think it's five or six hundred feet down to the river. Normally it's pretty shallow, but they're releasing a lot of water from the dam, and I guess it's possible . . . but no, I'm sure they're dead. They just flew off like—"

Westfield couldn't believe the story continued to get worse, but at least it sounded as if Chase was most likely dead.

Still, with no body . . .

"Tell me exactly where you are."

"This death squad dropped in from the sky and killed everybody," Tarsoni said in a desperate and vacant tone.

"Who were they?"

"I have no idea. Trained pros. Armed. Efficient. Killed everybody," he repeated.

"Tell me your exact location. The GPS is not reliable right now, for some reason."

"I'm less than half a click from the south side of the dam."

"Sit tight," Westfield said. "I'll have a couple of guys to you in about . . . " he plugged in coordinates into his program and saw how close Damon and Ryker were, "fifteen minutes."

Tarsoni looked at the still burning forest, thought of the killers on the dam, the sound of their choppers still echoing through the smoke. "I'm not sure I've got fifteen minutes."

Chapter Thirty-One

Chase's nostrils and mouth were seared by the intense smell of vaporized water as he plunged into the river so hard, he no longer had any doubt that he was alive. But for how long? The force of the jets unloading tons of water into the river pushed him into the depths of a cold, churning, torture chamber. The smoke and endless rolling layers of water obscured all but the faintest traces of light, and Chase lost himself in the opaque. He fought with dwindling strength to find the surface, but even if he had known which direction that was, the constant pounding kept knocking him sideways, thrusting him deeper, harder, over and over again.

He tumbled in a dream, the one where your legs won't move and it doesn't matter how hard you try, it's impossible to get anywhere. The thundering echoes, simultaneously muffled and amplified by the exploding water, betrayed his senses. Dizziness overtook him, his mind collapsing in confusion.

I must pick a direction, he thought, moving his arms, looking for any way out.

The pull of the current took over and sucked him downriver. Suddenly, the frothy white water seemed to lighten.

Daylight! Air!

He kicked to the rolling surface, breaking through, and gulping air in a convulsive coughing fit. The river carried him fast. He spun around, searching for Wen. Gasping, he tried to call her name, but only a weak wheeze escaped. A moment later, she appeared thirty feet ahead. Alive and looking back, scanning the river for him. He tried to wave, but couldn't get his arm high enough. It didn't matter because his part of the river was still moving faster than hers, and soon she was less than fifteen feet beyond. She finally spotted Chase.

He could see the elation on her face. Seconds later, they were embracing in the cold flow.

The current slowed as they came around the bend in the river, and the water grew shallow enough that they could make their way to the shore. But this was not a place they wanted to go. The Hellish landscape of orange and black, twisting flames, billowing and drifting smoke, offset against gnarled silhouetted trees in a devastated forest from some evil planet, seemed to offer nothing except the distorted realization that they were alive.

They exchanged a glance, each hoping the other had an answer, a solution that didn't exist.

"I need to get out of the water," Wen said.

"Maybe we can walk along the bank," Chase said,

trying to stand, surprised by how much effort it took, his body refusing to cooperate.

"We have to get as far away from the dam as possible," Wen said, stumbling toward the shore. "They'll still be looking for us."

He realized his leg had been injured in the jump. "No one could think for a minute that we survived that fall."

"But we did, and as long as there's a chance that we did, they'll keep coming." She coughed up water, holding her knees and bending over, her body convulsing while more water came out of her.

Chase nodded. "You okay?"

"I'll make it. I'm not thirsty anymore!"

The riverbank was blackened. The fire had been through there not too long ago, glowing coals and embers still littering the area. The hotspots made picking their way treacherous.

"At least we've still got the smoke protecting us," Wen said.

"How did you know we could make that jump?"

"I didn't. But I did know that we had less than a second to live if we stayed on the dam."

"Why didn't they just shoot us?" Chase asked.

"They wanted to be close enough not to destroy the antimatter machine."

"You think so?"

"It's the only explanation."

"Unless they wanted to take us into custody."

"Custody? Why?" She shivered in the heat.

"To find out what we've learned. They needed to know if we found out who the Fire Bombers are."

"Then who were they working for?"

"I don't know," Chase said, suddenly realizing the Antimatter Machine had gone into the pressured depths under the dam. "What about the Antimatter Machine?"

"The case the Astronaut included is shockproof and waterproof, but I don't know if it was built to withstand that kind of . . . "

"We survived," Chase said, still amazed and almost giddy with the realization, but limping.

"Your leg is hurt?"

"It'll be fine. *How* did we make that jump?"

She stared at his leg for a moment, then continued the conversation. "In China, we have many dams, and they are a matter of national security."

"Part of espionage?" Chase asked as they walked past a burning tree.

"Yes. The MSS is involved in taking trade secrets from Western companies to use in the design and manufacture of products, as well as military planning purposes. China is an important infrastructure expert. They know America, and American vulnerabilities."

"So you know dams?"

"They train us. I know what it sounds like when the jets on the spill ways are open."

Chase held out his arm to stop her as a large glowing branch fell into their path.

Wen smiled a thank you and continued talking. "Normally they never would let water out this time of year, but they must be doing it for the fires. Once I heard, I remembered seeing in China how far out the water goes and thought we might have a chance to land on the wave from the jets. It would cut our fall from five or six hundred feet to less than fifty. We might survive that. Then I hoped the wave would carry us all the way down to the river and soften our impact."

"All of that in a split second from the sound of rushing water," Chase said, stopping and taking Wen's hands. "You're amazing."

They kissed until their blissful moment was interrupted by a different sound. The whop-whop-whop of an approaching helicopter.

Chapter Thirty-Two

The IT-Squad Leader, still on the dam, couldn't believe what he was looking at.

"Targets are gone," he said to Tess after a long silence. "One of the hostiles had a chest cam. We've got film. Targets jumped off the dam."

"How big is that dam?" Tess asked, everyone listening, her heart sinking.

A technician on the plane with her, working a computer, answered first. "Six hundred and two feet, eighth largest dam in America."

"Any chance the jump was survivable?" Tess asked, knowing the answer.

"Even the best trained cliff divers in the world have never done more than two hundred feet," the same technician answered.

"Looks like suicide," the IT-Squad leader said, transmitting the footage to Tess. "They were surrounded and—"

"Who are they working for?" Tess broke in angrily, referring to the hostiles, already wondering how she was going to explain this to Flint. Worse, she was no closer to finding the Fire Bomber.

"The first facial IDs are just coming in," Travis said, watching the data feed into his laptop. At the same time the IT-Squad leader was uploading more data. "Classified."

"What?" Tess asked, knowing that meant US Government personnel or contractors. "Un-classify it!"

"I can't," Travis said. "It won't let me."

Tess pulled up her own laptop and began tapping the keys as if they were enemy agents. After several frustrating minutes, she grabbed her phone. "Get me the president."

Gunner hated technology, but begrudgingly utilized it whenever necessary. "You can't win the machine wars without using machines," he often said. "That would be like sending soldiers on horseback armed with muskets out to fight a brigade of tanks."

He kicked at a groove in the dirt as he waited for this particular gizmo, known as a Hatchet-680, to connect him to Powder. The relay device encrypted two-way communications through an eight-step process involving four satellites. What he would hear would not actually *be* Powder. Instead, it would be a computer-generated simulated voice that sounded completely human-like. Powder would hear the same technical translation on his end.

"Are you ready for tonight?" Gunner asked.

"I just made a pass," the digital-filter said. "I think we're good."

"Excellent. Since this one isn't on the list, and we've already hit this city once, I didn't expect any trouble. But tomorrow night is a different story."

"Do they know?"

"They definitely suspect we're hitting targets from the list, but they aren't certain. And even if they had the manpower, they can't risk stacking troops or agents at all the companies because every alternative news site and watchdog groups in the world would work overtime trying to figure out what all the businesses have in common and why the government won't tell us."

"You've said that before, and I still think it's a weak argument," Powder said. "I mean, it seems like an awfully big risk."

"For who?"

"For them *and* us."

"Don't worry," Gunner said. "Only a few more before we can go to autopilot."

"But I *do* worry. About. Every. Single. Detail."

"I know, my friend. You're a hero. One day the nation will understand and acknowledge the debt they owe you."

"I hope not."

Wen squinted into the smoke, looking back up toward the dam. "Do you see it?"

"I can hardly even see you," Chase said, coughing. "How am I supposed to see a helicopter through this stuff?"

"It's coming," she said, turning back to him. "Sounds like a Black Hawk."

"You can tell that from the sound? You really do have great ears. That's not what originally attracted me to you, but I'm learning to appreciate them."

"Sikorsky UH-60 Black Hawk, introduced in 1979, four blade, twin-engine, military grade medium-lift helicopter.

Utilized by the US Army. Sikorsky has also sold the Black Hawk to Japan and the Republic of Korea."

"What do you see in me other than a gorgeous, smart, rich, handy man with incredibly soft lips?" He shot a winning smile at her, and then turned serious. "If we weren't being pursued by ten or twenty men with machine guns and now a Black Hawk through a burning canyon, all your talk of 'four blades' and 'medium lift' might turn me on. But I'm more interested in finding a way out of this wilderness nightmare." Burning debris, embers, and sparks continued whipping past in the erratic wind.

The sound of the spinning rotors and large blades of the Black Hawk slicing through the thick, smoky air took on an eerie, ominous weight, as if a giant mechanical monster was gobbling up villagers one after the other. *Whop-whop-shuun-shuun, whop-whop-shuun-shuun, whop-whop* . . .

"How's your leg?" Wen yelled above the noise.

"Good enough."

"Good enough to outrun bullets?" she asked. "Or should we get back in the river?"

"Is there a third choice?"

"Not a good one."

"Let's find a place to hide," Chase said, picking up the pace to a painful jog. "One that's not on fire."

The air shifted into a different kind of swirl, pushing all the smoke and blowing fire remnants on top of them as the roar of the helicopter became deafening.

"Run!" Wen yelled as Chase dove for a marshy tangle of weeds by the river.

Chapter Thirty-Three

The next sounds Chase heard were the screeching of metal-on-metal, bursts of gunfire, and the desperate whine of a straining motor.

"They're in trouble," Wen yelled. "I Think they hit the power lines!"

Although they couldn't see it, the helicopter was so close that each excruciating, sonic-grinding sound as the craft tangled into the dozens of high tension power lines crossing the river, part of the dam's hydroelectric plant, gave them a clear idea of the catastrophe. Seconds later, when the helicopter crashed into the maze-like electric relay station, an explosion ignited yet another fire.

"Black Hawk down," Chase said.

Tess had been put straight through to the president, but he, in turn, had to speak with the director of national intelligence, who then pursued his own chain of command. Thirty minutes later, it was the director who called her back.

"The president asked me to try to explain this rather strange situation to you," the director began. "It seems that the crew you found on that dam have a classification that doesn't exist."

"That's crazy," Tess shot back.

"We don't know who they are, but we will. It just may take some time."

"Are you telling me that neither you, as the nation's *top* intelligence official, nor the *president of the United States*, have security clearance to find out who a dozen dead men on a California dam were?"

"It appears that way, for the moment. It's some kind of a glitch . . . maybe a former president or CIA director, somebody with full clearance, protected them for some reason. However, this is just a speed bump. I've got a team on it."

Tess, filled with a sense of dread, didn't like how the puzzle was coming together. Someone out there had procured the military's most advanced explosive, possibly discovered the CIA's most secret program, appeared to be working from a list so classified she could count on two hands the people who knew of its existence, and now a group of mercenaries who had been pursuing Chase Malone, were in the employ of someone with more clout than the president of the United States.

"We've got to know who these men were, and, more importantly, *who* ghosted them," Tess said. "And we need to know yesterday, so I hope you've got more than a team on it."

"The president said as much."

"You find who's shielding those men, and we'll find the Fire Bomber."

After the crash, Wen and Chase ventured inland, deciding it would be safer to make their way into what was left of the forest instead of sticking by the river, waiting for more choppers. Eventually, they happened upon an old logging road which, at one point, may have acted as a break-line for the fire.

"Hey, look," Chase said excitedly. "My Leatherman survived the jump!"

"Oh, wonderful. We're saved," Wen deadpanned.

"Make fun if you want, but this multi-tool has saved me many times."

"Shh, do you hear that?" Wen asked.

"Oh no . . . what do you hear now, incoming nuclear missiles?"

"No, it's some sort of vehicle."

Chase was about to ask her its make and model, but didn't think she'd see the humor in it. There wasn't anything funny about being trapped. One side of the logging road was still actively burning, the other was an open, smoldering moonscape where they would be easy targets. Running back the way they came offered nothing more than the prospect of delaying the inevitable. Chase wasn't sure his injured leg could take that kind of pounding anyway. After everything they'd been through, it seemed anticlimactic and frustrating to be caught this way.

Wen tightened the straps on her pack, making sure the Antimatter Machine, or whatever remained of it, was still secure. Chase wondered if she had one last miracle escape in her, and knew she desperately missed her guns. Wen's eyes continue to dart in all directions as the sound grew louder. He caught her looking at his leg and could see her calculating the odds about running back to the river. It was their only reasonable option. If they could outrun the truck and reach the water—both seemed highly unlikely to Chase—they might be able to get into the current and put enough distance between them and whoever would be shooting. But they both knew his leg wouldn't hold up to that kind of strain.

None of that mattered now as the truck rumbled into sight. Wen's tense demeanor relaxed a little as they both recognized the mint-green color of a US forest service truck.

"Hey, where did y'all come from?" the tired looking driver, his face covered in black sweat and grime, asked as they rolled to a stop.

"River," Chase said pointing back over his shoulder.

The man looked at their wet clothes, more than likely noticing a few of the burned spots. "Well, it's your lucky day. Get in back, you should be able to find some room."

Chase craned around to look in the back of the pickup truck, filled with maybe ten or more people. They looked like mostly hikers and campers.

"Where are you headed?" Wen asked.

The Ranger shot her an impatient look. "I wasn't making a request," he said. "This area is under mandatory evacuation. You have to come with me."

Chase knew Wen was thinking about doing a move on the Ranger and taking his truck. He put his arm on her shoulder and started guiding her to the back of the truck.

"Don't worry," said another Ranger, also riding in the back. "We'll get you to a safe staging area. From there, the sheriff's office is coordinating. They're working on providing transportation to the Redding airport. That's the regional shelter."

Wen and Chase exchanged a quick glance, not believing their luck—a safe, free ride back to their plane. They climbed in. Finally, something had gone their way.

Chapter Thirty-Four

Lenny and Skrunch, in their blood-stained, dirty, rumpled clothes, didn't talk much while her doctor friend patched both of them up. Not surprisingly, the doctor, one of those rich California suburban MDs whose patients never seem to have the type of injuries which Lenny and Skrunch displayed, didn't say much to them either beyond what was medically necessary. Lenny noticed the man seemed nervous, but he'd already assessed that this guy wasn't the type to give them any trouble, and certainly he didn't do any paperwork.

Once they were back in her old Volkswagen, Skrunch filled Lenny in on the details of the Russian attack—how she'd been beat up by another guy at the same time they were grabbing Bull and using Lenny's head for a sledgehammer.

He pressed Skrunch for how the Russians had gotten involved in the first place. She claimed they'd crossed paths when she hacked some information on a big real estate scam in Burbank. "Something about the information I'd stolen and sold had cost their clients over a hundred grand," she said, checking her rearview mirror as she took a turn a little too fast. "And ever since they've been trying to get the money out of me, only they kept increasing the amounts required to make them go away."

"Why didn't you just give it to them?"

"Damn, you must have got brain damage when they hit you. I never did make a hundred large on that deal. That's just what their clients supposedly lost." She turned the car onto the freeway and headed south. "It's all such a crazy, complicated mess. I don't even know how they lost money, but it was like only a three-k score for me."

"Did you tell them?"

She rolled her eyes. "These guys, as you can see, are not good listeners, and they can be totally persuasive about their position. Not at all reasonable, know what I mean?" She lit what he thought was a cigarette but turned out to be a joint. "I managed to scrape together six-k. Told Boris or whatever that's all I could get. They took it, but they were back the next day. Kept roughing me up, threatening to take my computers, but I convinced them my computers were the only way I was going to be able to make enough money to pay them." She checked the mirror. "I started pushing hard, did a bunch of jobs, had a big pay coming, and borrowed more money." She took a swig from a small, beige, plastic flask. "Our doctor friend back there even gave me ten grand. Then I made a deal with the Ruskies, told them if I could get fifty grand, would that end it. They said yes."

"And you *believed* them?" Lenny asked, as if she were an idiot.

"I had to." She knocked the cherry off the joint, left the roach in the ashtray, then lit an actual cigarette. "I got nobody. Fifty was as big as I could go. A few days later I got Boris the money."

"Impressive, but based on his visit this morning, I guess it didn't work."

She shook her head. "Nah. And it sucks, 'cause I still owe a bunch of other people. But for a while, like two weeks, they disappeared. Then one day they woke me up, pushed me on the floor, kicked me around, hard. Told me they wanted the other fifty grand. I said I couldn't. They said I did it once, I could do it twice. Gave me a week, or they'd cut off my hands."

"Geeze," Lenny said, wincing.

"Yeah, for real. But this time I was going to get all the money I could and get the hell out of town. I can do my work from anywhere."

"Where do you go to get away from the Russian mob?"

She shook her head and inhaled her cigarette like it was oxygen. "Flip if I know."

"When did we come in?"

Her stare lingered in the rearview. "My week is half over."

Lenny reached for the cigarettes and lit one for himself.

Skrunch went on to tell him some of what he'd already heard from Bull—that Skrunch and she had worked the same hack a few years earlier, and been impressed by each other's skills. Rather than compete, they split the job and went on to do seven or eight more jobs together before their connection faded as they got involved in different things.

"We'd occasionally flash each other online, or do a favor, but we hadn't had much contact in the last year or so."

"How do we save her?"

"If you can find a way to get to her stuff, I know I can find a buyer."

"You can find somebody with half a million dollars?"

"No problem," she said as a California Highway Patrol car passed them.

"You don't even know what we have," Lenny said.

"I don't have to know to answer the question of can I get half a mil for it, 'cause if Bull came all this way and was *that* worried about it, then it's worth at least that much." She took another long drag. "And once you tell me what it is, maybe we can even get more."

A lot more, Lenny thought. *But first we have to get it.*

Tess' plane landed in Albuquerque. She'd been planning on going to Los Angeles to meet with Chase, but now that he was more than likely dead, she'd decided to meet Flint in Taos. She'd tell him about Chase on the dance floor, a place where everything was easier, then she'd try to recruit him to come work for her at CISS. Flint had told her before he'd sworn off 'agency' work for good, but now that his client was dead, and with a chance to work on the biggest thing the CIA had ever done, maybe he'd reconsider.

"A new era," she would tell him. "We are defining the next century." He couldn't say no to that, even if he could say no to her.

Chapter Thirty-Five

Damon and Ryker arrived in the area approximately fifteen minutes after the Black Hawk helicopter crashed into the electrical substation beneath the dam. They traced Tarsoni, the last surviving member of Cox's ill-fated team, by using his phone's GPS.

"Tell us exactly what happened," Ryker said, still adjusting to the thick scent of smoke.

"We were on the dam," Tarsoni began. "Chase and his girl had just offed themselves swan-diving over the edge, and then these pros, probably dark ops, CIA, dropped down off choppers, a couple of Black Hawks I think, and some kind of gunship, maybe a Viper."

"And they just took you out?" Ryker asked. "No kind of warning or anything?"

"Nothing. We gave no provocation."

"Who does that? They have communications? Or maybe they were blacked out with the smoke, lost their connection or something? What I'm getting at here, Tarsoni, is were they acting on their own and maybe saw a bunch of armed guys on the dam as a threat that they should eliminate before they got into a firefight, or were they being directed by someone in Washington? And, if that was the case, who, and why this place?"

"Damned if I know," Tarsoni said as he climbed into the back of their SUV. "What's with this damn fire, anyway?"

"It's burning," Damon said.

"We had to use bogus credentials to get in here and find you," Ryker said. "Of course, initially we weren't really looking for *you*, were we? Lucky we came along or you'd be cooked, or on your way to jail, a lot of explaining to do. Back to the point, these spooks see Malone and the woman jump before they took you out?"

"They couldn't have. Those two went over the dam before we even heard the Blackhawks come in. And visibility was zilch, so no."

"Boss will find out who they were working for," Damon said as they began making their way back to the main highway.

"I don't doubt that," Ryker said. "Either way, Tarsoni, you're on our team now, and we don't screw up like Cox. Understand?" Ryker held eye contact with him in the rearview mirror until Tarsoni nodded. "Next time we get an assignment to take someone out, we kind of like to make sure we deliver a body as proof."

"I was wearing a chest cam," Tarsoni said. "I'm pretty sure it recorded them jumping."

"Turns out you're good for something after all. Let's get that transmitted to Westfield and then dinner's on me."

Chase and Wen spent a couple hours at a staging area near Summit City, which was neither a summit nor a city. It was a frustrating time among a swarm of at least three hundred hikers, campers, boaters, nearby residents, and whomever happened to be in the vicinity when the firestorm raged through. The winds had begun to subside, but the air was still smoky. Chase tried repeatedly to beg, buy, or bribe a ride out sooner, but Wen finally stopped him as one of the smoke jumpers, or firefighters, with some apparent authority, began to question him a little too closely.

"Sorry, sir," she said in her best sweet-little-girl voice. "He's just exhausted."

"We all are," the irritable man growled before hurrying off to head back out to the lines.

Finally, it was their turn for transport. Unfortunately, after a bumpy, claustrophobic, thirty-minute ride, they found themselves parked at the Gold Hills Golf Club instead of the airport.

For the first time since they went over the Shasta Dam, Wen was able to find a private corner where she could try the Antimatter Machine.

"Nothing," she said, fighting tears. Although they couldn't see any water, obviously some moisture had seeped in.

"The waterproof, shockproof case didn't protect it?" Chase asked.

"Apparently not."

"Then the Astronaut owes us a new one."

She looked at him, confused.

"This thing must still be under warranty."

"There's no *warranty* on an Antimatter Machine," she said incredulously. "This is a custom-built, one-of-a-kind piece of precision equipment. And even if there was a *warranty*, it most certainly would *not* cover being thrown off a six hundred foot dam into a waterfall only to be pummeled by millions of gallons of river water!"

"I don't think it was the jump off the dam that ruined it," Chase said with a straight face. "I'm pretty sure it was the smoke. The Astronaut neglected to install smoke filters. The thing was probably already dead long before we went over the dam."

She stared at him disbelievingly until he began to laugh. "You're being *funny*?"

"I thought so," he said.

She forced a momentary smile.

"Don't worry," he said, "when we get to my parents, we'll look at it. I can fix anything, remember? And if I can't, my mother definitely can."

An official came by a few minutes later and told them they couldn't stay there. "Turns out they aren't letting people sleep here tonight. Got a school bus leaving for the airport right now. They still have space."

Chase, whose clothes were still damp, couldn't wait to get to his plane. Wen's clothes had already dried, but she was anxious to get to the plane for another reason—she had more guns on board.

It took almost five more hours, but just after ten PM they were cleared for takeoff. The pilot, who had been well rested and waiting for them all day, assured them it would be a quick and easy flight. As Chase's Bombardier-8000 private jet climbed into the air, they looked down at the fires still devouring the forest.

"We're damned lucky to be alive," Chase said quietly.

"Lucky," Wen agreed. They had both showered, changed into fresh clothes, and eaten. Even though Chase never liked sleeping on planes, before they reached cruising altitude, both were asleep in each other's arms.

Less than half an hour later, as the Rifters played "Freight Train" to finish their set, Tess stepped off the dance floor at the Sagebrush Inn in Taos, New Mexico, to take a call. Flint watched her carefully, and after a few moments she looked up and found his eyes. "Chase is alive," she mouthed to him.

After the call she explained that he and Wen had somehow lived through the jump.

"They're on his plane en route to San Francisco as we speak."

Tess and Flint finished the dance. After talking the band into playing one more song, they too were on their way to San Francisco.

Chapter Thirty-Six

Westfield had watched the footage of Chase and Wen jumping off the dam twenty-three times. He'd even had it enhanced and analyzed multiple times. So when he got word around midnight that Chase Malone and the former MSS agent had boarded a plane at the Redding airport, at first he couldn't believe it. Everyone agreed surviving a leap off the Shasta dam at a height of over six-hundred feet was impossible—one hundred percent it could not be done. And yet facial recognition had positively identified the two of them getting on Malone's plane.

"Incredible," Westfield said out loud to the empty room. "These two really are superhuman. I sure wish they were working for me."

He pushed a button and waited for Ryker to come on the line.

"Turns out Cox really did screw this one up," Westfield began. "Chase Malone and his girlfriend are alive."

"But Tarsoni's film . . . I saw it."

"Maybe Malone can fly, and you had better learn how to yourself. His flight plan says he's going to San Francisco."

"As you know," Ryker said, "we just landed in DC."

"I know where you are. And I know you were at Redding airport at the same time as Malone! Now get back on a plane, get your asses to San Francisco, and finish this job."

Ryker broke the news to Damon and Tarsoni. Using special credentials, they'd previously gotten to the airport hours before Chase and had been fortunate to catch a well-timed nonstop flight to Washington.

Ryker was exhausted, and now they'd be on the red-eye all night and then they'd have to find Malone *again*. "We're starting with the parents' house," he told Damon as they headed back to the terminal. "I'm tired of this guy screwing up my life."

"What's his deal?" Tarsoni asked.

"You should have killed them at the dam when you had the chance. Man, they were like ten feet in front of you!"

"He didn't want the thing in their pack damaged, and hoped to question him if possible," Tarsoni said, wiping sweat from his face. Even at midnight, Washington's July humidity was sweltering.

"Well, none of that this time. We take every shot. We finish this job. Kill him and the woman. I don't care who or what gets hurt."

Wen woke from a nightmare and reached for Chase, waking him from his own tense dream. "What's wrong?" he whispered.

"I don't know . . . The running."

"We made it." He kissed her and felt her tears on his cheek. He'd rarely seen her cry. "What's really bothering you?"

"All the . . . killing people. I can't keep doing . . . "

Chase held her. "You've kept us alive." He knew she'd been trained since she was a teenager to kill, to do whatever was necessary to complete the mission. The paradox of Wen had baffled him. She was, at once, the warmest, sweetest, gentlest, woman he'd ever known, yet also a cold machine while in survival mode. Chase believed the Buddhist teaching that one should not kill a living being, but the world was not a meditation—at least not theirs.

"Buddha said, 'All tremble at violence; all fear death. Putting oneself in the place of another, one should not kill nor cause another to kill.' Then what am I?"

"None of us is perfect," Chase said. "Wen, you're a beautiful person. You've got to forgive yourself."

"I'm not beautiful." She cried more. "I'm an ugly killer."

"That's not how I see you," Chase said. "You're my hero. You stand up to the worst part of the world, the people who are trying to hurt others, trying to destroy things. You are a light in the darkness . . . We can't let the evil win."

She grinned. "Did you write for Hallmark in a former life?"

"Thich Nhat Hanh says, 'Yesterday is already gone. Tomorrow is not yet here. Today is the only day available to us; it is the most important day of our lives.'"

Along Route 360, night had long closed in on northwest Austin. Powder crouched, waiting. This job reminded him of the first one in Crystal City, except there were no fireworks—at least there wouldn't be until he pressed the detonator. But the similarities unnerved him for some reason—standing atop a multi-story building not far from a river, surrounded by similar structures, waiting for the fire crew below to finish evacuating the few remaining occupants. Even the warm breeze felt the same as that first night.

Powder shook off the strange feeling. *It'll be an easy repel*, he thought, looking over the ledge. He had to be in Phoenix tomorrow. It would be their first back-to-back strikes three days in a row. It was partly in an effort to keep law enforcement guessing, but also because a tight schedule needed to be maintained. Still, the constant pressure that someone in the government, whether they were admitting it or not, had the same target list that Gunner was using bothered him more than anything else. Gunner had said not to worry, but Powder could tell Gunner himself *was* worried.

Powder dropped over the side of the building and was on the ground jogging across the landscaped lawn almost before he even realized he was safely down. Halfway to the waiting vehicle he had a nagging feeling something wasn't right. There were only supposed to be three security people in the building, but as he recalled passing one of the windows he'd seen five people walking down the hallway. In the instant he blurred by them, his mind had assumed they were the security guards being ushered out by the firemen, but, as he got into his vehicle, he realized none of them had been in uniforms.

Might be time for plan b, he thought. The contingency, in case the bogus firemen were caught or couldn't get the building emptied, called for contacting the real police, who would evacuate the building and send in a bomb squad. But the Doomsday explosives they were using, coupled with their custom amplification system, had to be protected. The orders were strict: if their bombing methods were at risk of detection, the building had to be blown regardless of potential fatalities.

Crystal City had gone like clockwork, he thought, trying to figure out what to do, suddenly feeling this job was nothing like the first one.

Then the text came. His worries had been for nothing. The fire crew gave the "all-clear."

Powder immediately hit the detonation button. An explosion lit up the sky and built in intensity as the Doomsday was boosted. He pulled away from the curb and within a few blocks, Powder was already thinking about the Phoenix job.

In a few days we switch to auto-pilot, and then the war really begins.

Chapter Thirty-Seven

Trying to decide between two favorites, "blackstone scramble" or "banging pocket," during a late breakfast at Vovomeena restaurant, not far from Phoenix Sky Harbor Airport, Powder overheard a couple at the next table discussing the latest firebombing in Austin. Normally he would have tuned it out, but one of the diners said, "And this time they killed a lot of people."

Powder waved the server away, left a twenty on the table, and left immediately. Once outside, he didn't bother checking the news on his phone or heading back to his hotel, he just stood in the Arizona heat, already over ninety degrees, and called Gunner. It took a couple of minutes to get through the relays and encryption coding, but as soon as the connection to Gunner was made, Powder asked, "How many?"

"Media is reporting eleven deaths," Gunner said.

It was even worse than Powder had feared. "But I got a text, all was clear."

"Then it wasn't your fault, Powder. We knew this was possible. You gotta shake this off."

"I just killed eleven innocents," Powder hissed as he paced around the hot sidewalk of a parking lot.

"No one is innocent," the militia leader said, abandoning his soothing tone. "Especially people working at these companies."

"But that company wasn't on the list."

"They may not have been on *the* list, but they are on *a* list. I asked you, before this all began, if you trusted me, and you said yes. I don't tell you more than you need to know, and you like it that way. But our mission, this war, has more than one front. We are working multiple agendas. Every strike is critical in taking the country back."

"I saw those people. I knew something was wrong. I should have—"

"Collateral damage. You know how it goes."

"In war maybe, but we're making the calls here."

"This *is* war. This is a bigger war than you've ever been part of before," Gunner said, trying not to sound like the military history teacher he believed he already was and actually planned to be whenever this revolution was over.

"This is *your* war, Gunner. Your machine wars. AI, technology, every modern evil thing."

"I need you to do Phoenix."

"Then we go on autopilot?"

"We stick to the plan. Autopilot doesn't finish your job."

Powder wiped his sweaty brow. "I might be done after Phoenix."

"It's not over until we stop horUS."

"Can we ever really stop it without destroying everything?"

"Everything only matters if we can."

As the sun lifted above the horizon, Chase and Wen were already driving to his parents' house.

"I just received a message from WOLF," Wen said. "They've picked up information that a crew has been engaged to kill you."

"Wow, they really uncover some major secrets," Chase said. "We've been dodging bullets ever since we landed back in the States."

"Yes, but they know who."

"Who!?" He slowed down involuntarily, the sky red-streaked and intensely bright as they headed north to the accordion lovers town of Cotati.

"I thought you didn't care about WOLF?"

"This isn't something to joke about."

Wen laughed. "It's only a code name. Someone called Gunner ordered the hit. They are working on more. The dead man at Denver worked for him."

"Ask them to run with that. Find out if Gunner has anything to do with the Fire Bomber."

"Do you think WOLF works for you?"

"You're always saying we're on the same team."

She laughed again while typing into a phone.

"Is your phone safe?"

"Nothing is safe, only degrees of safety," she said while looking at the Antimatter Machine. "That's the best there is, but I was trained, remember? I take precautions."

"Maybe WOLF isn't so useless after all."

"Are you going to help them now?"

"Depends on if they find out who Gunner is before it's on cable news."

"One other thing—they say that the NSA is looking for a hacker named Bull."

"Another blind screen name. WOLF sure is consistent with tantalizingly useless information," Chase said, taking the exit. "And why would I care about this hacker?"

"WOLF believes the hacker has information related to the Fire Bomber."

"Really? And how do they know that?"

"They don't say."

"Of course not."

"They did say that Bull is now a target."

"Of the Fire Bomber?"

"No. Of US intelligence agencies. There are orders to eliminate Bull."

After the call with Powder, Gunner contacted his source, the person who had provided the list.

"How are the deaths playing?" Gunner asked.

"Not great," the source said. "Public opinion is going especially negative. Knocking out a bunch of billion-dollar tech companies when you were just doing property damage—people pretended to be upset, but no one really cared. In fact, some people, I think, were secretly rooting for you and how careful you were to avoid loss of life. Now that's out the window with cable news doing nonstop coverage of eleven families suffering and ripped apart based on the senseless act of violence by some horrible unabomber-like terrorist."

"One day they'll know the truth."

"If and when the public learns what you are doing and why, you'll already be dead or in prison."

"Not if I can help it."

"Come on," the source said. "There are so many people after you, I can't even keep track of them all. Most of these corporations you've been going after have their own security forces."

"More like private armies," Gunner said, kneeling by a fire pit, cleaning a gun. "That's the problem, the public is all caught up with right versus left, are we a democracy or a republic, when America is actually a Corporatocracy. The elites control the banks, who in turn control the corporations, who dictate all government policy."

"I've heard your sermon before."

"Do you disagree?" He looked down the barrel and blew into it.

"You know I don't," the source said. "But your little war just got a lot hotter. They're going to find you."

"Et primo consummare." He shot at a target.

"What's that?" the source asked.

The bullet pierced the exact middle. "Latin, for 'I'll finish first.'"

Chapter Thirty-Eight

Chase and Wen arrived at his parents' home in Cotati, the upscale little town about forty-five miles north of San Francisco, in time for breakfast. His father, Zack, famous for his pecan pancakes, doubled the batch when he saw how hungry his son was.

Wen and his parents had met briefly before she and Chase disappeared to Nuku Hiva. Daisy Malone was the type of mother that would have liked anyone Chase brought home. The family often teased that she'd never met a person she didn't like. His father, a bit more discerning, had been instantly captivated by the sweet, strong willed, highly capable ex-MSS.

Both parents were thrilled whenever one of their boys visited, with Zack shouting out his standard, "There's my boy! My boy is home." However, their moods slipped once Chase explained the situation in more detail than he had been able to on his last phone call.

"We've lived here more than thirty years," Daisy said, wiping maple syrup off her son's chin. "You can't just go run away every time someone's after you." Daisy had built a successful car repair business, and over the prior twenty-nine years, had probably repaired at least one vehicle for every resident of Sonoma County.

"Flint Jones, my head of security, is sending a team here today. I want you to do whatever they say. If you won't leave, at least do that for me. Any more flapjacks, Dad?"

"Yes," his father said, meeting Chase's eyes and flipping a few more onto his syrup-puddled plate. Zack Malone was much more practical than his wife. As an accountant, truly brilliant with numbers, he could take credit for that part of Chase's brain—although clearly the mechanical side came from his mother.

"Thanks, Dad." Chase, knowing his mother's stubborn independence, had been expecting pushback on his insistence that they accept a security team. But his father could see his pain and concern, and gave a look to Daisy before she could object further. Then she, too, took note of the strain on her son's face.

"We'll be okay," Daisy said. "Thanks for getting us safe, Convoy." She gave him a hug. "But what about you?"

"We've got all kinds of help," Chase said. "The government has our back, and we're not staying in one place long enough to attract any attention. Those were the best, Dad, I haven't eaten that much in a month."

Daisy looked at Wen for confirmation. She knew about her past with the Chinese MSS.

Wen nodded. "We're all over this. Really, Zack, I'd like the recipe for those one day."

Daisy smiled.

"Mom, I need you to do me a favor. Can you go see Mars and ask him to call me at this number?" Chase handed her a slip of paper.

"Sure, when?"

"I need you to go today, as soon as the security team gets here."

"I never need an excuse to see Jason," she said, using Mars's real name. He'd worked for her for years before winding up in prison. "I'd been planning to go see him today, anyway."

"You were?"

"Don't you remember? You told me yesterday to talk to him about all this crazy business."

"Oh, yeah," Chase said. "It's just that yesterday was a year ago."

They spent the next twenty-five minutes working on the Antimatter Machine. It fascinated Daisy, and after ten minutes with a can of air, they got the thing to power up.

The first button Wen pressed was the Astronaut's icon.

"The reports of your death were apparently exaggerated," the Astronaut's words came across the little window that had opened. "But I knew that . . . and so does everyone else interested in your whereabouts."

"Like who?" Wen typed back, fearing the MSS was on to her.

"Tracers all return to US Government agencies," he responded, as if knowing her concerns. "I see you are in Cotati. I hope you are not going to Balance Engineering. It is most certainly going to be hit tonight or tomorrow night. MatterTech was destroyed in Austin last night. It clearly establishes a second pattern, and Balance is next."

Chase, reading over her shoulder, took over the typing. "What is the second pattern?"

"I don't know yet, but there is one. The Fire Bomber has two objectives, and has woven the targets together like a long braid."

"Doesn't that make it more difficult to determine his motive?"

"Maybe for mere mortals," the Astronaut typed back. "But for me, the more patterns, the better, because a pattern of patterns leaves its own pattern that even the Fire Bomber isn't aware exists."

"How do we know the pattern is correct?"

"You can't trust words or people, but you can always trust patterns."

After they finished with the Astronaut, Wen did another adjustment on Chase's leg. She'd worked on it last night, but it was aching again.

"Where you'd learn how to do that?" Daisy asked.

"China. They teach us how to heal the body. I wish I had my acupuncture needles. That would fix him better."

Daisy asked Wen if she could do something with her lower back. Wen instantly obliged.

"That's like a miracle!" Daisy exclaimed. "My back hasn't felt this good in ages."

Wen asked Zack if he wanted a treatment, but he declined, instead insisting on taking a dozen photos in every possible group combination, of which he had thousands of his boys, filling more than thirty thick albums. As usual, his eyes teared as Chase said goodbye.

"Don't mind him," Daisy told Wen. "He's the sentimental one in this house."

Wen smiled and gave Zack a hug. "Stay safe."

Chapter Thirty-Nine

Bull felt like she was in a dungeon. The dingy, concrete block walled basement, which smelled of mildew and urine, looked like a modern-day version of a tower prison cell. She couldn't believe how these stupid Russians had screwed up not only her plans to get rich, but their own attempts to capitalize on her find.

Bull had spent much of her time in captivity agonizing over how to beat them at the game. First, she considered telling the Russians what a mistake they'd made by taking her prisoner and letting Lenny remain free. Their idea that he could sell her find was obviously flawed fifty different ways. But then she heard those awful words.

"Do not worry, sweetheart, we are only keeping you alive to make sure your boyfriend does what he is supposed to," the one who seemed to be the leader said. "Once he delivers the money, of course we are going to kill him and that Skrunch. But you, you are sorta almost pretty, and maybe young enough . . . if you do good sex with us, we will let you live."

She'd rattled off a string of profanities.

They'd laughed. "Ahhh, sweetheart, we will not keep you for ourselves. Nyet, nyet. We have clients we sell you to, but only if you are good. Are you good? You make us happy, we'll do you the favor. Otherwise, you go dead with boyfriend."

She pulled at the duct tape binding her to the rusted galvanized steel pipe that she'd already discovered was firmly bolted to the wall.

One of them smiled at her struggles. "Oh, sweetheart, it may sound not good now, but you wait. When you watch us kill your friends, you will change your mind. You will realize it is better to be alive than to be dead."

"I'm going to kill you!"

They'd all laughed again. The one who most liked to talk said, "What is big deal for you? It's only sex. You are made for that. Women make sex. And it is good for you. They take you and let you live in a clean, nice place. You sure will change your mind."

Bull wouldn't change her mind. All those hours of thinking had hardened her resolve.

She *would* kill them.

Her thoughts had been difficult to face, first having to admit to herself that if she had been the one on the street and Lenny had been the one held captive, she probably would've just kept going and not tried to save him. It was a terrible realization, especially because she knew he was out there this minute, trying to do everything he could to rescue her. And, now, knowing what she did about the Russians, she wished he would just forget her and run away. But she knew he wouldn't.

Bull also understood there was a chance Lenny wouldn't be able to access the find, and therefore not be able to sell it to get the money. What would he do if that turned out to be the case? Lenny was an incredible salesperson; he knew everyone, and he was smarter than she usually gave him credit for. He'd find a way. But then Lenny and Skrunch would come to her dungeon and she'd have to watch the Russians kill them.

Bull decided right then that she was going to figure out a way to save Lenny, Skrunch, and herself.

Maybe the find was the answer, or the Russians wanting sex, or something else.

It was new to Bull, thinking without her fingers attached to a keyboard, trying to find solutions without the help of the Internet. She'd forgotten one of the reasons that made her so good at hacking—Bull was also smarter than she gave herself credit for.

Chase arrived at the Balance Engineering headquarters building for the first time since he'd become a fugitive. He was there against the advice of the Astronaut. Wen agreed with the math savant, but went anyway, not wanting Chase to go alone. As soon as they walked in "the garden," a forty-foot high atrium filled with trees and plants that took up half of the first three floors of the BE headquarters, he felt calmer. He had spent countless hours there meditating.

His business partner, Dez, met him in a lush corner of the "forest" and took them up in a private elevator so they could get in undetected. Once at the top floor, Chase immediately went to the fifty-foot wall of windows to absorb the incredible view of the city and bay beyond—it was another meditation point for him.

Later he would visit the "lab," as they called the three

thousand square-foot room packed with monitors and computers with a direct feed into the underground servers located below the building, but for now they needed complete privacy.

Chase, still not used to seeing Dez with a prosthetic leg, turned back into the room and asked him if he'd made any progress on ALAI, a project Dez had begun the moment he'd been discharged from the hospital. Artificial Limbs controlled by Artificial Intelligence. The interface had been based on the super "Rapid AI" the pair had developed, resulting in their billion-dollar fortunes.

"Yeah," Dez, one of the brightest engineers in the country, responded. "I can stand and walk pretty smoothly, but I can't run yet."

"Is that the goal?" Wen asked. "To run?"

"Backflips, mountain climbing, no limits," Dez said. He showed them his leg, full of circuits and hydraulics.

"He's fearless," Chase said, truly admiring his old friend. Dez, already the most prominent African American in Silicon Valley, had been a huge influence on Chase. More than anyone, Dez had taught him that anything could be figured out, anything accomplished. Chase felt good being back at Balance and in the presence of the man with whom he'd worked side-by-side for so many years.

"Wait until you see what SEER spit out," Dez said as the elevator opened to a security station on the building's top floor. After they made their way through the biometric scanners, Wen saw, for the first time, what Chase had so often spoke of, the thing that had consumed him—SEER.

The entire floor was filled with the most advanced servers she'd ever seen. The MSS had several immense cyber warfare installations scattered around the globe, but none of them, even with the most sophisticated and advanced technology the Chinese leading edge firms could produce or steal, came close to the elegance and futuristic appearance of what lay before her.

SEER, an acronym for Search Entire Existence Result, was actually a super AI program that acted as a simulator which interpreted history, trends, and virtually all known data, to predict the future. Everything was sleek aluminum and glass, with indicator lights giving the appearance of the bridge of a spaceship right out of the latest sci-fi flick.

"You must really love me," Wen said, "to be able to stay away from all this."

Chase smiled as he nodded. "True."

The temperature of the room was kept low to protect the servers, and Dez handed them each a black down vest emblazoned with the Balance Engineering logo.

"Does SEER have anything on who is doing the bombings?" Wen asked.

"No," Dez said, moving toward the central command area, appearing in the dim light as if he had two normal legs. "Remember," Dez continued, "SEER is about predicting the future, and so far it has predicted the next three targets."

"You mean we know who's going to be bombed tonight?" Wen asked.

Dez nodded. "And tomorrow night, and the next night."

"We can be there waiting," Chase said. "I knew SEER could do this."

"There is one problem though," Dez said, pointing to the screen.

Chase stared, stunned. "Why would they bomb *us*?"

Chapter Forty

Although a typical, sticky summer evening in Washington DC, Tess' Pentagon contact had been to a meeting at the White House, and often, on his way home, he liked to stop at the Lincoln Memorial and walk along the Reflecting Pool on the National Mall, always taking a few minutes to stop at the Vietnam Veterans Memorial Wall. That's where his phone rang.

He checked the caller-ID and then looked around to make sure no one could hear the call. A man in a suit, about ten feet away, bothered him. In Washington, someone can always be a problem—a reporter, foreign agent, FBI, CIA, a hundred different agencies, a congressional aide, a thousand other possibilities. *"Trust no one in Washington,"* was a mantra often repeated in the nation's capital, and rarely heeded.

"Tess," he said, answering the call once he was a safe enough distance from anyone, including the suited man, who might be listening. "Where are you? I hope you have good news."

"Same place I always am . . . on a damned plane!"

"Where to?"

"Doesn't matter," Tess said. "We have a problem to solve."

"I'll say." Suddenly he was aware of the heat and humidity that hadn't bothered him until now.

"I'm not talking about the Fire Bomber. At least not directly. It's the victims."

"That can only be good. Obviously not for the families of the deceased, but now that we finally have some casualties, public sentiment will shift and pressure will build," he said, looking up at the Washington Monument. "We'll reach a tipping point."

"The FBI is closing in on the origin of Doomsday, and I'm told they have identified the remains of the Fire Bomber from India. He was an American, and they're working on linking him to anti-government groups."

"Damn," the Pentagon man said. "We need that information." His eyes darted around, scoping the area. He moved slowly.

"I'm all over it."

"The President has authorized the steps we discussed should the FBI find the Bombers first."

Tess knew that meant using a special team to make sure the Bomber(s) and any key people who organized the attacks were killed "resisting arrest" or while "attempting to escape." The President of the United States had implicitly ordered a cover-up. *Not the first time*, she thought.

"The FBI is only part of the problem," Tess said. "One of the people killed in Austin wasn't an employee of MatterTech."

Lenny's hands were shaking when the convict finally called him back. It had been at least six hours since he texted him the words "urgent life or death." He and Skrunch had been eating cold fast-food in an abandoned clothing store. The total darkness of the windowless interior space was broken only by the glow of their cell phones and an old LED flashlight Bull had given him—one of her few "gifts." The dampness and stale air left him cold and shivering, even though the outside temperature was in the upper 80s.

"Of course it's life or death," the convict said. "I told you that you should already be dead."

"It's not like that. We didn't even get a chance to try to sell it before—"

"Lenny, listen to me. Do. *Not*. Try. To. Sell. This. Information."

"Some Russian mobsters found out we had something really, really valuable, but they don't know what we have, just that we can get a lot of money for it. And they beat the hell out of me and kidnapped Bull."

"Then you got off easy. You're still alive."

"But don't you *get* it? They're going to *kill* Bull unless I get them half a million dollars."

"It's the Russian mob, they're going to kill her whether you get them a million dollars or ten million dollars."

"I can't let that happen. And I'm begging you for help."

"There's nothing I can do. You're in more danger than you can possibly realize. I've never seen anyone in this kind of peril. Danger-squared. It really is remarkable that you're still alive."

"Man, I got nowhere else to go. I don't care what happens to me, I just want to save her."

"You don't care what happens to you. Don't insult me with your melodramatic soundbites."

"Okay, I *do* care what happens to me, but you know what I mean. *Please*."

The convict was silent for almost thirty seconds.

"Hello, are you still there?" Lenny asked, afraid the convict had been caught with his phone by prison guards.

"Do you have the information?"

"I will."

"You will? Forget it."

"I really will. I just need a few hours."

"I know a guy."

As soon as Lenny heard those words from the convict, he knew he had a chance. For somebody like Lenny, who traded in secrets and lies and brokered between contacts at that shadowy intersection between crime and corruption, the only four words more important than "I know a guy" were "you got a deal."

Lenny told the convict where he and Skrunch were staying—a dark and dilapidated abandoned shopping center just outside Los Angeles. Once a prized part of the suburban culture, it had been a victim of the Internet success and now lay in ruin, caught in a web of endless litigation between the city, developers, landlords, and former tenants.

The convict agreed to set up a meeting between Lenny and a man who might be interested in paying him $500,000 for the dangerous information.

Lenny said thank you at least ten times as he signed off. "I mean it, I owe you my life, and Bull's life. I'll never forget this, Mars."

Chapter Forty-One

Tess and Flint never did make it to San Francisco. Minutes before their government jet was to take off from Albuquerque, Tess received word about the Austin bombing and its eleven fatalities. She immediately took the plane back to Washington while Flint caught another flight to Austin. They both felt a shift in the case. The world, already out of control and burning, was now bleeding.

Once in Austin, Flint received a confidential copy of a report from a CIA friend who was also in Austin. The general consensus was that the Fire Bomber was part of an organization attempting to destabilize the economy. That was nothing new. But there was another thread that surprised him—the CIA was receiving input from the NSA, who was covertly tracking the FBI.

"Alphabet soup," Flint said to his buddy.

"Yeah, this one is so hot—excuse my pun—that everyone is watching everyone else," the CIA agent said, sipping coffee as they leaned against a police car, watching teams scour the site. "If we don't catch this guy soon, we're in big trouble. Did you see the assessment from Red Envelope?"

Flint knew "Red Envelope," one of the CIA's most secret and reliable sections, was a group of about thirty analysts who in the "old days" had delivered their work to the Director in a red envelope. Although it was no longer done that way, the name stuck. He also knew they were seldom wrong.

"I skimmed it," Flint said. "But I got the gist."

"Yeah, war. Our enemies have the advantage and start hitting us with terror strikes here and abroad. Imagine if it isn't just the rag tag groups, but nation-states, even Russia and China, all covertly sponsoring attacks."

"Notre faiblesse cachée," Flint said in a perfect French accent.

"Exactly."

They both knew the story. Back in the late 1960s, as the Cold War grew increasingly hot, a member of Red Envelope coined the phrase after the Soviets "turned" several agents in France to be double-agents for the USSR. *Notre faiblesse cachée* translated to "our hidden weakness." The analysts painted several scenarios where if the US was hit by multiple small attacks while in the middle of a national crisis, such as Vietnam protests, assassinations, and, later, Watergate, the mighty United States could crumble.

Gunner, in the middle of preparing his rural Training Fields compound for an imminent attack, took a call from his source.

"How bad?" Gunner asked, instead of "Hello?"

"We didn't need Austin," the source said.

"Austin was an accident."

"There can be no more accidents."

"Is that why you called?"

"They are close."

"How much time do I have?"

"Thirty-six hours," the source said slowly. "Maybe less, depending on Chase Malone."

"Is he onto us, too?"

"Not yet, but he's a smart man. He'll figure it out."

"Can you buy us more time?"

"Not without raising suspicions."

"There's a way. This is the time to take chances," Gunner said, silently congratulating himself for authorizing the strike on Balance Headquarters.

"There'll be agents coming for you, Gunner. Make sure you aren't there when they arrive, or this will have all been for nothing."

"We're winning."

"Don't fight. Run and live to fight another day."

Being in Austin, Flint didn't feel out of place in his old white cowboy hat, and, once again, he remembered how comfortable he felt in dusty dance halls.

He'd accomplished a lot in a few hours. Austin, now the only city to have experienced *two* Fire Bomber attacks, was swarming with investigators and high level agents. He'd talked to all the regulars, plus local officials, about the firebomb strike on MatterTech, but he'd also been able to question the NSA's Fire Bomber point person about the Shasta wilderness fire and the attempt on Chase and Wen—did the NSA have any data on a connection to the fire and the

Bomber? He'd also grabbed an in-person conversation with the lead FBI investigator. Yet, even with all those important matters, as he stared down at his scuffed up cowboy boots, Flint Jones had to admit he'd rather have stayed in Taos with Tess.

In a happy coincidence, Flint learned that Michael Hearne was in Austin playing a gig and wasted no time getting there. Hearne's familiar picking style as he sang "The Songwriter," one of Tess' favorites, made Flint wish she could have been there.

He'd learned a lot about the case, and felt sure the ring was closing in on the Fire Bomber. Still, the connection and threat to Chase was as perplexing as ever. He watched Hearne on stage, eyes closed, singing out the line, "*. . . to a magical place where we feel we belong where secrets are safe and the medicine strong*," and he felt her in his arms going around the dance floor the night before.

Oh, Tess, he thought. But it might be weeks before he'd catch up with her again.

When Flint put down his beer and looked up to see Tess enter the room, she literally took his breath. He wanted to walk across that old wooden floor, take her into his arms, tell her everything he felt, all the things she knew anyway but they had never spoken, and then kiss her, the kind of passionate, never-ending kiss he'd imagined that neither one would ever forget.

There was too much at stake; not just the lives of Chase and Wen, or whoever the Fire Bomber's next victim would be, but something more. When she reached him he did get an embrace, not the one he wanted, not the one people write poems about, but it felt good. She felt good. They both held on longer than they ought to, but nowhere near as long as they wanted.

"Shall we dance, or do you want to talk first?" Flint asked.

Tess, wearing a rare skirt and not looking as exhausted as he knew she was, looked up at him as if he'd made a joke, then held out her hand.

Mike Hearne winked his recognition, surprised to see them so far from home. He was singing *The Girl Just Loves To Dance*. On the first sweep around the room, neither one spoke as they fell back into each other, like putting on that favorite old pair of faded jeans.

"Have you read the report?" Tess asked.

"Yeah."

"So you know?"

"Yeah. This one's different."

Chapter Forty-Two

Just after four AM on a warm, moonless night, Ryker, Damon, and Tarsoni left their vehicle almost a quarter of a mile away and moved stealthily toward Chase's parents' house. They had been studying the property and the movements of the two security officers via a live feed transmitted in real-time to a tablet computer. A cool breeze told them the prevailing winds were from the north. They knew every detail of the weather, the route, when sunrise would happen, and the exact distance to the neighboring houses.

Once they reached the Malone's property, each man concealed himself behind a large hedge and took one last look to orientate themselves. The three of them had been on countless operations such as this, facing far more opposition, in hostile environments, with zero intel.

"This," Ryker had said, "will be so easy, it might actually be fun."

They each snapped on a special wrist screen which, at the touch of a finger, would display high-altitude drone footage of the property—they would know where everyone was at every moment.

Flint had assigned three shifts to protect Chase's parents. Each two-person team were retired San Francisco police officers who knew procedures and the area well. The first pair had gotten off at nine PM, the two on now still had less than an hour remaining of their shift. The two officers were experienced, but it was their first night, and they were tired and ready to head home. However, they were also professionals and remained alert. One of them had just returned from their small van parked in the circular driveway. It was a makeshift headquarters for hot coffee and supplies. He headed to the front door of the house, where he'd spent most of his time patrolling. The officer didn't see the two men, dressed in black, waiting in the bushes.

In the backyard, Damon pulled the first officer down from behind and quickly injected him with a specially formulated anesthetic that would leave him out for at least an hour. Seconds later, near the front door, Tarsoni and Ryker jumped the other officer. Ryker thought they should terminate the security officers, but Westfield had given strict orders that this was a no-kill mission.

"Use the parents as bait to draw out Chase," he told them. Then "after having a talk with Chase" and extracting whatever information he had concerning the Fire Bombers, an operation codenamed horUS, and anything else relevant, they were to make sure that the billionaire should die in a staged accident.

They took the body of the second officer around back and laid the two unconscious men behind the shed, quickly cuffing their arms behind their back with zip ties and gagging them in case the drugs wore off early.

Entering the home with equal precision, again Ryker

and Tarsoni went in the front while Damon took the rear. Picking the locks almost instantaneously and, although they were prepared, hearing no alarm, the three men moved quickly up the stairs, silently entering the master bedroom with light-equipped guns drawn.

"Where's the husband?" Ryker asked as Tarsoni grabbed Chase's mother.

She woke with a terrified scream, a look of horror in her eyes.

"Sorry about this," Damon said, shoving a gag into her mouth and expertly binding her arms and legs.

"Bring her," Ryker hissed, leaving the room to search for the missing husband.

Damon threw her over his shoulder as if she were a sack of grain.

"Check those rooms." Ryker gestured to Tarsoni, touching his wrist pad to see if there was any sign of the husband outside on the grounds.

Damon, still carrying Chase's mother, followed Ryker down the stairs. A large foyer ran through the center of the house, leading to both the front and back doors. The living room connected to the back corner of the entrance hall across from the kitchen. Damon dumped Daisy on a leather couch in that room and, after a quick glance in the kitchen, rejoined Ryker, who was already heading down the hall opposite the stairs.

"Where is this guy?" Ryker whispered.

Damon pointed at two doors ahead, indicating he'd take the one on the right. Ryker took a couple of steps and reached for the door on the left. At the same time Damon disappeared into the room on the other side of the hall, Ryker reached for the knob.

Suddenly the door flew open fast and wide, slamming

him into the wall and smashing his head. As Ryker cried out a string of profanities, Chase's father bolted down the hall toward the front of the house.

Damon dashed after the father without stopping to see if Ryker was okay. Zack Malone ran full speed into Tarsoni, the two of them landing in a heap right in the middle of the foyer. Zack, twenty years older than his attacker, somehow came up with the gun. He jammed his knee hard into Tarsoni's groin, rolled, cradling the Heckler & Koch MP5SD 9mm suppressed submachine gun he'd just obtained from Tarsoni, and pointed it at Damon.

Chapter Forty-Three

Back at Sky Harbor Airport in Phoenix, Powder made a point, this time, to watch the news while waiting for his flight to board. The blast at CrownSight, a manufacturing plant located in Tempe, dominated the cable news displayed on screens throughout the departure gates. The bits of conversations he picked up while moving through the facility were also peppered with the story.

The Fire Bomber had struck again.

Powder continued to check other news sites on his phone, desperate for information. There had been no casualties. Powder had been so extremely careful he'd nearly been caught. CrownSight, like so many tech firms, had brought in extra security since the bombings began. The Doomsday explosives had been left, as usual, in a vehicle by a separate member of the militia hours before his arrival. CrownSight's team had spread a wide circle. Powder had to wait to pick up his pack and the rest of the gear until a patrol cleared the area.

The real trouble began once he'd planted the

Doomsday inside the manufacturing plant. He'd been unwilling to detonate until he was certain, beyond any doubt, that the building had been fully evacuated.

They hadn't been able to use the bogus firefighters because of all the added security roaming the building and grounds. Instead, the far riskier move of bringing in a legitimate fire crew led to police in full force, including a bomb squad and SWAT team arriving on the scene. Powder had no one to tell him if the place had been emptied out. He knew the bomb squad had three officers inside. He'd seen them go in with his night vision binoculars from a half a mile away. Finally, he used a call relay to telephone the local police and inform them that the bomb squad had ninety-seconds to vacate their position or they would become another statistic in the Fire Bomber's story.

Fifty-three seconds later, the first one came out. At seventy-seven seconds, number two showed. At eighty-nine seconds, nothing. Powder knew he needed to detonate—threats could not be made and not carried out, there was still too far to go until the mission was complete. Ninety—Powder hesitated, not wanting another innocent death. Ninety-one—his finger hovered only a millimeter above the button. Ninety-two—Power took a deep breath. Ninety-three, ninety-four—the two officers that had come out were looking back at the entrance as if contemplating going back inside. The police had widened the perimeter around the building, anticipating the explosion. Ninety-five, ninety-six —*Does this guy want to die?* Ninety-seven . . .

He couldn't wait any longer. *Sorry, buddy. You're a dead man.*

Powder pushed the button.

The epicenter was one-hundred-fifty yards from the entrance. The fireball formed like a small mushroom cloud and spread out in a melting radius of white heat and erupting smoke. The "dead man" ran from the building only a few feet ahead of the wall of fire exploding behind him, like a Hollywood-made finale. Cautiously, Powder made his way to the car, happy that apparently no one had died, but upset that he'd come just half a second from creating another victim.

People will die, that's the curse of war.

The airline announced boarding for his flight. He thought about the destination. The next bomb would be the most important since Gunner had lit the first match.

Chase yawned as Dez woke him around four-thirty AM. "We're still alive?" He glanced over at the HK MP5/10 submachine gun and the SIG Sauer 9mm pistol that security had given him last evening when they were expecting the Bomber or more assassins.

"Appears we're breathing, and the building remains standing," Dez said. "But the Bomber did strike . . . in Phoenix. CrownSight was the target."

"Ray Griffin," Chase said, naming the CEO of CrownSight whom he and Dez knew well. "Is he okay?"

"Yeah, no casualties, back to the Fire Bomber's regular M.O."

Chase got up from the sofa where he'd crashed. "So I guess we're off the hook tonight?"

"Apparently."

"Where's Wen?"

"She's waiting for SEER. I inputted the CrownSight attack into the system."

"Good."

"And she's on the phone."

"At four-thirty in the morning? With who?"

"I don't know. But she's talking about CrownSight and defending the fact that she's in this building."

Chase realized she could only be on with the Astronaut, who had predicted that the Balance Headquarters would be hit tonight. Chase had brought in nearly a hundred security people, activated and installed dozens of new surveillance cameras.

"All quiet here?" Chase asked, heading to the door.

"Nothing but our security people bumping into each other." He caught up to Chase in the hall, about to go into SEER. "It could still happen. Not now, but maybe when darkness rolls around again."

"I know," Chase said. SEER and the Astronaut had been wrong because the input data was flawed, or rigged, or something. "The Fire Bomber is smarter than we are, and that is the most terrifying thing of all. Whoever's doing these attacks has anticipated every possible method that would be used to find them or predict where they would hit next. But we're getting closer."

"Maybe too close," Wen said, as Chase and Dez joined her in the windowless inner SEER server room. "Way too close."

Chapter Forty-Four

Zack, having never fired any kind of gun in his life, squeezed the trigger as if he were a special ops soldier on his hundredth mission. Damon, with training and experience on his side, hit the floor, rolling back into the hall as the bullets lacerated the sheet rock wall above him. At the same instant, Ryker, nose bashed and dripping red from the impact of the door, spit blood and charged down the hall toward the Foyer. Tarsoni recovered enough to grab Zack's leg as he was struggling to escape into the living room. Zack kicked Tarsoni hard with his other foot while managing to flip onto his back and fire the 9mm submachine gun at his assailant. The bullets ripped into his chest and up his neck like red footprints in snow. Tarsoni, a bloody mess, died instantly.

Chase's father dove into the living room and scrambled around a big armchair. He spotted Daisy, who had somehow managed to roll herself off the couch, squeezed between an end table and the wall. Intent on nothing but her rescue, he lunged toward her. Their eyes met in an instant of panicked love and relief, then her expression changed to absolute terror.

Zack spun around in time to see Ryker's blood soaked face draw into an evil smile as he fired his gun. Chase's father squeezed his trigger at that same moment, but he never saw the results of his shooting, collapsing onto the hardwood floor in more pain than he'd ever imagined possible. Upon impact, his borrowed submachine gun fell from his hands and slid several feet. After that, everything became a paralyzing, muffled blur.

Damon scooped up the gun as he and Ryker flew into the living room. Daisy, no longer hiding, had kicked over the end table and a lamp while screaming through her gag. Rolling toward them, flexing like a snake, she groaned as if dying herself. Damon couldn't tell if she was trying to get to her dead husband, or attempting to attack them. Probably both. He swallowed hard, regretting that the mission had deteriorated to such a point—the needless death of Chase's father and Tarsoni completely breached protocol and compromised positions. But they were still in it, and had to still make it out.

"We're exposed. You're going to have to get the car," Ryker said. "We can't stay here, and we sure as hell can't carry her a quarter of a mile without attracting attention."

"It's not light yet. Let's risk it," Damon said.

"No," Ryker said, kicking Daisy, who had by now reached him and was contouring her body in an attempt to knock him over. "Look at her, she'll wake the world."

"We could give her a sedative."

"Go! Now!"

Damon, not in the mood to argue anymore, went to the front door. He tried to look out the narrow window next to it, but it was that frosted and distorted-type of decorative glass that let in light but nothing more. Damon slowly pulled the door open and stepped out. The window he'd just tried to look through exploded, sending glass and metal shards across the foyer. He fell back into the house, kicking the door shut as two more shots splintered the wood trim.

"We've got company!" he yelled, tripping over Tarsoni's body.

"I can see that," Ryker shouted as he kicked Daisy again and then tossed her over his shoulder.

"You're going to bring her?" Damon asked incredulously as Ryker joined him in the foyer, both heading to the back door.

"She's the damn mission!"

In Training Fields, Gunner awoke with the sun, and already a full day's events had been packed into the thirty minutes since his ham and cheese omelette breakfast. Fallout from Austin continued, updates were pouring in from Phoenix, tonight's plan—the most important yet—was being altered by a steady stream of last-minute data, and the prior evening two FBI agents had checked into a motel in Clokeysville—the closest town to the training fields and the compound where he now stood, issuing a command to prioritize the kill order on Chase Malone.

The man with the mission took his leave, and would soon be on a plane to California.

"Fight or flight?" his second-in-command asked Gunner once they were alone.

"The Feds don't know about us yet," Gunner said, sipping coffee and pacing the edge of a stream, inhaling the coolness of the morning.

"Two agents in a cheap motel definitely isn't what they'd send against this," the man said, sweeping his arms to encompass the heavily fortified training field compound that at any given time could include more than one thousand well-trained, well-armed men.

"That, and our source assures me we are still clear."

"Still, it's only a matter of time. And those agents are certainly going to pay us a visit today."

"After tonight, it will matter less," Gunner said, staring above the tree-line as if he could see the drama unfolding out west. "And before we have to decide whether to fight or disappear into the underground, they'll have their hands full."

The second in command nodded and warmed his hands on his own paper coffee cup. He knew of the many contingencies Gunner had in place, knew what was at stake, that the enemy had to be stopped. They were trying to save the country they loved and nothing had been left to chance. Gunner, a smart and thorough strategic planner, had spent years preparing for this war.

"We're ready . . . " Gunner said, pausing as if the words caused him physical pain, ". . . ready to burn Washington if necessary."

Chapter Forty-Five

A security woman from the next shift crouched, waiting in the backyard behind a small stone retaining wall that Chase's mother had built when her two boys were still in elementary school, which now held a wildflower garden that always delighted visitors. The woman was ready to fire until she spotted Daisy Malone in the silhouetted light from the open doorway. Her training told her the shot was too risky with the presence of Daisy.

Speaking quietly into a radio, she relayed the information. "Two intruders, armed, carrying hostage, coming out the back door."

Ryker, tired of wrestling with Daisy, bashed her head with the stock of his submachine gun. Her squirming, which had prevented him from hearing the woman behind the retaining wall, ceased immediately.

In the silent predawn stillness, Damon heard the last crackle of static from the radio and pointed. Ryker tossed a smoke canister into the flowers as both of Westfield's men advanced toward the wall. The smoke had its effect—just as

Damon reached the house-side of the flower garden, the female officer emerged, coughing and apparently still afraid to shoot, more so with her stinging, watering eyes.

As she waved her gun in their direction, Damon fired multiple shots, and the woman folded into the flowers, dead. Damon and Ryker never slowed as they made for the back of the property.

A second security officer reached the rear gate as Damon and Ryker entered a stand of trees about seventy feet away. He fired repeatedly, forcing Damon and Ryker to dive for cover.

"Damn," Damon said, catching a glimpse of blue flashing lights shining through the windows of the house. "Westfield isn't going to like us killing a bunch of cops."

"Too bad," Ryker said, struggling to his feet with Daisy still on his shoulder. "Westfield ain't here."

"Leave the woman," Damon said.

Ryker, as much as he hated to admit it, knew he was right. Depending on how many law enforcement officers were responding, they might not make it out of there at all, but without Daisy, at least they had a chance. She could have been used as a shield, or a hostage if they'd been run-of-the-mill burglars or kidnappers.

"Too much at stake," Ryker said. "We're on our own. Westfield can't save us on this one. We've got to escape or die trying, brother!" He dumped Daisy on the ground as if discarding a load of garbage. At the same time, Damon launched another smoke canister and the two men sprinted through the trees. An unlucky Cotati Policeman, who was actually a close friend of Zack Malone, crossed paths with the two thugs.

"Stop! Drop your weapo—" he tried.

Ryker, in full stride, squeezed the trigger of his submachine gun. The man's body, mangled by bullets, hit the ground as Damon passed without a glance. The two men doubled back to their vehicle and completed their escape.

After being reamed by Westfield, they headed toward San Francisco for an unscheduled meeting at Balance Engineering. Their boss made sure that a wave of confusing tips and sightings slowed the police enough to let his men slip through. Furious that his A-team had botched another mission, leaving a bloody trail that included four dead—one of his own people, Malone's father, a security guard, and a police officer—while not even achieving their objective, Westfield was forced to consider more drastic measures to protect horUS.

Tess and Flint's phones rang simultaneously. The sun had barely risen in Austin, but they'd been up since receiving word three hours earlier about the Phoenix bombing. "Must be more bad news," Flint said as they each reached for their devices.

Both calls were about the same thing—Chase's father was dead, his mother was in the ICU at Stanford Hospital.

Afterwards, Tess and Flint shared details, including the death of one of his security people.

"I let Chase down again," Flint said remorsefully.

"His mother will live," Tess reminded him. "It's the same as us having people inside the MatterTech building in Austin. Four IT-Squad members. The best." Her voice was rising, referring to why Austin had been different from the others, on why the "war" was looking so bleak. They'd discussed it well into the night. Tess, in command of herself at all times and in charge of one of the most powerful CIA divisions, was experiencing more worry than she'd ever known. The Fire Bomber was winning, and it appeared they wanted more than just to stop horUS. "Four of them trained in every counter-intelligence and military technique we have," she continued her rant, dressed in one of Flint's shirts, loosely buttoned at the top, showing her shapely legs and tanned skin. Flint loved this woman, her rage, her softness, her uncaring attitude toward him most times, but savage passion in fleeting moments like this one. "And they couldn't even stop him. They were there waiting. *Waiting!* And just like with your person in Cotati, we lost an agent and let the suspects escape!"

"I know." Flint had been shocked that CISS had been able to anticipate the Bomber's next target in advance and put people into the building, knowingly risking their lives.

He handed her a mug of coffee. He'd pressed Tess on how they'd figured it out, but she'd waved him off. She hadn't any warning on Phoenix, or where the bomber would be next.

None of that mattered to Flint at the moment. He had to call his client and tell him his father was dead.

Chapter Forty-Six

SEER's servers hummed almost silently as Wen, two submachine guns still hanging across her body, pointed to one of the large monitors. "It's as if the Astronaut can see this," she said as data rolled across the screen.

"What did the Astronaut say?" Chase asked, noticing the guns and knowing she had a couple of pistols and extra cartridges in her pack. One of them was a Glock 19 that one of the security people had managed to find for her after hearing it was her favorite pistol.

"The Astronaut knows why he and SEER got it wrong about last night."

"And?"

"The Bombers are definitely pursuing parallel tracks—two missions—and Balance is in the second one."

"SEER was wrong," Chase said, still hardly believing it.

"What's it say now?" Wen asked.

"Still the same," Dez replied. "Now the Fire Bomber will strike here tonight."

"Maybe our show of force scared them away," Chase said.

"SEER had Phoenix in three days, but it happened last night."

"What do we do?" Dez asked.

"The Astronaut told me that there is a pattern of patterns," Wen said, looking deliberately at Chase. "That the Fire Bombers are trying to stop technology."

"Which technology?" Chase asked, well aware of the common goal. He and Wen were working for a similar objective—to make sure technology benefited humanity instead of polarizing it, or even destroying civilization. Chase and Dez had remade Balance Engineering, and its ultra-secret SEER, to predict the future and anticipate how technology could spin out of control and get ahead of society. According to Wen, WOLF was pursuing paths that would use technology to wrestle control of the world away from the one-percent—the global elites who had risen to dominance by manipulating the masses with technology.

"The irony isn't lost on me," Chase said. "The Fire Bomber, Balance Engineering, WOLF, us . . . we're on the same side."

"What is WOLF?" Dez asked.

"A subversive group," Chase replied.

"They are only subversive to the corrupt governments that they are fighting," Wen argued.

"Why haven't I ever heard of them?" Dez asked.

"They want it that way. WOLF believes what you do," she said, pointing to Dez and Chase.

"I don't want to be a part of a revolution," Chase said.

"You have created one of the most revolutionary programs in the world! What do you mean you don't want to be part of the revolution? You *are* the revolution. One day we will all have to choose sides," Wen said coolly.

"Okay," Dez interrupted. "Enough of that. We can worry about someday another time. Right now we've got to deal with tonight. Do you still not want to move SEER?"

"Look around. It's an armed camp here. We'll bring in even more forces today. The Bomber won't get near the place."

"Okay," Dez said reluctantly.

"It's one thing for the Astronaut and SEER to find these patterns and predict things," Chase pressed, "but it shouldn't be that hard. We've been looking at this from the beginning. What do all the target companies share? How are they connected? If we sort them into two groups, there must be a common denominator."

"Possibly just as important," Dez began, "is how are they bringing down these buildings? Almost complete destruction. The Pentagon insists even they don't have explosives that compact and powerful."

"They claim there's nothing yet in development," Chase said.

"Don't believe the Pentagon," Wen said. "If we find the method the Fire Bomber is using, we'll find the people behind the Bomber."

"Let's look at the list of bombings again and overlay all the products each company makes."

"With the new data from CrownSight . . . " Dez began. "Look at that, CrownSight sells almost exclusively to the federal government."

"Why didn't I think of this before . . . " Chase said. "Pull out all the companies that sell to the government."

A few seconds later they were looking at two lists—one with government contracts, and one without.

"Could it be that simple?" Wen asked, studying the seventeen companies.

"Maybe," Dez answered. "Let me just have SEER break out what they sell to the government."

"And parse that out to Defense and Intelligence agencies," Chase added as his phone rang. "Hold on, it's Flint, I have to take this. Keep going. It shouldn't take long."

He headed to the hall, but never made it. Wen turned as Chase wailed and dropped to his knees.

Chapter Forty-Seven

Chase didn't feel Wen's arms wrap around him, but he instinctively collapsed into her.

"What?" she asked. "What's happened?"

"They killed my dad!" His voice cracked, as if hearing the words from his own mouth switched on a full thrust of fury and rage. He stood up, still tightly clutching the phone like a weapon. "Where's my mom?"

Flint had begun the call with the news that she was alive, but in the hospital. "Stanford."

Chase headed for the elevator.

Wen and Dez, speechless and stunned, followed.

"Chase, you *cannot* go there!" Flint shouted from the phone. "It's too risky!"

He put the phone back to his ear. "No one is going to stop me from going to that hospital!"

"I am," Wen said from behind him.

Chase turned and shot her a wounded, disbelieving look.

"Whoever did this was after *you*," Wen said. "They'll be waiting there for *you*."

"I hope so," Chase said, holding up the HK MP5/10 submachine gun.

"No!" Flint shouted again from the phone. "This is classic walking into a trap."

"You'll never see them," Wen said. "And they won't miss."

"Flint, we've got more than a hundred security guys here," Chase argued back into the phone. "I'll take them all to the hospital with me, and—"

"You don't understand," Flint interrupted. "These people, whoever they are, will not play this like you think. They've already proven that by going to your parents' house. Remember the Denver airport? And there's some real evidence now the fire in Shasta was deliberately set."

"This is different," Chase growled. "I have to—"

"What if they wait until you're in that hospital and then they blow it up?" Flint asked. "Your mother, you, and everyone else in that building will die—*thousands* dead."

"Damn it!"

"Look, I know you're destroyed by what happened," Flint said. "But don't help them make it worse. Don't go on a suicide run. Your mother needs you alive."

Chase turned to Wen, his desperate, tortured expression searching for answers.

"I promise you," she said, taking his hand and staring directly into his eyes, "we will find the people who did this, and we will kill them."

Chase stared back silently for a moment. "I'm sorry. I still have to go," he said, turning away. "I need to go to her. Don't you see? She would come for me. Through fire and hell, she would come."

Wen took a deep breath, knowing his mind was made up, she began to do what she always did—make a back-up plan.

Chase told Flint he'd call him from the hospital and continued his march toward the elevator, not pausing as he called the man in charge of security for the building and asked him to assemble a team of fifty. By the time he reached the lobby it was a chaotic scene, with dozens of security personnel assembled and different leaders attempting to decide the best way to continue to secure the premises with less staff. Chase spent more than ten minutes helping his head of security work out a plan.

Dez caught up with him and argued that if Chase took half their force to the hospital, Balance's headquarters would be at risk. "This could all be an elaborate diversion to strip our defenses," Dez said. "We're doing just what the Fire Bomber wants."

Chase nodded. "Maybe you're right. I should go alone. They won't be expecting that. I'll slip in and—"

"No," Wen said, appearing out of the crowd. "Here." She handed him a phone.

"Who is it?"

"The one person you might listen to. Your mother."

Tess kept busy on her flight back to Washington. She dispatched a CISS IT-Squad to the Stanford Hospital, took a call from the President about Phoenix, and spoke to the FBI Director about the status of the hunt for Fire Bomber suspects and backing their organization. The Director expressed optimism that they were closing in and told her about several organizations they were probing in Training Fields, Idaho and Texas.

Concerned that the FBI was going to find the Bombers first and unravel the entire horUS project, she phoned Travis. "Where are we?" Tess asked. "The FBI is close."

"We're not," Travis said. "The decision to put IT-Squads in all these potential targets has spread us too thin to effectively pursue other leads."

"That decision was *yours*."

"And you agreed with it," Travis said tersely. "We thought we could catch the Bomber in the act and follow him up the food chain."

"I know what the plan *was*, but we're out of time. What about the investigation into the source of their Doomsday?"

"It's a dead end."

"How could they walk out with one of our military's greatest weapon's secret?"

"And make it substantially more powerful," Travis added.

"The same way they got their hands on the list! It's time to do another check on every one of us."

"By 'us' you are referring to the nine of us on horUS?"

"Yes."

"I don't have the manpower for that."

"Then pull an IT-Squad out of the field and examine every one of us, including anyone close enough to have access."

"That'll take at least four IT-Squads, maybe five."

"Do it!"

"You're going to leave an awful lot of prime targets exposed."

"I'd rather those buildings be exposed than horUS."

"Done."

Chapter Forty-Eight

Wen had called Chase's brother, Boone, at the hospital with their mother. She told him what Chase was about to do. Boone agreed that for his mother's protection, Chase needed to stay away.

Chase stared at the phone, his mother's bandaged face and thousand-year-old eyes staring back at him. Her pained look was almost more than he could handle after learning of his father's murder.

"Convoy," she said weakly.

"Mom, I'm *so* sorry."

"Not your fault, honey, I should have listened. We . . . "

"I should have—"

"We should have left like you told us," she finished.

"Mom, save your strength. I'll be there soon."

"No. You can't come. I don't want more trouble. Boone is here. Those monsters could come back and hurt you, or Boone, or kill me . . . "

"But—"

"Do *not* come. Don't look for those monsters. Promise me you'll stay safe."

"Okay, Mom."

"Stay safe," she repeated. "I love you."

"I love you, Mom." He wanted to tell her how sorry he was about his father, but worried the emotional toll would be too much in her condition. He could tell she'd been crying. There'd be time later.

She tried to smile, but the pain held it back. Boone, who'd been holding the phone, took it away from her.

"Chase," his brother began, "you be careful." Boone gave Chase a knowing look, understanding that nothing in the world, not even a promise to his mother, would stop him from finding those responsible for his father's death. "Anything you need, you call me."

"I will. Love you, man."

Boone nodded, a hundred words and emotions conveyed between brothers in that unspoken instant, chief among them—resolve. "Love you, too, Chase."

Then his mother was back. "I forgot to tell the police," she whispered. "Your dad had a camera thing."

"You mean a surveillance system?"

"Yes. It was hidden, but you can see footage online. Maybe it will help." She gave him the website.

"What's the access code?"

"Boone's birthday and yours." She began to fade again. "If there's something there, you decide what to do with it."

"I will, Mom. Thanks. You should rest."

Boone appeared again. "Use your tech-magic."

Chase nodded. "You'll stay with Mom?"

"Every second. Police are right outside the door."

"We're sending some backup."

He whispered so Daisy wouldn't hear. "Get me a weapon."

"You got it."

As Chase ended the video-call, Dez looked at him. "You okay?"

"No."

Dez nodded.

Wen reached for Chase's hand.

"That wasn't fair," he said to her.

"I know."

"But you were right."

They stared into each other's eyes for a moment.

"Let's go see that footage," Chase finally said.

"Are you sure you're up for that?" Wen asked.

"No."

The head of security walked up and asked for the game plan.

Chase told him to send ten of his best people. "Coordinate with the police and make sure to get my brother, Boone, a semiautomatic pistol."

A few minutes later, Chase, Wen, and Dez were alone in the elevator, heading back to the upper floors.

"After you left," Dez began, "I asked SEER where the next strike would be based on the companies with government contracts. It came back as Las Vegas."

"What's in Vegas? Chase asked.

"Lipton Innovations. Major defense contractor. Supplies a ton of stuff to the intelligence community."

"Sounds like a fit," Wen said.

"Let's go to Vegas," Chase said.

"SEER still says, based on the data from the other track—"

"The non-government contract targets?"

"Right," Dez continued. "Balance Engineering is one of the next three strikes. Most likely the first, most likely tonight."

"Two strikes in one night? That would be a new pattern," Chase said. "Vegas seems the most probable. Wen and I will go there. Let's keep the full force on guard here tonight. We'll get Flint to find some more people and we'll have this place covered."

"What are you going to do in Vegas?" Dez asked.

"It's our chance to be there, waiting."

"And?" Dez asked. "What do you do if a Fire Bomber shows up?"

"Wen is a lethal agent, one of the best in the world."

"I'm not worried about *her*," Dez said, wanting to simultaneously hit and hug his distraught friend.

"Oh, don't worry, I'll think of something," Chase said as he pulled out his ringing phone. "I think this is Mars."

Chase clicked the speaker button and told him about his parents. Mars, who had worked for them for fifteen years, was as devastated as if it had been his own parents. More so because Mars had lost his parents as a teen, and kind of adopted the Malone family as his own.

"Tell me what you need," the prisoner said, "and I'll find a way."

"Thanks, brother."

"I wish I had longer to talk, but I'm in one of those limited windows. The reason I needed to reach you is, after your folks were here yesterday . . . geez, yesterday . . . they were *just* here . . ."

"Yeah," Chase said, remembering laughing with his dad twenty-four hours earlier.

"This hacker contacted me," Mars went on, "with information about the bombings."

"Yeah, one of probably thousands the FBI is sifting through."

"No, this is different. I've worked with them before. They have something. It's scary big."

"I'm listening."

"They want to sell. Half a million dollars."

"What?"

"It's worth it, but I can't say more over the phone. I'll get you a message on the meeting place through one of our normal channels. But it needs to be *tonight*—they're low on time. You need to be in that town where we once had the best milkshakes you'd ever tasted."

"Okay," Chase said, knowing Mars meant Los Angeles.

"These two are okay, but someone is bound to know they got this high octane stuff, so be careful. This is as dangerous as you've ever stepped in."

"The information they have, does it implicate the people who killed my dad?"

"It implicates everyone."

Chapter Forty-Nine

Chase, Wen, and Dez worked for the next two hours, fine-tuning the inputs for SEER and planning on how they would approach Las Vegas. Chase was convinced that San Francisco would be safe if the Fire Bomber hit Vegas. Chase let Wen and Dez know he was going to skip out for a moment. He looked at Wen, and she knew where. On the roof there was a Zen garden. He went and sat by a fountain, meditating for a few moments. Chase cried, breathed deeply, and let go—at least for a moment. A searching look through the clouds gathering on the bay, he mourned his father.

"What if we go to Vegas and no Fire Bomber?" Wen asked Chase once he'd returned. After a concerned glance, she decided he looked better.

"Then we'll alert Dez," Chase replied. "He'll have time to evacuate."

"I think we should move SEER," Dez said for the sixth or seventh time.

"You're absolutely right," Chase said. "Get all the priority stuff out."

"It's time to call the Astronaut," Wen added, noticing the time. They'd arranged to check in with him earlier.

Chase laid out the latest information from SEER and their frustration at not being able to find the Bombers.

The Astronaut appeared on the screen, smiling, almost child-like, as if delighted by their confusion.

"I don't understand," Chase said again.

"Of course you don't, because you are just focused on the question, 'What do all the companies that were bombed have in common?' Instead, you should be looking at the answer."

Chase glanced at Wen as if they were talking to a crazy man. She nodded back to the screen.

"But we don't *know* the answer," Chase said. "That is why we're asking the question."

"Of course you don't, because you are asking the wrong question."

Chase let out an exasperated sigh. "Then who would want to bomb all these companies and why? How's that? Do you like that question better?"

"It doesn't matter what I like. Patterns don't care about likes, dislikes, or preferences of any kind. Patterns don't want anything. They exist only because there is a pattern, a sequence, a repetition . . ."

"It's technology," Chase said out of his frustration. "The common denominator is technology."

"Good," the Astronaut said, "but technology is an enormous subject. One could travel in that subject for a long time, a lifetime, and never see the same thing twice. In fact, one could say that every company is involved in technology of some kind or another, couldn't you?"

"The companies that have been bombed on the first track don't make anything similar," Chase said, staring off into the distance. "That's one of the clues. They make all different products . . . It's components. Each company is contributing a component to make something else." He looked back at the screen for validation from the Astronaut.

"Yes," he said, pleased. "Now, what is the question?"

"What are the components used for?" Chase asked, as if he'd conquered a great math equation for a cranky old professor.

The Astronaut frowned disappointment.

"What?" Chase asked. "That's not the right question?"

The astronaut said nothing.

"Why would somebody want to destroy what all the components are making?" He glanced at the Astronaut, who remained silent.

Wen watched Dez continue to enter data into SEER, then checked out the security monitors on the opposite wall. They were well protected, but she knew at any moment a breach could occur. Wen had been trained what to look for—anything different or anything too normal. She scanned the forty-two monitors for what she expected could come at any minute.

"If it's not what they're making, or who would *not* want them to make it," Chase began, "then it must be why is it secret?"

The Astronaut smiled slightly.

"Why is it secret," Chase continued, "and who wants it secret?"

The Astronaut's full smile returned. "Good boy. Now put that into your SEER and see what it tells you. See if it doesn't answer all your other questions first."

Dez began typing faster.

"But you know already, don't you?" Wen asked the Astronaut. "Why don't you just tell us?"

He winked at her, pleased she'd figured that out. "I only know what they're making with the components," the Astronaut said. "But, as we've just established, that is not enough to find our answer."

"Well come on," Chase said. "Tell us what the hell they're making."

"Drones. The components are used to manufacture drones." The Astronaut said 'drone' as if saying the word 'evil'. "They are making the most sophisticated drones you could ever imagine."

"Drones?" Chase repeated.

"For surveillance?" Wen asked. "Or for bombing?"

"Both," the Astronaut replied. "And, I'm afraid, even more."

"This is the most important puzzle of our lives, and we must continue putting the pieces together. Time may be on the side of the bad guys."

"Before we set the hour for our next call," the Astronaut began, "Chase, I want to tell you, I'm sorry they took . . . that your father is gone. Kahil Gibran once wrote, 'For life and death are one, even as the river and the sea are one.'"

Chapter Fifty

As the Bombardier-8000 jet leveled off to its cruising altitude for the fifty-six minute flight between San Francisco and Los Angeles, Chase logged into the security site his mother had given him and entered his and Boone's birthdays as the password. He'd tried doing it while they were still at Balance, but wasn't ready for what he was about to see. Chase stared out at the ocean of clouds stretching below the sapphire sky into the infinite, and whispered mostly to himself, "It's hard to lose someone you loved, and doubly hard when you liked them so much."

The motion-activated footage began with the men entering the home. Chase could tell by the time-stamp that his father would have already been in the basement. He woke every morning at four AM to work-out for about an hour. His computer would have given him an alarm when the cameras were triggered, at which point Zack Malone expanded the view by activating cameras in the foyer.

The incredible scene of the three thugs going upstairs and then returning with his mother left him gasping. Wen rubbed his shoulders. He could only imagine what his dad was going through in the basement. The tension pulsed through them as they saw the men go out of camera range, obviously searching for Zack. Then the rumble exploding into the foyer.

Chase and Wen watched, riveted, as the battle between Chase's father and the men raged. A thousand emotions gripped Chase as he sat miles above the earth, stunned—both proud and furious—while his father fought Tarsoni and managed to come up with the weapon. Like Chase, his father didn't like guns, but smoothly turned Tarsoni's submachine gun on the other two men as if he'd been trained in the special forces. As the footage rolled, it didn't seem real, looking more like an action movie than something happening in his childhood home. Yet the high-drama of the attack zoomed by in real time. Suddenly, Zack shot Tarsoni, and Chase let out a, "Yeah!" It was more a nervous reaction than anything else.

He felt nauseous even before watching Ryker fire endless rounds into his dad. Wen, noticing Chase's whole body trembling, paused the video and hugged Chase, holding him until he said, through gritted teeth, "I want to finish it."

She clicked the button to resume.

The angles and lighting made some of the action impossible to clearly make out, but when Ryker carried his mother out of the living room, Chase involuntarily lunged at the screen. Watching her fight and yell as the two men left the house, he wasn't aware that his hand, clenched into a fist, was pounding his thigh in a wild frustration he could hardly handle.

The back-door camera caught Ryker bashing Daisy's head and then shooting the female police officer. After that, the lack of light left only grainy shadows as the monsters disappeared into the darkness.

Chase switched back to the interior camera to take one last look at his dad. They were shocked to see that although left for dead in the empty house, his father was crawling through his agony across the floor. Watching him with labored breaths, pulling his bloody body inch by inch, Chase was desperate to go help him, as if it were still happening.

"Where is he going?" Wen asked.

"Don't know," Chase whispered.

Zack Malone struggled with a purpose and urgency that belied his brutal injuries, leaving a trail of blood.

"What's he doing?" Wen asked.

Chase said nothing. His father's progress grew slower as more blood drained from his dying body with each move. They watched for three-and-a-half torturous minutes until he reached his apparent goal—a large bookshelf. He took another forty seconds fighting to pull a heavy book from the bottom shelf and trying to open it.

"I don't believe it," Chase said, tears falling.

Wen was about to ask what he meant, but then she saw the thing Chase's father had been after. Through his fatal injuries, with the determination of a wild animal protecting its cubs, Chase's dad pulled open a photo album filled with beautiful childhood pictures of Chase and Boone. Wen almost cried herself as Zack became clearly upset when he got some blood on one of the pages. He carefully turned two more pages, looked, smiled, and cried before he collapsed, dead.

Chase, silent for a few long moments, finally stood up, walked to his pack on the other side of the cabin, pulled out the HK MP5/10, and said, "This one gun isn't going to be enough." He pointed it to the computer, where a photo of Ryker still occupied one section of the split screen. "I'm going to need a lot more weapons!"

"An eye for an eye, is that what you want?" Wen asked softly, staring at him dead on.

A thousand words filled Chase's eyes. A thousand images. He knew about revenge. He knew it would not satisfy. He knew it would be wrong. He *knew*.

"Damn it!"

Chapter Fifty-One

Inside Mission Control, in the basement of the Vienna, Virginia CISS building, Tess and Travis watched the wall-sized monitors while technicians worked the computer terminals. The monitors, populated with live images from several points in Austin, Phoenix, New York, and the other Fire Bomber strike locations, were divided into horUS and non-horUS targets. They still couldn't be sure *what* the Fire Bombers were targeting. The horUS companies represented between forty-four and fifty-three percent of the attacks, depending on the most recent hit. Travis argued that there was a good chance that the Bombers were after something other than horUS, and the number of victim-firms involved in that project was mere coincidence.

"Are you willing to gamble the security of the country on that assumption?" Tess asked. "Or, the reputations, freedom, and even our lives, of all nine of us?"

"Of course not. That's why we have IT-Squads in every operational theatre of this thing," Travis said. "I'm just saying that it would explain why we haven't been able to discover the backers or apprehend even one of them. We may be looking in the wrong place."

"So you're back to Chinese economic terrorism?"

"Statistically, it's just as likely as someone going after horUS. How possible do you really think it is that someone uncovered the operation? The background checks, although still ongoing, have so far cast no suspicion on any of us. And they're not going to."

"Tess," a senior analyst said, walking up to their station and interrupting the conversation. "We just got a line from our point at the Bureau. The FBI is planning a raid on a militia compound in about ninety minutes."

"Where?" Travis asked, knowing they wouldn't have much time to get an IT-Squad there before other federal agents descended.

"Idaho. Place called Cedar City."

Tess, who had been hoping that Chase, or the internal investigators at CISS, would ID the suspects long before now, and certainly before the FBI, had also been relying on an illegal, yet thorough, CISS network monitoring the FBI, and other federal agencies, to provide advanced warning of an imminent arrest of Fire Bomber related suspects. In addition to electronic surveillance of computers, servers, and other devices, the network utilized eavesdropping on nearly all government personnel. CISS agents were also covertly employed at the FBI, Department of Justice, and Department of Homeland Security. It was one of these high-level moles who had provided the early warning on Idaho.

"Where's the closest IT-Squad?" Tess asked.

"I'm checking," Travis said. "Las Vegas."

"Can we beat the FBI?"

"It'll be close," Travis replied, looking at the 'minus-twenty-three minutes" already displaying on his screen.

"Close isn't good enough," Tess said, heading to "Secure," the area at the end of Mission Control which housed direct encrypted lines to the White House, Pentagon, NSA, and CIA.

Travis contacted the IT Operational Officer and ordered him to move the IT-Squad from Las Vegas.

The senior analyst looked at him questioningly. "Isn't Tess requesting authorization to order a strike on Cedar City?"

"I suspect she's doing just that," Travis said.

"Then why send an IT-Squad?"

"As you know, she already has the standing-authority to use CISS resources to take out those we deem necessary to protect our interest, but once she involves the Pentagon, anything could go wrong."

"You don't think they'll deny her request?" the analyst asked.

"Not a chance," Travis replied, knowing with horUS at stake, the President would give Tess anything she needed. "We just have to be sure."

Armed with full authorization from the President, Tess bypassed her normal Pentagon contact and went straight to the Secretary of Defense.

"Tess, we can do this," the former Army Colonel and Texas congressman said. "But damn sure, if there isn't a lot that can go wrong with this. Who's gonna catch the fire?"

"There won't be any fire," Tess replied.

"Hell if there won't. If we send in ordinance and evaporate somewhere between three and six hundred American civilians in the middle of the great state of Idaho, it's gonna be a lot more than fire. We'll be dealing with what those in the Navy call a 'ship-storm.'"

"Don't worry, Mr. Secretary," Tess said, addressing him more formally than she typically did. She'd known him for more than fifteen years, and the pair shared plenty of secrets. "We can cover this at least ten different ways. We're talking about a militia that has been terrorizing the country, blowing up tech companies, and killing Americans for weeks. We'll release evidence which shows these people were preparing to mount a full-scale revolution once they'd shattered the economy. The line will be that we went in with a respectable show of force, and, by their own mistakes, all those nasty explosives they've been unleashing on everyone ended up destroying the entire compound, which, by the way, was loaded with weapons. Need I say more?"

"This is all above my pay grade anyway. The president wants to go forward, as long as you've thought this thing through and cover our collective butts. You got the media playing along with this?"

"As usual."

"All right. I'll greenlight it. You realize we'll either retell this old war story when we're retired, proud and strong, or maybe we'll be crying about it in a prison cell. Either way, I will follow orders and make the problem disappear."

Back in mission control, Tess linked into the Pentagon feeds and watched live as a thirty-two hundred acre compound in Idaho, home to two-hundred-seventeen men, women, and children, loosely affiliated with the "Come Freedom Militia," disappeared off the face of the earth.

Chapter Fifty-Two

After landing in Los Angeles, Chase and Wen stayed on the plane and continued to research the companies that had already been hit by the Fire Bomber, scouring SEER results and other data to identify the potential future targets.

The Astronaut had told them of his theory that the drones had advanced tracking capabilities and could be coordinated with satellites. He'd said, "If these things are built, the CIA or NSA would be able to watch a man who wakes up in Yemen and follow his every movement until he meets a group in Syria. Maybe that seems okay in the age of 'the war on terror,' but what about watching a woman who leaves her home in Beijing in the morning until she checks into a hotel in South Africa, and then do it all again the next day?"

"Or what about when this technology gets into the wrong hands, or is hacked, or . . .?" Wen had questioned. "Because it will."

"Exactly," the Astronaut had replied.

"Maybe that's what the Fire Bomber is doing?" Chase had asked. "Trying to get the technology and cover his tracks, or . . . trying to stop it?"

They had a list of leads for the Drone project, but still didn't have much on the "second track," the one that targeted Balance Engineering. Chase tried to focus, but couldn't stop thinking about the footage of his father's killing.

"It's time to call the Astronaut," Wen said.

"To see if he's cracked the pattern of the second track?"

"That would be nice," Wen said. "But he may be able to tell us how to identify the people in the home-security video, since our facial recognition attempts are coming up blank."

"'People?'" Chase asked rhetorically.

Chase transferred the security footage of his parents' home from his laptop to the Antimatter Machine, and then Wen uploaded it so that the Astronaut could access it.

"Know that I will continue to do everything I can to help you identify and locate these perpetrators," the Astronaut said across the encrypted video conferencing window.

"Thank you," Chase said, relieved the Astronaut was committed to his case, feeling a warmth toward him he hadn't felt before..

"I am tied into every facial recognition and biometric system in the world, including the Chinese MSS, FBI, and NSA, and it shouldn't take long to produce a match. We've got good images from the security cameras. Men like these will be known—past arrests, military service, even a stop at their local bank will get them in the database. We'll find them."

"While we're waiting," Wen began, "can I ask you about Lipton Innovations?"

"Of course," the Astronaut said, smiling. "I anticipated your question, and I've just sent you a summary data report on the company, its ownership, corporate affiliations, vendors, clients, customers, and, even more important, their products. If you tap into that second section, you'll see an analysis of which product could be used in surveillance or weaponized drones. It's broken down into three parts, color-coded—I think color coding is important with this kind of process."

"Yes," Wen said, used to his precise ways.

The Astronaut continued. "In the next section on the other tab—the green one—you can see how these components match with the other target companies in the past, beginning with Tri-Knight Avionics in Crystal City. I've prepared a second report on the same companies intersecting with the potential future targets that we've identified. You definitely will want to cross reference that with what you are seeing with SEER."

As they began looking through the material, they quickly spotted one specific component that the Astronaut had highlighted in many sections, and they asked him about it.

"Yes, there are actually two critical components," he replied. "One is a flight evasion solenoid transistor energy resister, often referred to by its acronym 'FESTER.' It makes the drone virtually invisible."

"Really?" Wen asked.

"Is that possible?" Chase added. He looked out the window for a moment as he felt a slight tremor. The tarmac was busy. In fact, an ambulance whizzed by. He thought of his mom, wondered how she was, and made a mental note to try to call her shortly.

"Impressive engineering. Then there is the CSR, which stands for "capture sort relay," also quite an advanced piece of technology. The CSR is a high-resolution still camera and super hi-def credit-zoom-capable video-capture system. This little marvel enables the drone to record and process endless live feeds, then sort and prioritize data images onboard, in real time, before instantly sending them to either satellite or ground-based computer enhancement facilities that provide the intelligence agencies with the acquired assets, short only a microsecond lag when viewing high priority targets of literally infinite streams."

"Amazing," Chase said, returning his focus to the screen. Wen noticed his minute of daydream and knew where he'd went.

"That's not all Lipton Innovations manufactures in this little drone project. They make the hardware and software that can process the image data coming in from tens of thousands—potentially hundreds of thousands—of sources, enabling them to composite, again, in real time, all these images."

"You mean they can put these 'invisible' drones over China in sufficient numbers to record everything going on in Shanghai, or a Chinese military installation such as Zhurihe Combined Tactics Training Base?"

"You're thinking too small," the Astronaut said. "They can watch the *entire* People's Republic of China, including the South China Sea, Taiwan, and anywhere else. They get enough of these up there, they'll know everything that's going on in the world."

"Unbelievable," Chase said. This represented everything he feared about misuse of technology. "Why is it whenever we create a beautiful, life changing new invention, governments figure out a way to weaponize it?"

"Or," Wen added, "to use it to control the population?"

Chapter Fifty-Three

Westfield continued his rage on Ryker and Damon for botching the raid on Chase's parents. "Now we've got another investigation to deal with, and you missed Chase yet again!" His anger was made worse because they weren't in his office where he'd be able to berate them in person, maybe even unleash some violence of his own. Although more than twice their age, Westfield still proudly maintained his prowess.

"We'll get him in Los Angeles," Ryker said, having just received word that Chase and Wen boarded a private plane at the San Francisco Airport with a flight plan filed for Los Angeles.

"No," Westfield said. "You stay in San Francisco. We have people in Los Angeles who can handle them. I want you monitoring the hospital and Balance Engineering."

Ryker pleaded their case, but Westfield would not be swayed.

After the call, Westfield checked the latest internal reports. The FBI was getting closer. There were three strong leads. Arrests were expected within the next twenty-four hours. "Damn it, I'm too old for this," he said to himself. "Time to elevate." Westfield called a number he had not used in many years.

"Hello?" the man on the other end said.

"Three-six-three-JH," Westfield replied.

"Yes."

"Fourteen-three," Westfield replied, after referencing a chart that informed him Washington DC was number fourteen.

"Three?" the man repeated, verifying the number of people to be killed.

"Correct."

The man then gave him a series of numbers which indicated the time and place to deliver the files of the people to be eliminated.

Westfield double checked the names and the order of their executions—Tess Federgreen, Travis Watts, the Secretary of Defense—then he sent the dispatch, thanked the man, and hung up. One way or another, within twenty-four hours, his worst problems would be solved.

Gunner watched as the trucks were loaded. He hadn't been sure until an hour before if he was going to give the order to fight or to evacuate. However, with the success of the Phoenix strike and Powder still going undetected, ready to hit the critical target in Las Vegas, the difficult decision became an easy choice.

The expected call from Gunner's source, someone who had never understood the full extent of the militia's capabilities, hadn't come. The leader of the resistance pondered the possible reasons; the source could have been discovered, a government clampdown could have occurred in the face of an imminent raid on the training grounds, or the pressure could have finally proven too much. After the deaths in Austin, the source had become more reluctant to provide information.

In their last conversation, the source told him that the authorities were hours from putting it all together. "As soon as the FBI identifies you," the source had said, "the operation will be over."

However, Gunner had informed the source that "The militia were prepared to fight 'the final standoff,' long into forever."

"It's a suicide mission," the source had countered. "Your people may be well-trained and well-fortified, but there are what, a thousand of you? Be realistic. You are no match for the US government's full might, which will swiftly be brought to bear against any insurgents. They will mop you up in a day. Don't let it get to that."

But there was something the source didn't understand, Gunner had no intention of fighting at the Training Fields. He had trained in guerrilla tactics. Having prepared for this moment for years, this fighting machine of a man was ready to fight everywhere.

As the last truck filled, the vehicles began to depart in a staggered operation designed to attract little attention through varied routes. Gunner nodded knowingly to the sky. *We are on the move now.*

His phone vibrated. The source.

"The FBI is going to knock on your door in less than sixty minutes."

"Good for them," Gunner said. "I'm happy they're not completely incompetent, as it turns out."

"You're not still thinking of taking your final stand now, are you?"

"No, we're not going to be around when those friendly agents show up. I'm afraid they'll just miss the party, but we'll leave them some beer."

"I'm glad to hear that. But they have other ways to find you, and they'll be looking."

"Are they sure it's us?"

"No. If they were, there would already be a thousand personnel surrounding the Training Fields. But when they arrive to find it empty, they will know you fled, they will know it's you, and a fury the likes of which you cannot begin to imagine will be unleashed on you."

"Likewise," Gunner said, pressing his lips together in a maliciously repugnant grin. One couldn't be sure if this surly backwoodsman was as confident as his words, or crazier than hell, and would absolutely follow through—and win. In either case, one would want to be on his side.

Chapter Fifty-Four

The Astronaut reported that the men in the videos were either ex-military, ex-agency, or some other similar type. "Because only someone like that can scrub their record. And there is a link—US Government."

"Whoever is behind the drones . . . " Wen began.

"Is behind the attack on Chase's parents," the Astronaut finished.

"And the ones trying to kill us," Chase added.

"Exactly."

"Then you can't get their identities?" Chase asked.

"I did not say that. It may take another hour. I have programs running as we speak, pulling and dividing data. They exist, they work for the government—or did—there is a trail, and I'll find it. Don't worry, we'll get them."

"Thank you," Chase said, instinctively wincing from the silent pain within his gut every time the thought of his father surfaced in any form.

"Of course," the Astronaut said. "And while I've been searching across Heaven, I discovered drone footage of the two of you after you left Shasta, at the dam, and of your parents' home."

"They've been tracking us with drones," Wen said, as many things suddenly became clear. Constantly amazed by the Astronaut's abilities, Wen was especially impressed by how he could move through Heaven, the ultra-classified intelligence computer/satellite network of the US spy agencies.

"Footage of my parents' place?" Chase echoed.

"The morning of the attack," the Astronaut explained. "It would seem that they were checking the security guards' movements."

"*Bastards*. That proves whoever is behind the drones are the same ones after us."

"I've taken some precautions," the Astronaut said. "If all goes well, they won't be able to use their drones to track you for at least twenty-four hours."

"How can you do that?" Wen asked.

"Remember CSR?"

"Lipton Innovations. Capture-Sort-Relay."

"Very good," the Astronaut said. "The drones' CSRs are linked into a secure section of Heaven for updating, maintenance, and merging, so that it can work with the other programs, applications, components, and necessary equipment. That made it easy to disable. Not completely, of course, but sporadically there will be issues, making it unreliable and, therefore, they will ground for repairs."

"Brilliant," Chase said.

"I certainly hope so," the Astronaut said, "because I can't dance and am not good at sports."

"Okay," Wen said. "But we're after the Bombers, not the Drones."

"We're after whoever killed my father!"

"Yes, yes, but we have to unravel this whole thing."

Chase didn't respond, because at that moment he received an encrypted message from Dez about the meeting with Lenny. Someone had dropped a handwritten note at Balance with names and meeting details.

"It is all connected," the Astronaut said. "Including the mystery of how the Bombers are able to inflict complete destruction on their targets."

"I've been working on a theory," Chase said.

"Wait," the Astronaut interrupted. "Allow me to introduce you to Paul Ryker and James Damon." Ryker and Damon appeared on the Antimatter Machine's monitor. "These are the men who killed your father."

After the total annihilation of the Come Freedom Militia in Idaho, Tess prepared for the media storm. Although the remoteness of the militia's compound meant it might take a day before the story snowballed, she needed to be well ahead of it.

As it turned out, as with all things related to the Fire Bomber, it took mere hours before the media began harassing Washington contacts. And among the powerful in Washington, the most well plugged-in ones called her. One of them was the Deputy Assistant Secretary of Defense.

"Are we done? Were they the group?" he asked.

Tess, who assumed the Secretary of Defense, who had approved the mission, had already briefed the Under Secretary, was annoyed by the question. But he was one of the horUS nine, so she told him what she'd just said to the President.

"We won't begin to know until morning. If there is no

Fire Bomber strike tonight, that'll be quite a good sign. But even if something *is* hit tonight, that doesn't mean we got the wrong group because orders could have already been in place."

"Then the Bomber, or Bomb*ers*, are still a problem."

"They'll be taken care of. Recent intel tells us there may only be one. Either way, he, she, or they, will be found."

The Under Secretary didn't trust Tess, the CIA, or the President, for that matter. He knew that the most powerful entity on earth was the Pentagon. He trusted the US military and its multiple internal intelligence agencies, and horUS.

"Meantime," the Deputy Assistant Secretary of Defense began, "I've got a meeting this afternoon with Google."

"Bad timing."

"They're worried."

"For good reason," Tess said, knowing that the Deputy Assistant Secretary of Defense was in charge of Platform and Weapon Portfolio Management for the Pentagon, meaning more than anyone, he had the point on horUS. She also knew he didn't like her—or anyone, for that matter.

Google had helped the Defense Department with Project Maven, a controversial program employing AI to automatically tag cars, buildings, and other objects in videos recorded by drones flying over international conflict zones. But after pressure from employees who claimed the search firm would be, in effect, aiding "the military 'track and kill' with greater efficiency," the company did not renew the contract. Google's involvement in horUS had, therefore, been kept a highly classified secret. Normally it would have been handled by the Office of the Under Secretary of Defense for Intelligence, the Defense Department directorate that oversaw such programs, but when horUS was conceived, the top officials, including the Secretary of Defense, knew only one man inside the Pentagon could handle the project and keep it secret: the Deputy Assistant Secretary of Defense. He'd been a fixture behind the scenes in Washington for decades, and there were not many covert operations of note in which he did not have a hand.

Chapter Fifty-Five

After an eighteen-minute drive from Los Angeles Airport, Chase pulled into an endless parking lot outside the abandoned 800,000 square foot shopping mall where they were set to meet Lenny. The mall, closed for more than twenty years, appeared dilapidated, a relic of the pre-internet world, something out of an urban war zone—a place that could easily be haunted, if one believed in such things.

"How do we get in?" they asked simultaneously.

Circling the massive edifice twice before selecting the most promising section, Chase parked and gave a sad look back at their rental car, wondering if it would be there when he and Wen returned.

They scoured the area and found some old pipes and a piece of rusty culvert that looked as if wayward teens, vandals, and gangs might have used the artifacts for the same purpose when trying to gain access to the abandoned mall. Propping the pipes and bracing the culvert in such a way, Chase was able to climb up to a narrow ledge, pulling Wen up behind him. The barriers to keep people out were challenging, but they served only to slow more determined intruders.

They shimmied along the narrow ledge until reaching a hole in the wall they'd spotted from below. Wen slipped through easily, but Chase had to do a few contortionist moves to squeeze in, where he joined Wen on the remnants of a bent and twisted catwalk.

"I don't really have a good feeling about this," Chase said as he swung down on the bottom of the steel grid and dropped nearly twelve feet to a dusty concrete floor, instantly being painfully reminded of his leg injury at the dam site.

Wen touched down, cat-like, next to him, springing into a defensive pose, as she'd been trained. "Where's your sense of adventure?" she asked, really meaning where was his sense of humor. She worried that the rage and anger he'd been holding onto so tightly would get in the way if they encountered trouble tonight.

"The only adventure I'm interested in is finding the son of the bitch who killed my father."

Wen shined a light into the vast darkness. "Just remember this is all part of that. If we do this right, one step at a time, it'll lead us not just to Ryker, but whoever employs him."

"Then let's find this hacker weasel and get out of here. They're supposed to be at the four fountains at the bottom of the two big escalators."

"There's not exactly a mall directory handy," Wen said. "And obviously the fountains aren't going to be running."

"Never underestimate a Malone," Chase said, pulling out a computer tablet. He tapped the screen a few times and a map of the mall's interior displayed.

"Impressive," Wen said, patting his back. "I don't suppose it has a little red *you are here* arrow on it?"

"No, but I think we can figure out where we are based on—"

"Hey! Who the hell invited you to my house?"

Wen spun her light and illuminated a scraggly old geezer leaning against a wall of graffiti. She quickly assessed his threat level to be low. Obviously he was homeless.

"This cannot be our hacker," Chase said under his breath, praying it wasn't.

"Get that light out of my eyes," the man shouted, pawing his hands into the air, trying to shoo the light. "No room here for you!"

"We have reservations," Chase said, moving away.

"You got nothing!" the man yelled, throwing an empty cardboard box at them. "This ain't no hotel. Get out of my house, or I'll call the cops!"

Wen laughed. "Call them. We might need them."

"Bah!" The man tossed an empty bottle at them. It shattered a couple feet in front of Chase, who turned as if he were going back.

Wen grabbed his arm. "We've got enough battles."

They made their way through the winding corridor into one of the main hallways, this one filled with old rusted shelving units and stripped-down display stands that now resembled dangerous medieval torture devices. Finally, they reached what they'd been searching for—the top of the main escalator.

"It's a long way down," Chase said, shining his light into the inky blackness.

"Do you think there might be sharks down there?" Wen joked.

"You never know," Chase said as they descended into what felt like the murky depths of an underwater shipwreck.

Chapter Fifty-Six

Wen kept her finger ready on the trigger as they reached the last still-steps at the bottom of the busted escalator. Chase held a gun pointed ahead, more ready to use it than he'd ever been, although still not sure which hand to keep it in.

"Who's that?" came a voice from the darkness.

"Who are you?" Wen asked.

"It's Lenny."

"Mars sent us," Chase said impatiently.

"Okay, okay." A light shined up at them.

"Get that damn light out of my eyes," Chase snapped, remembering the homeless man's protests.

"Skrunch, move the beam away!"

Lenny and Skrunch stepped out from behind a collapsing plywood wall near the gritty, forgotten fountain basins.

"Thanks for coming," Lenny said, holding out his hand.

"This had better be worth it," Chase said, ignoring Lenny's offer.

Wen held the light close to Lenny, and then to Skrunch.

She stared at the hackers, deciding quickly they were no physical threat. In fact, they looked awful, and it concerned her.

"Follow me," Skrunch said, heading toward a small, empty store sandwiched between two cavernous vacant spaces, one of which might've been a department store.

"Where are we going?" Chase asked.

"Somewhere a little more private," Lenny said, limping.

"No," Chase said, waving his arm around. "We don't mind the crowds out here."

"Okay, okay," Lenny said. "Skrunch, grab the other laptop."

She ran into the store and disappeared through a door in the back. Expanding the illumination of the flashlights each of them held, additional light filtered down through massive skylights that had once made the mall a modern, cheery retail palace instead of a Draconian maze. Strangely, a glow from the parking lot's lights reflected in, casting an eerie, pale green hue to the dystopian chambers.

"Freeze," Wen said as Lenny reached into a canvass messenger bag on his shoulder.

"Okay, okay," he said, holding up his arms. "I was just getting my laptop."

"What's she getting?" Wen said, pointing in the direction where Skrunch had gone.

"Another one."

"You need two?" Chase asked.

"Yeah, because we—"

"Just get it," Chase said.

"Slowly," Wen added, still aiming her gun at him.

"Okay, okay," he said, reaching in carefully and pulling out his computer." He held the machine in his hands, pushed a few buttons, and sighed, in apparent relief, as it came to life.

"What's the other laptop for?" Chase asked.

"Like I tried to tell you," Lenny began. "This one's got your data on it. The other one is for your payment."

"I'm not paying anything until you show it to us."

"Didn't Mars tell you I'm cool?"

"Mars vouched for you, but seeing how he's in prison, I need a little reassurance."

"Same here," Lenny said, backing up, as if to protect the data. "I just can't go all the way with that. If you see what I got, then you might know enough to not need the rest."

"You're telling me one peek is worth half a million?"

"Easily." Lenny stared at Chase.

Chase looked at Wen.

"I can shoot you now, and we can just take it," Wen said.

"That's not how we play this. Until I type in the password, you got nothing."

"I'm pretty good with computers," Chase said. "Not sure I need you."

"You do." Lenny stared again, almost pleadingly.

"Then I'll trust you," Chase finally said, deciding the guy might be legit. "But if I'm not completely amazed . . . "

"You will be, you will be," Lenny said, relaxing a bit. "As soon as I see half the cash hit my account, I'll give you the data. Then you check it and send the other half."

"No deal," Chase said.

"It's fair, man. I'm trusting you halfway, you trust me halfway."

"Mars said this man has something," Wen said. "We've come all this way. Let's trust him and see what he has. She raised her gun inches from Lenny and pointed it at his head. "If he doesn't have anything, or he tries to cheat us, I'll kill him, and then her." Wen moved the gun away toward Skrunch, who was now jogging back to them with a laptop, its screen already glowing.

Chase fished a phone from his pocket and tapped the screen. "Adya, it's me. I want to send that two-hundred-fifty-thousand-dollars to this account." He looked up at Lenny.

Skrunch traded laptops with Lenny, who then read the account number to Chase. After Chase finished telling Adya the information, she asked him three questions that only he could answer. If he was under duress, she'd know.

Chase asked Adya to hold on while he looked at the data.

"Wait, I can't seem to—" Lenny said.

Wen cocked her gun.

Chase was growing impatient. He already knew why the Fire Bombers had declared war. SEER was busy narrowing down the list even further. They even had the next three targets. "We only came here because you're supposed to have this earth-shattering information," Chase said. "You've got ten seconds to produce it."

"Hold on, hold on, I'm not the computer guy. I just can't find it. But it's here."

Mars told me this guy had critical data I needed, Chase thought. *But Mars is in prison, and although he has his finger on the pulse of criminals and the shadow worlds, this is way above him—espionage, government conspiracies, trillions of dollars at stake, and potentially a revolution.*

"Can you help?" Lenny asked Skrunch. She leaned in and began offering suggestions.

Yeah, this is all theatre, Chase thought. *Mars might've gotten this one wrong. I probably just blew a quarter million on a pair of grungy hackers. This is just a high tech shakedown. I'm going to let Wen waste this guy.*

"Just a few more seconds," Lenny said, working the keys with Skrunch.

Suddenly, the musty silence was shattered by a series of loud crashes.

Wen spun just in time to take a blow across her chest.

Chapter Fifty-Seven

Wen realized immediately that the object that had hit her chest was an empty bottle, but it still hurt. Her initial impulse to shoot the homeless man throwing bottles gave way to rational thinking based on her training. Less than ninety seconds later, she had him subdued, tied up, and after his constant rants, taped his mouth shut.

Chase never took his eyes off Lenny and the laptop. He knew Wen could handle things, and wasn't surprised that she carried a small roll of duct tape and zip-ties in her pack.

"Here it is," Lenny finally said, tilting the laptop toward Chase. "Read right there."

Chase scanned the first two paragraphs quickly, not expecting anything more than what the Astronaut had already provided. However, it didn't take long to realize this was something more.

"Oh my God," Chase said, in a voice he could barely recognize as his own. "How much is here?"

"All of it, man."

Chase began opening files and clicking on documents.

His eyes filled with Defense Department memorandums, CIA strategies, covert studies, cross agency deep-data, classified aerial photographs, vendor lists, and more. It was astonishing, and worth millions, even billions, more than he'd paid.

Yet with all that, the items that caused him to look over his shoulder as if he were about to get shot were a cache of previously encrypted—now unencrypted—emails. The correspondence, seemingly lengthy and detailed, was between nine people—the President of the United States, the Defense Secretary . . .

I can't believe the power behind this thing, he thought as he quickly read through several of them. *What the hell?*

He saw two names he knew well—Tess Federgreen and Travis Watts.

No wonder Tess is desperate to find out who the Fire Bomber is. The Bomber's trying to stop this—trying to stop them. The Fire Bomber knows their names, and can blow up a lot more than just buildings.

And then he saw the critical code word, the thing he most needed to know in order to rip it all apart: horUS.

"This looks good," Chase said, playing it cool. "You got a flash drive for me?"

Skrunch handed him a flash drive.

"I'm going to have to keep the laptop, too," Chase said, slipping it into his pack.

"Hey, man, for half a million bucks, you can have the laptop *and* my Nikes if you want them."

Chase pushed a button on his phone. "Adya, go ahead and send the remaining two-fifty."

Skrunch handed the other laptop to Lenny. After a few keystrokes he had the screen up waiting for confirmation that the funds had transferred.

Wen heard a noise and fanned her gun in that direction.

"It's cool," Skrunch said. "Probably your homeless dude again."

Wen, ignoring her, took a few steps and clicked on the flashlight she'd attached to her gun with electrical tape.

"What's taking so long?" Lenny asked nervously.

"Adya?" Chase asked into his phone. He listened for a moment. "She says it's gone and she has a receipt number, it should be showing up on your end already."

Lenny continued to stare at the screen.

"Refresh your damned browser," Skrunch muttered.

"That did it," Lenny said. "Confirmed. We're golden. Pleasure doing business with you."

"Yeah," Chase said. "One word of advice: *don't* try selling this again. You somehow lived through this one. If you raise this to anyone else, you won't be so lucky."

"Are you threatening us?" Skrunch asked.

"I'm promising you," Chase said in a deadly tone.

"Let's go," Lenny said.

"My bag's in the storeroom," Skrunch said, walking in that direction.

Chase found Wen ten feet into the darkness. "Anything?" he asked.

"Something isn't right. Get your gun ready."

"The deal was true. They weren't screwing us."

"Good, but that's not what I'm talking about."

They heard another sound—empty beer bottles, perhaps accidentally kicked, spinning on the concrete floor. Broken glass—maybe one hit a wall.

"She's right, it's probably that homeless guy."

"No. He won't come back."

"Then let's just get outta here," Chase said.

Wen pointed her gun and light in an arch ahead of

them as they passed an old shoe store, and then what was probably a jewelry kiosk, the outline of block letters spelling "GOLD" and "SILVER" still visible.

They hustled toward the escalators. She spotted a shadow move inside a space called something "ATTIC" and nudged Chase to look.

"We're about to get hit," she said.

They began to sprint.

Five feet from the escalators, just as Chase was thinking they were going to make it, something fast and invisible hit them. They both went down on their backs.

Wen managed to keep one of her weapons, but Chase's gun popped out of his hands as he hit the hard floor. For a second, with the wind knocked out of him, he couldn't breathe, and wasn't sure if he'd been shot. Before he could recover, a heavy, wet canvass tarp landed on top of them.

Wen fired through the dank material, but it was too late. She kicked and screamed. However, the fight made no difference, as all reference and sound quickly faded. Soon there was nothing but forever dark silence as their bodies floated in nothingness.

Chapter Fifty-Eight

Chase awoke to burning pain across his cheeks, feeling as if a giant dog was biting his face over and over again. He tried to reach up and stop it, but his hands were trapped behind him. His wrists also stung, feeling as if they were on fire. He tried to speak, but his tongue seemed glued in place in the worst case of cotton mouth ever.

A few seconds later, although he couldn't be sure if it had been ten minutes, maybe even longer, Chase finally realized that somebody was slapping him repeatedly across the face. In the startling pain, he suddenly opened to his situation and the suffocating odor of heavy cologne and thick smoke—cigarettes, maybe something else.

Is it burning flesh?

"Where's Wen?" Chase finally managed to say in a raspy, stuttered voice.

"Where is when? What is what? Who is who? Who is on first?" a man, smelling of vodka, mimicked in a Russian accent. "You should shut up, you pathetic dog,"

Chase tried to focus on his surroundings. They were still in the mall. He looked out and could see the main hallway where more light was coming in, but it wasn't a natural hue, and gave no clue as to its origins. The store across the way had giant, once brightly-colored letters that spelled out "TOYS" and then some other missing letters. For some reason this depressed him even more.

Then he saw Wen in the reflection of a broken mirror. She was behind him. They were both in old folding-chairs, hands taped at their backs.

Two stocky men were at one end of the space. Lenny stood near them with his hands tied in front of him. Skrunch paced nervously fifteen-feet away. She was definitely free.

"What do you want?" Chase asked.

"Money, Mr. Malone. Lots and lots of money," the Russian said, holding up Chase's wallet. "You are wealthy man. Seven hundred twenty-nine dollars in your wallet is nothing. I want ten million dollars."

"I'll bet you do," Chase said with a laugh.

The man kicked Chase's chair out from under him. Chase's head slammed against the floor.

"There is nothing funny happening here Mr. Malone. If I do not get ten million dollars, you are going to die very quickly."

"If you want ten million dollars, maybe you should start acting a little nicer," Chase said. From his new vantage point on the floor, he could see the contents of his and Wen's packs piled up on an old, tipped over display counter, including the Antimatter Machine, which he hoped they thought was just another laptop. Not far from their stuff he saw another woman, also tied up. He didn't recognize her.

While the media tried to unravel the mysterious end of the militia in Idaho and how it connected to the Fire Bomber, Gunner continued with his master plans. At about the same time the FBI was arriving at the Training Fields, his militia's compound in Michigan, he was getting off a small plane in West Virginia. The man greeting him shared the news about the Idaho militia. Gunner immediately made a risky call to his source.

"This isn't proper," the source whispered into the phone.

"Idaho," Gunner said.

"I was powerless to stop it."

"But you knew they had nothing to do with this."

"I don't think you would have escaped without them hitting Idaho."

"This is typical. They destroyed innocent people without any evidence they were involved with the bombings."

"We can't predict how every aspect of this will go. There is always the possibility for collateral damage."

"Remember those words in the coming days," Gunner said, hanging up. He pulled out a handwritten list from his pocket. One side of the worn yellow sheet listed the horUS companies. The back contained many more names, including most tech titans that had anything to do with artificial intelligence, and their companies. "Autopilot," he said to the man who had met his flight, "starts tonight."

Flint, now in San Francisco, personally checked on Chase's mother at the hospital, reorganized the security detail, then went to Balance Engineering to make certain the building was completely secure. Before he left town he met with his agents who had been at the Malone home during the attack and paid his respects to the husband of the officer who had lost her life. Flint, frustrated by his inability to protect Chase and his family, or discover the identities of those pursuing them, called Tess.

"What about Idaho?" he asked after they exchanged greetings.

"We're not confident."

"Bad intel?"

"We don't know yet."

"Do you have Chase?"

"No, he lost us in Los Angeles. We'll get him on-screen again. It's LA, not the wilds of the Shasta wilderness."

"I've tried to pull him away from this, but even before they killed his father, he was not backing off. He's not much of a surrenderer."

"Is that a word?"

"Apparently not to him."

"We're trying to ID the attackers. The FBI found hidden web-based surveillance cameras in the house. They're trying to access the feeds."

"I want to know," Flint said, already planning to check with Chase in case he knew how to get in.

"I'll see what I can do."

"If not Idaho?"

"We have another group," Tess said. "They're going in now."

"Where?"

"Can't say."

"Come on, my guy is a target of the group. His dad is dead. His mom is not out of the woods."

"I'll tell you when I can."

"What else aren't you telling me?"

"More than you can ever imagine."

Chapter Fifty-Nine

The narrow space allowed only enough light to show the silhouetted figures of the others who were present. Chase strained his eyes to identify them and figure out his chances. In the darker shadows, the areas outside his line of sight, there could be more thugs, which made planning an escape challenging.

I know Wen is going to try something, but without seeing her, I can't know the timing, he thought. *I've got to get into a position to help her.*

"You dumb dog," the Russian said, suddenly kicking Chase in the leg. "I am tired and would like to go have a drink. But you are wasting my time. So I will have to settle for the half-million dollars you have already given my friend over there." He pointed to Lenny. "And then, I will give you something in return. How about five bullets. One for each of you. I am a decent fellow, so I will do it. Quickly. In. The. Head. Boom." The Russian laughed. "I do not think it will even hurt."

"You're not a good fellow!" Wen shouted. Chase knew

this was just to make sure he knew she was alive and her location.

"Perhaps you are right. Maybe if I am not a good fellow, I should use you first. I like Chinese food."

"Try it, you impotent oaf," Wen taunted.

"Do not worry, little Chinese slut, I will give you some of this Russian bear before you die. But first, business. Always business before pleasure. So, Mr. Chase Malone, brilliant billionaire, one last chance."

Chase said nothing.

"Tsk, tsk, tsk," the Russian said. "But if you do not want to spend ten million dollars to save five lives, I do not care. I am tired and thirsty." He turned away from Chase and began talking to someone else. "Shoot them one at a time."

"In the head?" the man asked.

"No, I have changed my mind. The China girl insulted me, so shoot them in the gut, slow bleeding, painful death. But shoot the famous Chase Malone last. I think he might reconsider his selfish position once we are about to kill his girlfriend."

"Who first, then?"

"Start with Skrunch girl. We need to get rid of her anyway."

"Hey, I helped you!" Skrunch yelled. "We had a deal! I wouldn't owe you anymore. You're going to let me go!"

The Russian laughed. "We were never going to let you go, stupid girl. You should know better. I cannot let people go."

"You made a *deal*!?" Lenny yelled. "You idiot! They're going to kill us all!"

One of the other men grabbed Skrunch and dragged her over in front of Chase, pushing her up against the wall. Someone lifted Chase's chair off the floor.

Chasing Fire

"Try to keep your seat this time, Mr. Malone." The Russian laughed. "Are we ready now? We will give you three seconds to stop this unfortunate event, Malone. Kill her when I count to three."

The man holding Skrunch tied her to a post and held a gun against her head.

Skrunch cried and pleaded, "No, no we had a *deal*."

"One," the Russian snapped loudly.

Three seconds? What the hell? Chase thought. *Come on Wen, spring into one of your action moves.* He couldn't tell if the Russians would actually kill Skrunch, and he definitely wasn't sure if it was up to him to try to save her after she'd betrayed them and set up this trap. But he couldn't just let somebody . . .

"Three."

The gunshot was deafening in the small space and seemed to echo forever. The man let go of Skrunch's arm. She dropped to the cluttered floor. Chase saw blood running from her head and turned away.

"Ohhh!" Lenny screamed. "What happened to two?"

"Okey-dokey," the Russian said. "Who is next?" He shined the light at the other woman Chase now assumed was Bull. "How about we let Mr. Malone choose who dies next."

Why is Wen being so quiet? Chase wondered.

"Okay, if you aren't going to choose, I will," the Russian said. "Let's kill the stupid dog, because I would like to maybe play with this girl while Mr. Malone watches because he looks like he might like that."

Two guys dragged Lenny over in front of Chase while the leader absently fondled Bull.

"Should we do three-seconds again?" the Russian asked. "That seemed to work well the last time. One . . . "

Chapter Sixty

He's going to do it again! Chase thought frantically, looking around the dark space inside the abandoned mall, searching for any way to stop the nightmare. *I don't really care about Lenny, but he didn't seem to know any better, and he's no more than thirty seconds from killing Wen . . .*

"Two," the Russian said, as if it had a second syllable, while eying Chase.

"All right, wait," Chase said.

Lenny let out a moaning sigh.

The Russian smiled. "You cracked sooner than I expected. That is good. Maybe I will have time for another drink."

"What do I have to do for you to let us out of here?" Chase knew the Russian would never release them—he'd just heard him say to Skrunch a minute earlier that he couldn't let people go—but he had to buy time.

"Transfer ten million dollars to my account, and then you will be free," the Russian said in his best innocent voice. "That is all you need to do, my friend."

"You're not my friend, but if you let my friends go—the two women and Lenny over there—I'll transfer the money. But you have to let them go first."

"You are confusing me, Mr. Malone."

"One—release the two women and Lenny. Two—Transfer the ten million. Three—confirm the funds are in your account. Four—you let me go. We're done."

"No, dumb dog! It is not working like that. First, you give me the money. Then my friends and I will leave this pig sty. You will remain here, tied up, until someone finds you."

"No deal."

"Shoot funny Lenny!"

"Okay, wait!" Chase said as Lenny whimpered. "How about this? We do everything your way, but you don't leave us tied up. We'll stay here until you've been gone twenty minutes. If we leave earlier, you can shoot us."

"I can shoot you now. I do not need permission," the Russian said, firing his pistol. Lenny collapsed, screaming in pain. "Ahhh, sorry, I did not hit his face. Next time I will not miss." He pointed his gun again.

"All right, stop, *please*," Chase snapped. "I'll take the deal."

"That deal is no longer available," the Russian said, lowering his gun and smirking. "Now it cost you eleven million."

"What?"

"Best deal you can have." He pointed his gun at Lenny, who was curled up on the floor holding his leg, moaning. "Count to three with me. One . . ."

"Okay, eleven million," Chase said. "Untie me. Bring me the laptop."

"No, you call someone. You have them do it."

"Then I'll have to give them my access code, and as

soon as I do, they'll know that I'm in trouble, and it will start a GPS trace and alert my private security force, state and local police, and the FBI. All my accounts will instantly be frozen. That's the way my system is set up."

"I do not like you Mr. Malone, and I truly do not trust you."

"The only way you can get this money is if I type the access keys in right now. I'm the only one with the authority."

The Russian looked at one of the other men, who shrugged. "Okeydokey. Keep the guns on them. Anything funny, kill them all."

Now what the hell do I do? Chase wondered. Still worried about Wen, hoping she'd decided to play opossum; that she, like Chase, was counting on the Russians being oblivious to her dangerous capabilities. He didn't care about the money. Everything was to buy time.

One of the men cut the tape from Chase's wrists and pushed him to the counter where the register had once been. Another shoved a laptop in front of him.

Chase looked at the computer. "This is the wrong one."

"It came from your bag," one of them argued.

"I know, but it doesn't have the right access. I need the one he had. That's where we transferred the money."

It didn't make sense, but Chase figured they might not argue with a tech genius about computer issues. Chase held his breath, hoping the bluff would work.

The first Russian nodded to the other, who went to get the second laptop, put it in front of Chase, and turned it on.

"Happy?"

"Yeah, thanks." Knowing this could be the last minutes of their lives, Chase went to a banking site and keyed in some numbers. They watched him closely as his account information appeared on the screen.

"It will take a moment," Chase said. "It requires three-part validation."

"Kill the girl if it does not validate in thirty seconds," the Russian said, setting a timer on his phone. "Twenty-nine, twenty-eight . . ."

Chapter Sixty-One

Chase knew how to signal Wen. He took a deep breath, then said in a loud, deliberate voice, "I feel like I'm about to jump off a dam!"

Wen instantly let out an excruciating scream that could have shattered glass.

Everybody turned their attention to her. "Shut her up," the head Russian said.

In that same moment, Chase took the laptop and swung it with all his strength into the Russian's face. Wen stood up, still taped in her chair, and managed to jam the metal backrest under the chin of the man closest to her. As she crushed his Adam's apple, she continued pushing backwards with her momentum. She landed with the chair full force onto his chest as the man slammed into the floor, knocked out. Wen sprang back to her feet and charged another man. Just as he was about to fire at her, she turned sideways and leaped at him, smashing his head and sending him reeling. Before he could recover, Wen had him pinned against the wall. She produced a concealed shard of broken mirror and efficiently cut his throat without ever slowing her movement.

Wen continued moving, spinning out and heading back into another attacker. Lenny, leg still bleeding, somehow got up long enough to tackle a man running toward Chase, who was trying to get to Wen. Lenny, outmatched, was able to knock the man's gun into the darkness before the Russian worked him over as if pounding a heavy bag hanging in a gym. He left Lenny back on the floor, curled in a fetal position, before resuming his charge toward Chase.

Bull flew in between them, tripping the ape and even getting a half-kick into his eye as he went down. It wasn't enough to stop him for long. He staggered back into the fray, picking Bull up off the ground, planning to slam her down, before Wen suddenly appeared, spinning backward and thrusting javelin-style two of the metal chair legs into his stomach and face. The strike hit perfectly, impaling one of the steel legs into his mouth and out his jaw.

The successful assault left Wen tangled on the floor with the massive man screaming. Another Russian stepped in, pointing a gun at her. She rolled back, inflicting further agony onto her self-connected victim and kicked the incoming man hard in the face, wrapping her legs around his neck and twisting until his spinal cord snapped and he collapsed onto her. Wen, completely trapped under the two Russians, and still bound to the chair, tried to claw for the gun the second man had dropped. Bull, who had somehow freed herself, pulled the second attacker off Wen and helped her free herself from the chair, leaving it stuck into the first man.

The small space erupted in gunfire. Chase, wrestling the

lead Russian for an automatic pistol, slammed his elbow into the man's nose while the bullets sprayed in all directions. The others dove for cover.

Bull and Wen both had guns, and crawled along the floor, trying to get position. The last two Russians not tangling with Chase returned fire. Debris, drywall dust, splintered wood, plastic, and flying glass created a toxic cloud in the middle of the darkened space as bullets shredded everything.

Chase scooped up a handful of dust from the floor and jammed it into the Russian leader's eyes. Instead of releasing the gun as Chase had hoped, the enraged Russian swung around with renewed strength and fired at Chase. Several rounds escaped the chamber, but fortunately the temporarily blinded man couldn't see well enough to aim, and instead glittering, eggshell-like glass from the long fluorescent tubes in the ceiling rained down on them.

Chase squirmed out from the weight of the Russian's legs and was able to knee his already tortured face. After the laptop slamming, dust to his eyes, and fluorescent storm, the blow from Chase's knee had extra impact, weakening him just enough. Chase grabbed the man's wrist while repeatedly pumping his knee into the Russian's face, snapping his wrist against the hard floor several times, which allowed him to finally pry the gun from the Russian's strong hand.

Now in possession of the firearm, Chase was left in an awkward position. All he could do was push the gun against the Russian's gut and pull the trigger. A messy explosion of blood and flesh coated Chase's chest, face, and arms, but the man still wasn't dead. He flailed about menacingly, yet ineffectively, as Chase crawled away and sat against the wall, exhausted, shaking from the strain. He wished for more light so he could see where everyone else was because he didn't know where to shoot.

Wen, figuring there was no more than one opponent remaining, stopped shooting. The space became eerily quiet except for the angry moaning of the leader, slowly dying as he bled out. Wen crawled along the side of the wall where she could see Chase's silhouette faintly backlit from the main hall outside. Along the way, beam-down in pile of wood scraps and sawdust, she found one of the bigger flashlights that had belonged to the Russians, still powered on. She held it against her gun and spun it into the room, searching for enemy targets. There were none.

She yelled out, "How many Russians were there?"

No answer.

"Damn it, *how many Russians were there*?"

"Seven," Bull answered. Wen shined the flashlight around the room again, counting dead Russians. She got to six, not counting the moaning man. Then the light crossed Lenny, still alive, but badly injured, not far from Skrunch's body.

Wen stood up, shining the light toward Bull. "I guess you're the real hacker who found horUS?"

"Yeah," Bull answered.

"You want me to finish this guy off?" Wen asked Bull, pointing the light toward the Russian leader, who gave a defiant grunt. "Or do you want me to let him suffer? Or maybe you want to shoot him yourself?"

While Wen continued to shine the light at the Russian, Bull walked over and pointed her gun at his head.

"No, I'd rather him die slowly," Bull said, looking at the pool of blood.

Chase joined Wen. "That was not fun," he said. "And you're going to need to put my leg back in again."

"I think the fun is just beginning. These weren't even the people who have been trying to kill us."

"Good point," Chase said, limping over and grabbing the Antimatter Machine and the laptop with the horUS data on it. "Let's get out of here before someone else shows up."

Chapter Sixty-Two

A conference call between, Tess, Travis, the Deputy Assistant Secretary of Defense, the CIA Director, and the head of the NSA had not gone well. Each of them were part of the nine horUS originators, and as the CIA Director said, "The odds of our program leaking have increased with each bombing. That means even with all of our protections in place, the possibility of one or all of us going down with the drones is very real."

The pressure had been mounting for days. Tess believed they could end the nightmare as soon as the identity of the source could be revealed. "Who the hell is giving this information to the bombers?" she asked them all again. They each agreed it could not be one of the nine, but possibly someone in their respective departments. Tess had been working through lists and had even set several traps, but thus far had nothing. She told them that her top analysts believed the source was at the Pentagon, to which the Deputy Assistant took great offense.

"My people believe it's someone in the intel community," he shot back.

The call deteriorated after that, and each agreed to double their efforts at finding the source.

In the weeks since Tri-Knight Avionics became the Fire Bomber's first victim, the firm had leased a new building and moved all their employees. A few days earlier, they'd started producing components for horUS again. Gunner had been expecting the news, but it forced him into a difficult decision—one which would mean probably losing Powder. He realized the only way to stop the program long enough would be to kill the employees, too.

"Buildings and equipment can be replaced almost instantly," he told a subordinate. "People take a long time to replenish."

"Agreed," the man said.

"Phase one is nearly complete," Gunner continued, scraping mud off his boot. "Phase two, although much shorter, will make that look like a picnic."

"And phase three?" the man said. "When do we start the daytime strikes?"

It was an excruciating decision for Gunner, killing Americans, but he believed the employees were complicit in the betrayal of the country by its leaders.

"The killings will start in forty-eight hours."

Lenny and Bull headed to the doctor who had helped him before. Afterward, the plan called for them getting out of the country. Wen had hastily arranged for WOLF people to hide them, at least until horUS was exposed, because that's exactly what Chase planned to do as soon as they found out who the Fire Bombers were, and they had tracked down Ryker and Damon.

Back aboard the Bombardier-8000 jet, en route to Las Vegas, Chase and Wen reviewed the data from Lenny.

"It's called horUS," Wen said, reading from the Anti-matter Machine, where they'd transferred all the material, as well as sent them to the Astronaut. "The acronym stands for High Optics Reconnaissance United States. Horus is the Egyptian god of the sky, meaning 'the distant one' or 'one who is above all others.' He is depicted as a falcon headed man. The eye of Horus . . . " She paused and looked at Chase. "The all-seeing eye."

"They're watching every American."

"Why?" Wen asked, already knowing the answer. China had been doing the same thing for years with their mass network of hundreds of millions of cameras.

"It's by far the most invasive surveillance system in the world. Privacy is gone and no one even noticed. They'll claim, like they always do, that this is about terrorism or protecting the population, but it's not. These drones are about one thing: controlling the people," Chase answered.

After landing in Vegas, they headed toward the Bellagio to meet up with a team of fifteen hired guns that Flint had put together to help them. Although, at Wen's insistence, Chase had not informed his head of security *why* he needed the extra force. Flint had pushed, and speculated that they were on the trail of the Bombers, but, in the end, he gave in and arranged for the unit to join Chase and Wen at the casino, figuring a busy, crowded, central location would be safest.

On the way from the airport, while Wen drove the rental car, Chase called the one person other than Ryker and Damon who he blamed for his father's death.

Chapter Sixty-Three

"When were you going to tell me about horUS?" Chase said as soon as Tess answered the phone.

"I shouldn't be surprised you discovered it," Tess said, at home, hoping for an early evening after a long day trying to pinpoint the Fire Bomber's next target, searching for Chase, and trying to uncover the Source. Now that was shattered. The wall, carefully built around horUS, was cracking before her eyes. "After all, it was your brilliance and tech-savvy experience that made me want to bring you on board."

"Really? It looks more like you got me involved so you could use me and my connections to further your agenda."

"No, I thought you could find the Bombers. That was the reason." She was growing impatient with Chase. Her home was her refuge—a mini-estate overlooking the Potomac River just outside Washington. "I needed to stop them."

"Before anyone found out."

"Yes. I needed them found before the FBI, before the media, or anyone else, discovered their motive."

"To *protect* horUS!"

"Of course. Can you imagine the outcry if horUS got out?"

"Oh, it's going to get out. I'm going to make sure it gets out."

"Think that through, Chase."

"What are *you* thinking? What are you people trying to do?" He motioned to Wen to slow down.

"Don't be confused about horUS," Tess said. "It's not a bad program."

Chase laughed. "I think you might actually believe the garbage you're spewing."

"The program is designed to save American lives. To *protect* us. This isn't the world where you grew up. It's changing astonishingly fast because of technology, some of which *you* helped to create."

"Wait, this is *my* fault?" Chase asked, reminding himself to sound calm. The Vegas strip was blazoned with its lights, billboards, casinos. The reflected images danced on the windshield, as if tattooing their opulence, cheap dates, and easy money on his life. It disgusted him.

"Do you think the Chinese, or Russians, or any number of the thousands of extremist organizations around the world care about your right to privacy?"

"Oh, is that how you're going to frame this? Defend it by saying all we have to do is give up a little bit of our rights to protect everyone? Do you recall what Benjamin Franklin said about that? Let me remind you: 'Those who would give up essential liberty, to purchase a little temporary safety, deserve neither liberty nor safety.'"

"Benjamin Franklin died more than two hundred years ago. He couldn't have even remotely imagined the world as it was a century ago, let alone what we are dealing with now."

"Then tell me, I really want to hear how you think spying on Americans twenty-four seven, their every move, helps protect them."

"In case you haven't noticed, and I would've thought with your relationship with Wen you might have, Communist China is bent on taking over the world. They've managed in just a few decades to steal most of our technology and a huge portion of our economy. Their influence in the world is growing by the day while ours wanes. And it's not just them. It's all the criminals and other hostile governments and groups that are becoming increasingly sophisticated. Our traditional military is becoming less effective. If we're not watching the country, we're going lose it." She started pacing back and forth in bare feet, loose pajamas and a glass of wine, which she'd just topped off for the second time.

"Orwell was right in *1984*, Big Brother is—"

"Don't be so dramatic. This is no different than people putting security cameras around their home."

Chase thought of his father crawling to the photo album and the cameras that had allowed him to see that horrible image. The cameras that had allowed his father to see the intruders, had shown him the monsters Damon and Ryker. Chase was thankful for that footage.

He clenched his fist.

Wen pulled into a convenience store lot and quickly went inside.

"It's a hollow argument, Tess. Maybe, just maybe, you, and the other eight people involved, have wonderful intentions and are doing this for all the most noble reasons, but who comes after you? What will the next excuse be to tweak it, to push it just a little bit further, to arrest a potential revolutionary who may or may not have ever committed a crime, but entertains it out of frustration or simply to explore all the possibilities?"

"You have no idea what we're facing every day. There are militias in all fifty states. Membership estimates exceed seventy-five-thousand revolutionaries, Antifa, dozens of anarchist groups, right-wing extremists, left-wing, NorthBridge, MS-13, domestic terror organizations too numerous to list, the Inner Movement, the Inner Force, the Aylantik, the Fire Bombers . . . "

"I don't need a laundry list—my point is how do you tell the *difference*?"

Wen returned with bottles of water and bags of trail mix. She offered him a handful, which he waved off.

"We will have safeguards in place."

Chase laughed again. "Like we have safeguards in this country with the Constitution, the most incredible document ever written. It's packed full of safeguards, and yet it's now riddled with holes. It's become a prop used by the elites in the overreaching governments, and the military, to control us."

Wen smiled, thinking he sounded like a member of WOLF.

"Spoken like a true billionaire."

"Hey, I earned my money by trying to make the world better."

"Funny, that's how I earn my paycheck, too."

"What about the hackers?" Chase asked, getting back on track. "Even your most secure, sophisticated network, guarding the most prized secrets in the world, wasn't enough to stop a twenty-something girl from getting in. I didn't learn about horUS because of my wizardry and technology. I got it from a burned-out hacker."

Wen continued driving slowly through the insanely chaotic town.

Tess stuttered something incoherent as she apparently realized the dangers she faced now weren't just from Chase, but there was a hacker out there—maybe many of them—who knew. Suddenly, everything became unstable, as if the ground beneath her was shaking in a rippling earthquake that might never end. Still, Tess was Tess, and had been operating for years in the middle of an explosive battlefield. She recovered quickly, but her tone had turned icy.

"You've proven my point about hackers, dissidents, *anyone* trying to undermine the security of our great nation. And if you don't think it's great, look around for what system you would rather have, and don't quote some Scandinavian country the size of Pittsburgh. There is no better place. We've got flaws, and we're trying to fix them. But anybody, like these Bombers, who disagrees so strongly they're willing to break the law . . . HorUS will let us find them and bring them to justice."

"Anyone who would break the law?" Chase shot back "Like you, the president, and the others? How many laws have *you* broken Tess? What should we do with *you*?"

Chapter Sixty-Four

After ending the call with Chase, Tess poured herself another glass of Pippin Hill Cabernet Sauvignon, her favorite wine from a Virginia vineyard. As she enjoyed a long taste, she gazed out the window and watched a young fawn and its mother graze lilac leaves on the edge of the meadow of her two-acre back lawn where it met the woods. The innocence and simple presence of the doe and her fawn were like a salve to her mind, burning with turmoil of the Fire Bomber, horUS, and the missing Chase Malone.

Suddenly the two deer, clearly spooked, took off running. At the same moment, she heard a snap, as if a branch had broken, and slight scraping by the front door. Her gun was at the far end of the sprawling, one level ranch house. Instead, she reached for a large chef's knife and tiptoed toward the front of the house.

Tess chose a spot where the French doors opened to the back patio—still visible, but giving her the best chance to surprise anyone coming through the front entrance. A four-story square tower at the other end of the home would have given her a commanding view of the property, but it would be too risky to get there.

Reminding herself to breathe, she waited, recalling the description of the attack on Chase's parents. *I'm imagining all of this,* she told herself. Yet she knew the Fire Bomber would target her. Perhaps that was the next stage, killing the nine orchestrators of horUS.

She pulled her cell phone from her bra, about to dial 9-1-1, when a shadow moved across the front veranda.

The police will never make it here in time, she thought. *I've got to get my gun.*

She crouched to make her way to the bedroom while staying out of the line of sight of the windows. She dialed 9-1-1 as she went.

Startled by a sudden knock on the door, Tess accidentally dropped her phone as she darted into the guest bedroom. Its window had a view of the front of the house.

"Son of a . . . Flint!" she said in a relieved sigh, jogging back around to open the door. "What on earth are you doing here?"

"Surprising you."

They laughed about her being worried as Flint checked around. She gave him a full tour, including the unique tower that a prior property owner had built, attached to the house so they could see the river and part of the DC skyline. Their walk ended with a dip in the pool to deflect the afternoon's humid heat. Tess, being competitive and an excellent swimmer, challenged him to a race. Flint came up from their final lap the winner, but just barely.

"I'd better stick to dancing," he said, laughing while getting out of the pool and trying to catch his breath.

"You didn't do too bad for an old cowboy," Tess teased, climbing out and sounding not winded at all.

He took her in his arms and kissed her.

"Why, Flint Jones, I do declare," she said in her best Scarlett O'Hara voice. "You do make a woman blush."

"I aim to do more than that." He pulled her toward the house. "Let's get you out of these wet things."

Tess laughed.

Out of the corner of his eye, Flint caught sight of an armed man dressed in black emerging stealthily from the trees. Even while processing and instantly planning his reaction, he turned slightly away, as to not let on that he had seen the man, while he searched for options. Fifteen feet away, his gun, along with his clothes, lay on the large glass dining table. He put his arm around Tess and appeared to kiss her cheek.

"Laugh like I just said something funny, but we've got trouble," he said under his breath.

She laughed nervously, her eyes searching.

He grinned, as if amused, and continued talking low. "I'm going to try to make it to my gun. Anything happens, don't worry about me, get into the house." He glanced back at the man to see how much room he still had, but the intruder was gone. Flint picked up his pace while subtly but quickly scanning the perimeter. Instead of finding the man he was looking for, he saw a different man.

The second darkly dressed killer and Flint made eye contact. Flint shoved Tess into the manicured shrubs landscaped around the pool as he hurdled a chaise lounge, heading toward the table with his gun. Before he reached it, the table exploded. The second man, seeing what Flint was going for, had shot the glass-top table. The flying crystals of glass were compounded by incoming machine gun fire.

Flint rolled, hitting the concrete and broken glass with his bare shoulder, desperately searching for the gun as his back hit shards that tore into his flesh. The pain didn't even register as blood oozed from his still wet upper body. He kept moving, partially concealed by oversized-pots filled with tropical trees and heavy patio furniture. The gun was nowhere. Imported trees created a mini forest, giving Tess' pool area a small island resort look. Flint stooped as he ran along the edge of the house, taking his first glance back to check on Tess. *Damn it, where is she?* At the same time, he attempted to calculate the moves of the two gunmen. *Are there more?* He frantically took in the entire area. *Where have they gone?*

Chapter Sixty-Five

Flint made a break for the tower, figuring it could give him the advantage of the high ground and because he knew, from their earlier tour, that he could also access the main house in case Tess made it that far. As he reached the tower's door, he spotted one of the men following him. Flint bolted up the narrow steps which wrapped the inside walls of the four-story, ten-foot by ten-foot square structure.

The pursuing man climbed the stairs cautiously. Flint, having already decided the man was a professional, anticipated his careful movements and knew the man would be leading with his weapon, holding it close, expecting surprises. He also predicted the man to figure Flint had to be at the top of the tower. Still, the locked door connecting to the house, which Flint had checked, would bother and distract his pursuer. He'd wonder if maybe Flint had slipped into the house. Flint was banking on the fact that the man knew Tess, his target, a highly placed CIA official, and the man with her, might also be trained with prior field experience.

Flint, keeping one eye on the stairwell, glanced out the window, saw Tess dash into the back door of her house as the other intruder fired several shots at her. It appeared he missed, but Flint couldn't be sure.

The trick was convincing the assailant that he'd made the wrong guess, that Flint had actually gone into the house and locked the door behind him. Flint deduced that there would be no other way to get enough of a surprise on the man to make up for the fact that he was armed and Flint was not.

The man reached the top step, tentatively peering into the open space, anticipating an ambush. When he didn't see Flint, he climbed all the way up into the small room and quickly looked at the ceiling, searching for a hatch or opening into an attic. Nothing. He smiled when he saw a wardrobe cabinet against the far wall just large enough to conceal a man. A stack of hastily discarded clothes, still on hangers, dumped on the otherwise clean and uncluttered floor, told him what he needed to know. Deciding it would be foolish to attempt to open the door, not knowing what kind of weapon the hiding person had, he aimed his gun midway up the thin pine door of the wardrobe and fired.

In that same instant, Flint pounced from behind, grabbed the man, and snapped his neck. The gun fell from his now limp hand. In addition to dumping the clothes from the wardrobe, Flint had opened the four windows, one on each side of the tower, and had been silently waiting on the roof. Wasting no more time, he snatched the man's handgun, submachine gun, and extra ammo, ran downstairs, darted out onto the patio, and quickly scanned the area for additional intruders.

As soon as Flint crossed the threshold, he went completely stealth, having no idea where Tess or the agent could be. A moment later, the agent revealed himself with footsteps and a closing door. Flint knew it was the agent and not Tess because she, being the one pursued and highly trained, would never have given herself away like that. It told him two more things—Tess was still alive, and the man's location. Still in just swimming trunks, barefoot, wet, and bleeding, Flint tiptoed toward the sound.

The noise from a gunshot blast forced Flint to cast away all caution. He flew down the hall, knowing she'd be in the master bedroom suite because that was where she most likely kept her gun. The shot he'd heard had been fired from a gun fitted with a suppressor. Tess would not have a silencer on her pistol. Trying to control his personal feelings, afraid he might already be too late, Flint thundered into the room.

Tess stood in the corner next to her king-sized bed, hands in the air. The man, about to shoot her, spun around, firing when he heard Flint. The bullets cut across Flint's stomach, but as he fell, he managed to get a shot off.

The shooter fell back as Flint's bullet clipped his shoulder. It took him only a moment to recover, but by then Tess had retrieved her gun.

With Flint down, the man spun to face Tess, ready to fire. She beat him to it. Her shot, from a .44 magnum, hit him in the center of his chest, a perfect kill shot. His gun fired as he went down, the bullet lodging somewhere in the ceiling.

Running to aid Flint, she fired another round into the man's head to be certain he would not be coming back to life. Tess crouched next to Flint, knowing it was too late to call for help. She pulled the bedspread off and used it to try to staunch the blood, but there was too much. "I love you," she said.

"Could. Be. More," Flint said in a low, hoarse voice.

She held up her gun as if to assure him she was prepared. "You'll be okay," she said, lip quivering, trying to convince herself.

"No," he said weakly, then, finding her eyes, added, "I love you. Always have."

She nodded, her battle with tears failing now.

"You must. Take. Care of Chase. Promise. Me."

She looked confused.

"It's a debt. I owe."

"I will," she said. "Promise."

"Thank. You."

She nodded, wiping her cheek.

"Call the company," he said, meaning the CIA. "Could. Be more."

Tess didn't want to leave him to get her phone. She knew he could be gone any minute.

"I want another dance," she said.

He started to smile.

"Flint? *Flint?* Oh, Flint . . . I'm so sorry."

Chapter Sixty-Six

The call between Chase and Tess had left Wen concerned. "Tess isn't going to just let us walk around with this horUS information," Wen said. "This is kill-data. There are drones up there right now, watching us."

"They're always watching," Chase replied, letting it sink in as they arrived at the Bellagio Casino.

When Flint's crew still had not shown up more than twenty minutes after the appointed time, Chase grew impatient. "Something isn't right."

"We don't have unlimited time," Wen said. "But we could use backup, so maybe we should give them a little longer."

"I can't reach Flint," Chase said, looking at his phone after trying a second call in the past five minutes. "I'll keep trying, but they'll just have to catch up with us later."

As they headed out to the entrance of the Bellagio,

Wen, as always, scanned the area. "Look over there," she said quietly. "And there."

"I see them, but we can't do this here."

"Do what?"

"These guys are most likely with the same group that killed my dad," he said, clenching his jaw.

"We don't know that."

"There's one way to find out. They are a link. We can get one of them to talk, tell us who they work for."

"Ryker isn't with them. Let's wait for Ryker. If we try to take out these four guys right here, you'll have every cop in Vegas on us."

Chase stopped, assessing options.

"We don't need that," Wen said slowly. "Remember the mission."

Chase closed his eyes for a moment and tried to drown out the bells, bings, and bustle of the casino. When he opened them, the four men had moved closer. "What do you want to do?" he asked, deciding to leave it up to her expertise.

"Follow me," she said, moving quickly onto the street. Chase stayed close.

The four men were now less than thirty feet behind them.

Wen pulled a startled valet out of a waiting copper-colored Lamborghini convertible. "Get in!" she shouted to Chase.

He jumped over the door and had barely hit the leather seat, as Wen floored it. "You want to talk about Las Vegas cops after us? Could you have picked a more conspicuous car? This is a Lamborghini Aventador Superveloce Roadster. Five or six hundred thousand dollars," he shouted over the roar of the engine. "The owner won't be happy."

"It goes fast," Wen said, trying not to smile.

"That doesn't help in strip traffic," Chase admonished as they reached a red light intersection. He turned around and surveyed the lineup. "The 'goon-squad' is six cars back. At least let me drive."

"Okay," Wen said, knowing she was better riding shotgun and he was better driving. "But remember, this is not a race. We have to get to Lipton Innovations by midnight." She slid across the front seat as he climbed around and dropped into the driver's seat.

"Lipton Innovations is eighteen minutes from here," Chase said as he tapped in the address to the GPS and the light changed to green. "Meanwhile, there's a case of liquor." He pointed to a box labeled "Booker's Rye" whiskey wedged between the seats. "Maybe you can fix me a drink."

She wasn't amused as she looked behind them. "Five back now," she said.

"Moved up one already?"

"Yeah, you see them in the dark blue SUV?"

Chase checked the rearview mirror. "Yeah, but our car is way faster." He used the congested strip to their advantage. Nine or ten blocks later, after some quick turns on to and out of side streets, he declared, "I think we lost them."

"Maybe," Wen said, looking slowly all around. "Then let's ditch this car. It's too flashy."

"I was kinda getting used to it," Chase said with a smile, which had been almost completely absent since his father's murder. "When we're all done with this, I might have to pick up one of my own."

Wen shook her head. Suddenly, the blue SUV pulled out of an alleyway just ahead of them.

They raced in and out of lighter traffic, alleys, parking lots, and the occasional sidewalk for fifteen more minutes.

Every time Chase thought they were clear, the SUV showed up again.

"They have to be using horUS," Wen said after they lost them again. "That's the only way they could keep finding us."

"Which means these guys work for whatever government agency is managing horUS."

"CIA?" Wen asked. "Tess Federgreen?"

"Would she have arranged this before I told her we knew about horUS?"

"Maybe she thought you already knew something she needed to know. Maybe Flint's team was never coming."

Chase thought about those theories while he searched for another vehicle they could trade the Lamborghini for. The SUV squealed out of a street they had just passed. Now on the edge of town, Chase punched the accelerator and watched as the speedometer topped two hundred mph.

"There," Wen said, pointing to a long, wide underpass.

"Good idea." Chase pushed the car faster, praying the airbags worked in case they met an oncoming vehicle, but otherwise hoping they could lose these guys for good. Halfway into the underpass, orange and white reflective construction barrels blocked their way. "Damn! Who put those there?" Chase yelled. "Too late to turn back now."

They plowed ahead, smashing through the barrels, and found themselves in a lengthy tunnel created by the underpass with eight lanes above them. Parked cement mixers and dump trucks totally blocked any exit.

"We're boxed in!" Chase danced his feet in a rapid combination of gas pedal and brakes, putting the car into a 180-degree spin, turned on his brights, and headed back the way they came. A split-second later he slammed the brakes again.

The SUV was stopped crossway at the entrance of the tunnel. Eight armed men climbed out and took cover behind the vehicle and the few construction barriers still in place.

"Got any ideas?" Chase asked.

"Back up slowly. We can go out the other side on foot."

"So can they. How long do you think it'll take him to catch us?" Chase asked, nodding toward one of the men setting off on the outside of the concrete tunnel. "He's heading around there now to meet us."

"Then we'd better get there first."

Chase, glancing into the rearview mirror to check how far they still had to go as the Lamborghini slowly crawled back into the darker section of the tunnel, saw something. "I've got an idea."

Chapter Sixty-Seven

Damon and Ryker, with two others, had been standing by in the SUV while the other four approached Chase and Wen back at the Bellagio. They'd learned how slippery the pair could be, but as Damon ran around to the back entrance of the tunnel and took position, they thought they might finally have their prey.

"What's the status?" Ryker asked into his wrist to the group on the other side.

"The Lamborghini just burst into flames," one of the men responded.

"It's a distraction," Ryker said. Watching the tunnel entrance with night vision, Ryker communicated directly to Westfield in his Washington office. "Do you see us?"

"I got you," Westfield said, looking at the screen displaying a live feed captured by horUS. The drone's CSR filtered in night vision heat patterns, and the program could remove all vehicles.

"Remove all vehicles and show me just people," Ryker said, staring into real-time visuals on his tablet.

"The CSR is acting up," Westfield said when the image failed to change right away.

"The what?"

"It's a critical imaging sorting component," Westfield said. "Has anybody left that tunnel?" He made more swipes with his finger to rewind the view until he saw the copper-colored Lamborghini enter the tunnel.

"No one has left. They're still in there," Ryker said.

"Make sure he doesn't leave."

Ryker spoke into his wrist to confirm with Damon on the other side. Then he spoke to Westfield again. "Can you make sure the local heat stays out of this?"

"I'll do it now," Westfield said, pointing to an assistant in his office to get the Las Vegas Police Department to back off. "And Ryker, you've got to finish them."

Ryker acknowledged, then told Damon to send someone in. At the same time, he pointed silently to the two men still with him to proceed inside.

He radioed Damon as they approached the burning car. "I've got a bad feeling that Malone and that Chinese chick slipped out."

"Not out this side. Did they get past you?"

"No, but what the hell is with the fire?"

"Blinds our night vision."

"Maybe. Or what if they get one of those dump trucks started, plow it into the flaming car, and cruise out that way? Check the dump trucks, now!"

"Let's go," Damon said, as his men ran to the trucks. "If you're right, they can only come out your way. Too much equipment and piles of sand and stuff back here."

"I'm ready," Ryker said.

Ryker's earpiece buzzed with static, and then Westfield's

voice came through. "What's happening?" his boss asked, unable to see inside the tunnel.

Ryker ignored him.

Damon and the others each took a dump truck, approaching slowly. Then a frantic search, cab, bed, underneath . . . nothing. Empty. Ryker and his men ran to the two cement mixers. Nothing.

"Damn it!" Ryker barked. "Where *are* they?" His shouts echoed inside the tunnel. "Check every inch of the place!"

Noxious smoke from the burning Lamborghini began filling the area with fumes and black clouds. They rifled through two portable storage cabinets, lifted tarps, double checked underneath, behind the tires, and fired shots into several sand piles. The heavy smoke continued to close in on them.

Ryker tied a bandanna around his mouth and nose and approached the vehicle, looking for bodies, studying the scene. "Unbelievable!" He ran as close to the car as he could, then screamed every profanity he knew.

Damon arrived next to him as Ryker pointed to what had upset him.

"Get the dump trucks started!" Ryker yelled to one of the men. "Push this damn car out of the tunnel, *now*!"

One of them climbed into the closest truck and went to work. He used a Jack key, which could start any ignition, and ground gears until the big truck lurched forward. He slammed the truck into the burning vehicle, and at first it struggled to move the half-a-million-dollar melting hunk of metal and rubber. A long five seconds later, and a relic of the Lamborghini began sliding toward the entrance.

"Ryker can you hear me?" Westfield asked repeatedly.

As the smoke cleared, Ryker saw what he was looking for and cussed again.

"They're gone."

Chapter Sixty-Eight

Chase and Wen found themselves in a suddenly silent world. The smell of cold, stale air and wet concrete greeted them. Chase shivered as they stood in the damp, dark space, lit only by their small flashlights. They'd just climbed down the rusty metal rungs of a narrow, built-in ladder beneath the manhole cover Chase had backed the car over. Prior to their descent into the storm drains, Wen hastily made a series of alcohol bombs from the Booker's Rye whisky left in the Lamborghini. Chase went down first, before Wen moved the car the final inches into position over their escape route. Wen's slim frame allowed her to slip under the car after tossing two lit Molotov cocktails into the vehicle.

"It won't take long for them to discover our vanishing act," Chase said, shining his light up where Wen had slid the cover back in place. He had recently read an article about the scores of "mole people" living in the hundreds of miles of storm drains under Las Vegas.

"We can get lost down here for hours," Wen said.

"More like days," Chase answered, still second-guessing

the decision to run from the fight. "This feels like the ancient catacombs, or a tomb."

"It could become one for us if we don't keep moving." They took a second to debate which way to go.

"Lipton innovations is south of here," Chase said. "Which direction is south?"

"You're pretty optimistic," Wen said, shining a light down both tunnels. "I'm calculating the odds if we can make it out of here alive, and you're still planning to get to our destination on time."

"It's impossible to tell, because these tunnels can just wind and turn," Chase said, ignoring her. "We may think we're heading south and wind up actually going northwest."

"We've already waited too long. They could drop down on top of us any moment. Let's just go this way."

They ducked into the round concrete corridor and did their best to move fast through the cramped space. After what seemed like a long time, they slowed to catch their breath, now completely disoriented.

"How long have we been down here?" Chase asked.

"Seven minutes," Wen said.

"That's nuts, it feels like an hour."

That far underground, there was no cell coverage, no wireless, and definitely no point in trying the Antimatter machine. Wen pointed her light up ahead. "It seems to widen," she said, starting to jog again.

Chase had to stoop to keep from scraping his head on the concrete ceiling, and was relieved when they reached the area Wen had seen, because it opened into two rectangular tunnels crossing theirs.

"Left," they said in unison, having no interest in continuing down the narrower round drainage tunnel and figuring left was the most likely tunnel to be heading south. Making better time, a few minutes later they came upon a side opening, which looked to be somebody's bedroom—a stack of blankets, stacks of paperback books and magazines, a shopping cart filled with dirty laundry and jackets, an open sleeping bag, crumpled bedding, a cardboard box overflowing with empty food containers.

"Mole people," Chase said. "Supposedly there's hundreds of them living down here."

The area seemed otherwise abandoned. They kept moving.

They passed three or four more encampments before Wen suddenly grabbed his arm. "Shh do you hear that?"

Chase stilled himself for a moment and strained to listen. "It's definitely footsteps," he whispered.

"A lot of them," she hissed.

"I can't tell what direction it's coming from." The long, vacant stretch seemed to offer no place to hide, no way out.

"We probably should've stuck to the round tunnel. Gone up one of the manhole covers."

"There was a round tunnel back a little ways, do you remember?"

"I think that's where the footsteps are coming from," she said, pushing him forward. "The men followed us into the tunnel."

They started running faster, knowing their footsteps could be heard as well. It wasn't long before they ran into a group of homeless people—eight men, two women.

"Hey, hey, hey, where you going in such a hurry?" one of them asked.

"We're trying to find our way outta here," Wen said breathlessly.

"Aren't we all, honey," one of them said, as most of them laughed. "Aren't we all."

"Can you tell us the quickest way to get out?" Chase asked, looking over their shoulders and trying to determine if this was going to turn into something ugly.

"The fastest way to get out of here is to get yourself a good paying job, save enough money to pay rent—oh and cable TV, you'll want cable," one said, to more jeers and laughter.

"But to get a good place, you'll need good credit," one added. "No credit, no place—no place, no job. The casinos aren't going to hire you once been down here in—"

"Okay," Chase said, cutting off the man's rambling. "Have a nice night." He tried to weave his way past, but they blocked him.

"There's a toll to get through here."

"I don't see any tollbooth," Wen said.

"There's been signs for the last mile, but it is kinda dark in here, honey," a big lady said.

"We don't want any trouble," Chase said impatiently, still hearing footsteps behind them. He'd had a brief hope that the footsteps had belonged to this group. Now he knew they were all about to get slaughtered.

"How much is the toll?" he asked.

"Your wallet, everything in it, and your backpacks," the largest man said.

"Last chance," Wen said in a firm, even voice. "Let us pass."

"Pay the toll and—"

Before he could finish, Wen had knocked him and three other men to the ground with a combination of round kicks and flying punches.

The others came charging at them. "Why you little—" Before he got out his insult to Wen, she'd slammed him and another one into one of the walls. Chase pushed two more out of the way and kept moving with their forward momentum. None of the homeless followed. But it wasn't the downtrodden and derelicts they were worried about it, it was the crew from the surface of heavily armed, highly trained men who still had them trapped underground.

"The dirty dozen back there came from this direction," Chase said. "Oxygen shouldn't be much farther."

"As long as there aren't any turns."

"Nice work back there."

"They were just down on their luck, looking for an easy score," Wen said. "Normally I wouldn't have gone at them that hard. But those men from up top can't be more than a minute or two behind us, and you know they heard the commotion. They'll be moving faster now."

Chapter Sixty-Nine

The echoes of approaching trouble reverberating through the concrete maze warned Chase and Wen that they were down to seconds. The footfalls had been growing louder until they became a constant rumble. The living quarters where they had chosen to take their stand were similar to the dozen they had already passed—littered with trash, worn and stained clothing, and strange collections of urban artifacts that the occupant thought might be useful. Unfortunately, the occupant was also present, and somewhat inebriated. In the thirty or so seconds that they'd been trying to convince the poor fellow that they were not going to hurt him or take his belongings, Chase had given him two twenty dollar bills, and continuously begged for his silence, saying they were just there "to play a joke on friends."

The man moaned and repeatedly asked if Chase had any liquor. "You sure as shocks smell like a distillery," the man slurred.

Chase, who had spilled quite a bit of the Booker's Rye

on himself while they set up Molotovs for torching the Lamborghini, couldn't deny the familiar aroma that the homeless man was drawn to, but informed him, with apologies, that he'd already drank it all.

"Now that's not fair, I—" the man whined, starting to get up.

Chase gently pushed him back and reminded him of their deal. "Please be quiet for just two more minutes."

The footsteps' drone became deafening. Wen readied her weapon and aimed it at the opening. Chase thought of his father and steadied his arm, knowing they'd have to begin shooting as the men arrived or they'd lose their element of surprise.

The stampede amplified more, telling them that the pursuers could only be a couple of feet from the opening, and then they suddenly slowed.

"Another one," a gruff male voice announced.

"Ransack it like the others," came a different voice.

Chase and Wen, barely concealed behind an old cardboard box and an overstuffed shopping cart, remained completely still as four men ran by and only two remained to search their dwelling.

As soon as the two men climbed into the cavity, the homeless man began to protest.

"Hey, what the flip! This is not a party, you get the surprise?"

Two men shined the light at the man.

"Yow, get that light outta my eyes! Do you got twenty dollars for me to shut up, too?"

The men looked at each other.

"But I don't want any of that blinding light," he slurred. "Tell him, Distillery Man, tell them our deal."

The men suddenly realized somebody else might be in there. "You got friends visiting?" one of them asked.

"Not friends, they just busted in here and took over like they own the place. I don't got no landlord."

"Where are they?" the man asked as he ripped a large piece of cardboard down.

Wen grabbed his head and snapped it so fast he never even saw her. The other man spun and raised his gun just as Chase toppled the shopping cart onto him.

The homeless man began protesting loudly, flailing about, complaining they'd messed up his home.

Before Chase could make another move on the man struggling to get out from under the shopping cart, Wen twisted his arm until it snapped, grabbed his gun, and did some sort of move on his neck that instantly silenced him.

Chase grabbed the other man's gun and tried to get a look at his face.

"I already checked," Wen said. "Neither of them."

Chase knew she meant that the two dead weren't Ryker or Damon.

He nodded and followed her out.

"You freaks!" the homeless man yelled. "I can't— You get back here! What am I supposed to do with these two bodies and this crazy, messy house?"

They hit the tunnel running as fast as the space allowed, heading toward the men who were already at least fifty feet ahead. Once they were within twenty feet, one of the men yelled back. "Is that you Bowker? Anything in there?"

By now, Chase and Wen were only ten feet behind the men, and could see four clear silhouettes.

"Now!" Wen shouted, opening fire with the men's weapons. They dropped all four men before even one of them could turn around. As they stepped over the bodies, they shined a light onto each man's face to see if Ryker and Damon were among the dead.

"Two in the house, four out here . . . Either Ryker and Damon are still back there," Chase said, pointing back the way they came, "or they didn't come down."

"They could be waiting for us at the exit."

"Wherever that is." Chase noticed one of the men was still moving. The man reached a bloodied-arm toward his dropped weapon. Without hesitating, Chase squeezed the trigger and blew the man's head apart. "That's for my dad, you piece of trash."

Chapter Seventy

Ryker and Damon were coping with the maddening experience of trying to anticipate when and where either their crew, or Chase and Wen would emerge from the tunnels. Westfield had secured a map of the storm drains for them; however, it came with the caveat that it was not necessarily complete or accurate.

"We should have heard by now," Ryker said. "If Malone and the woman escape again, Westfield's going to have us shot."

"Maybe," Damon said as he read the GPS on his tablet. The display was now overlaid with the schematic of the storm drains thanks to a nifty piece of software.

"All we can do is guess," Ryker said. "If I was down there and came out of that small little round tunnel, I would surely not crawl back into it on the other side of that nice big wide comfortable tunnel. But which way would they go? Assuming they had no knowledge of the drains, the tendency is to go right. But according to our data, the tunnel eases slightly downward there in that direction. In the natural tendency then, I don't think they'd be inclined to go deeper, so they went left."

"Possibly," Damon said, manipulating the screen with his fingers so that the map would follow the tunnel to the left.

"And it just so happens that the tunnel to the left gets them to fresh air fastest."

Damon nodded.

"Assuming they don't take a wrong turn somewhere." Ryker studied the various tunnels. "Let's take another guess that it's one of those two openings. Which one is more logical for them?"

"Flip a coin?"

"I'm not making a decision like this on a coin toss. There's an answer in there on that map about which way they'd go. Of course, if our boys get the . . . " But Ryker had a bad feeling the "boys" weren't up for the task. "Chase Malone has some sort of lucky totem or something, and that girl is like a magic weapon"

"Like chasing the wind," Damon agreed.

The amount of graffiti and its colorful elaborateness increased as they continued down the tunnel. "That's a sure bet we're nearing the outside world," Chase said, pointing to the urban artwork.

They had made a series of choices left and right, big tunnels, small tunnels, rounded, rectangle, using everything from the temperature of the drafts, intuition, and listening for sounds of any kind to guide them. All the while they stayed vigilant for Ryker, Damon, and whomever else they might bring with them.

Wen hoped they'd avoid the confrontation she knew Chase wanted. The indelible images of his father struggling with his last breath to take one final look at his boys had destroyed part of Chase. She knew there was no repairing that. A different man was down there with her now, one new to killings and revenge. It wasn't the right time yet, but over the course of the next few weeks, she would have that conversation with him. The one about no matter how hard he tries, how much he might be able to make Ryker and Damon suffer before they die, before he kills them, even if he finds their bosses and their bosses' boss and kills all of them, he's not going to feel any better. It's not going to make that pain ache any less. Only time does that, and it takes a very, very, *very* long time for it to heal that kind of wound.

And then she would hold him, and kiss him, and tell him the worst part of all is that it never truly heals. The healing that people feel is really just the numb covering of years, the fading rawness of the wound, but inside, those scars would always burn.

Chase checked the time—eleven forty-three. It was still possible to make it to Lipton Innovations before the Fire Bomber, but not by midnight—unless they got lucky and escaped the underworld in the next few minutes, then figured out transportation to the tech center.

They passed a few straggling homeless people, each walking alone. The men didn't make eye contact, but they were certainly observing Chase and Wen, who each, as much as possible, held their weapons out of sight.

They asked one where the entrance was, but he just grunted and ignored them. They came across a couple, a man and woman in their forties, definitely looking out of place down there—clothes still filthy and frayed, but just a little nicer than the others they'd seen. Maybe they were more recent arrivals. Maybe they didn't have substance abuse issues or mental disorders.

"Is this the way out?" Wen asked.

They slowed and took a few moments, apparently deciding whether to engage or not. Finally the woman answered, "Yes. The opening is just about two or three minutes that way." She pointed over her shoulder.

"Did you happen to see any men out there?" Chase asked. "People with guns?"

The couple looked at each other in the glow of the four flashlights. "No," they both said in unison before hurrying along.

"Let's go," Wen said.

"I can't wait to breathe fresh air," Chase said as they started to jog again.

"Yeah," she agreed, wondering what they would encounter.

"Between the mall and down in these storm drains, I've read so much graffiti I can almost understand it. In fact, I think I'm becoming fluent in Graffiti."

"That just makes you more dangerous."

"Right," he said in a sad voice.

"They could be out there, you know."

"I hope so. We've got guns."

Chapter Seventy-One

Powder kept reminding himself to focus while he waited to move on the Lipton Innovation building. Concentration hadn't come easy since the Austin catastrophe and the close call in Phoenix. Part of the months of training had included clearing his mind, staying in the zone. They'd known all along that the further the mission progressed, the more risks would close in on them. Yet knowing and dealing with it were two different things. It didn't help that this one came with even more challenges.

Lipton Innovations, part of a massive conglomerate, utilized every modern measure to safeguard the facility and employed the largest private security force in the world—some even referred to it as a corporate Army.

Knowing this was going to be perhaps the most difficult strike on their list, Gunner had made secret pacts and enlisted the help of a number of questionable and surprising parties. Powder didn't know what deals had been cut, or the extent of the maneuverings that had been done to facilitate his gaining access, but he knew what to do, and what would be waiting for him.

The timing on this job was absolutely critical because of the presence of such a significant and well-trained security force. The details were down to the minute. He waited until one twenty-nine AM before cutting through the first fence. Sixty yards later, he cut through another one just as the surveillance cameras swung away. Once on the other side, Powder timed his movement to six minutes, then sprinted along the fence line until he reached a white rectangular rock, the marker telling him to turn right and head straight to a high barrier wall along the closest perimeter.

He reached an impressive metal door which looked like it belonged on a bank vault. From memory, he keyed in a sixteen-digit code and was amazed, but not surprised, when it opened. A flood light drenched the area. He couldn't avoid it. A surveillance camera would have zeroed in on the gate as soon as he touched the keypad if it hadn't been "conveniently" caught in a software glitch.

Powder slipped into the shadows and made it to a small annex attached to the main building. He ran a magnetic keycard through the slot and the lock clicked open. The immaculately organized space appeared to be a maintenance shop. Tools filled one wall, stacks of supplies and equipment were neatly arranged around three aisles marked with yellow safety paint. In the corner were two of the three things he needed to complete the bombing—a ladder going up, and stairs going down. Both were made inaccessible by heavy, padlocked steel plates. Fortunately, he knew where the key was hidden, and quickly he unlocked both.

I need one more thing, Powder thought, pleased with how easily the job he'd been dreading was falling into place. He scanned the room. *There it is.*

Underneath one of the counters, two crates marked "SPRINKLERS, HOSE BIBS, & FITTINGS" actually contained enough Doomsday to completely flatten the entire facility. It was just sitting there, as planned, waiting for him. A turning point in the war.

Chase and Wen had emerged from the "lair of the mole people," as Chase had taken to calling it, and found nothing but a handful of derelicts. No one knew it at the time, but Damon and Ryker were less than fifteen-hundred feet away, waiting at another opening. While Chase was checking around to see if his nemeses were nearby, Wen miraculously hailed a cab. It let them off at a donut joint a few blocks from Lipton Innovations. Hidden behind the trash area, amidst the smell of donuts and old coffee grounds, they powered-up the Antimatter Machine and connected with the Astronaut, who provided fairly accurate reconnaissance for their mission to take out or capture the Fire Bomber.

Wen instinctively concentrated as she stared through the scope. "I've got a shot," she whispered, even though there was no way Powder could hear her more than two hundred yards away.

"If we kill him, we'll never know what he knows," Chase said.

"There's no way we can get there in time," Wen said. "We don't know his process. Taking this shot is the only way we know we can stop this."

"I'm not sure it's a bad thing if we fail to stop him."

"What are you talking about? Wen asked, still tracking Powder's every move through her infrared scope.

"You know what I mean."

"You want to let him blow the building?"

"Lipton Innovations is the only company that makes the FESTER and the CSR."

"I know."

"If he blows the building, it could set horUS back a year, maybe two, possibly even longer."

"But it'll just be a setback." She watched as Powder took a few steps. *What's he doing?*

"Sure, but during that setback we can bring this thing into the light. Show people what's going on."

"*If* we let him go, *if* we can catch him after the explosion, *if* it really sets them back, *if* the public believes the information, *if* they do anything about it . . . that's a lot of ifs." She saw Powder glance into a device, maybe a phone.

"Why wouldn't the public believe us? Why wouldn't they do something about it?"

"Ask Edward Snowden."

"This is different," Chase said, yet he couldn't help but recall when NSA whistleblower Edward Snowden, who went public about mass government surveillance on US citizens through emails and phone calls, famously said that his greatest fear was, "*That nothing will change*," and indeed, the public seemed to shrug off the government's intrusion into their privacy . . . and soon forgot.

"Not really different at all," Wen said, studying Powder's hands through the scope. "We've got to decide right now—do I shoot him or not?"

Chase stared off toward the Lipton Innovations building.

"I'm pulling the trigger."

"No, let him go!"

Wen released her finger and watched as the Fire Bomber went around the edge of the building and disappeared into the darkness.

"What now?" Wen asked.

"We still need to catch him. Let's go."

"Hold on," Wen said, keying in a message to the Astronaut. "Maybe he can hack into horUS to help us track the Fire Bomber."

"I don't want to lose this guy," Chase said as they stood to exit their hiding place. "We need to move!"

BOOM, BOOM, BOOM-BOOM. Lipton Innovations blew in a massive series of explosions. Chase and Wen were both knocked to the ground.

Chapter Seventy-Two

Tess didn't allow herself to mourn Flint just yet. Once an agency crew arrived, she'd left immediately for Mission Control—her home more than anywhere now, since her house and property had become a battlefield. Tess knew she would never return to it. The place would be listed on the market as soon as agency people finished the clean-up, boxed everything, and sent it all to storage.

Tess stayed up all night on coffee and adrenaline. In the previous hours she'd discovered the identity of the source, and they were tracking the mastermind—the head of a large militia in Michigan, although he was now somewhere in West Virginia. For the first time, the Fire Bomber had also struck three targets in the same night. Raleigh, North Carolina, Harrisburg, Pennsylvania, and Las Vegas, Nevada.

"Travis is on his way in," an assistant told her at around four forty-five AM east coast time.

"Good, I need his help handling the source," Tess answered.

"Las Vegas," a technician said from across the room. "Fire Bomber."

"Lipton Innovations," Tess said, knowing it had to be the target—the key contractor for horUS.

"I don't know. Pulling it up now."

The big screen switched from a dynamic map of the United States to a massive fire in what had been a major manufacturing and corporate facility.

"Confirmed," the tech said. "Lipton Innovations."

"Total destruction," she said. "Any word from our team on the ground?" Three days earlier, she had ordered an IT-Squad to be stationed there.

"I'll check."

"San Francisco," another tech said as a different screen lit up with the Balance Engineering building imploding.

"Seattle," someone shouted before Tess could respond to Balance Engineering. "Looks like Boeing." Another screen confirmed the site.

"Six in one night," Tess said, wondering how the Fire Bombers could be doing it.

"The president," a tech announced.

"I'll take it in Secure," Tess said, but even before she could make it there, four more strikes were announced—Los Angeles, Bellevue, Washington, and Denver. While on the phone with the president, two additional bombings occurred in the San Francisco Bay area.

"He knows we have them," Tess said to the president, referring to the leader of the militia. "That's why this is happening. The Fire Bombers are unleashing everything they have left."

"I don't care about the reason," the president said. "We haven't had this kind of destruction since 9/11, and even then . . . we're talking about dozens of buildings now that this group has destroyed with impunity. Thank God we haven't had a comparable loss of life, but . . . "

"I'm telling you, it ends *today*. The source will be in custody in the next thirty minutes. This Gunner character, who's the Fire Bomber mastermind, will be dead or in custody possibly even sooner. And right now there's a crew about to apprehend the Las Vegas Fire Bomber."

"What about all the other explosions tonight and those fire bombers?"

"Working on it, but it appears to be some sort of automated attack. We have teams in many of the locations. This militia was ready for war."

"What set them off?"

"It appears to have been horUS."

"Should I be worried?"

She knew he meant about his exposure with horUS.

"I'm about to implement Rolling Wave," Tess said, knowing the president would understand. "Rolling Wave" was the final back up plan, the "hell has frozen over" contingency plan. "We have no choice."

"Then do it."

The president ended the call. She knew he trusted her, partially because she was excellent at her job, and also because no alternatives existed. People were about to die, but the larger good would be served, and that had always been the president's first priority. He'd told her once, "Tough decisions have to be made to assure the continuity of not only the government, but the country, and its place as the world's premier power."

She remained in Secure, alone, watching live feeds from Vegas, San Francisco, Seattle, Raleigh, and the rest. Nineteen separate tech companies had been hit. Her anger at the night's events was tempered only by the satisfaction that she could finally see the end. There were still difficult issues to deal with, and if horUS—and, more importantly, the people who had created the program—were going to survive, the next few hours would be the most critical.

A minute later, the information she'd been waiting for came across her private screen. The two people who'd attacked her home had been identified and traced.

"Cane Westfield," she said to herself, after reading the history of the men who had, for the past several years, not officially existed but, in fact, reported directly to Westfield. "I never particularly liked you, but I didn't see that coming." She keyed in several lines of text, sealing his fate. "But it's almost convenient after tonight's events." She couldn't bring herself to silently thank the man who'd tried to have her killed and was ultimately responsible for the death of her dear Flint, but his actions had made a certain part of her job simpler. "You will be dealt with in hell Westfield."

Someone knocked on the door of Secure. Tess checked the monitors, relieved to see Travis. She buzzed to allow him access.

Westfield learned of the failed attempt on Tess and cursed, knowing she was one of only three people with the clearances to find out who the men were. He also knew that she was now safe in the fully protected and hardened CISS building in Vienna.

Perhaps only the Fire Bomber would be able to get her, he thought. *The irony.*

However, such an outcome would be impossible. He prepared for the worst. Tess would have a team sweep her home, pick apart the bodies of the two assassins he'd sent.

Soon, if not already, she'd uncover their identities, the CIA would uncloak their erased existences, the connections to certain programs would be linked, and then traced back to Westfield himself. She couldn't prove it, but she wouldn't need to. Tess Federgreen was a fierce warrior, as powerful as himself, but younger, more cunning. There was nowhere to hide.

She will come for me.

Even so, he still sought to achieve the same goal as Tess—protect horUS. That meant Chase Malone had to die, and he believed there was a great chance that Tess would not do it. Ryker and Damon needed to succeed.

He pulled up the feeds from Vegas, checked all resources, and tracked the pair. "Ahh," he said, watching back-feeds of Chase and Wen. "You had your sights on the Fire Bomber and then lowered your gun. You let him blow up Lipton Innovations. Chase Malone, you are part of this. You are the enemy. I sentence you to death."

Ten minutes later, the coordinates of Chase's exact location were in Ryker's tablet, and a dozen more men were on their way to finish the mission and carry out the death sentence.

Chapter Seventy-Three

After the explosion at Lipton Innovations, Chase and Wen tried for almost an hour to find Powder, but finally, exhausted, not able to recall the last time they'd slept, they made their way back to the strip and got a room at the Mirage using one of Chase's aliases. They had to sleep. Flint's team, who they'd missed earlier at the Bellagio, had finally made contact. They would all leave Vegas together at five AM, the destination yet to be determined.

They turned off their phones and crashed. Two hours later, the wake-up call they'd left brought them back to the brutal reality. Once back on, Chase's phone rang instantly.

He recognized the number and was hoping to get an update about his mother. "It's Boone," he told Wen, pressing accept.

"Chase, I've got some horrible news," Boone said.

Chased gripped the phone, fearing his mother had died.

"The Balance Engineering headquarters building has been completely destroyed," Boone said in a dire tone.

"What? How could that . . . What about Dez? Adya? *What?*"

"We don't know to what extent, but there were definitely casualties. Dez called me when he couldn't reach you. He's okay. No word on Adya."

"What happened?"

"The Fire Bomber."

"Yeah, but . . . we just saw the Fire Bomber hit Las Vegas. We saw—"

Wen hit him on the leg, reminding him they didn't witness anything. She pointed to the phone and then the sky, a signal that "they" could be listening.

"How's Mom?"

"Improving. Asleep now."

"Good. Does she know about Balance?"

"No."

"Let's not tell her. It'll only upset her more."

"I agree," Boone said.

"Which happened first? Balance or Las Vegas?" Chase asked.

"Right after Dez called, I turned on the news. Both Lipton Innovations in Vegas and Balance were all over the coverage. They say it's the first time the Fire Bomber has struck twice in the same night. I think I saw that Vegas happened first. You're in Vegas? Are you okay?"

"How do we know it was the Fire Bomber that did Balance?" Chase suddenly asked Wen. "We're not on the horUS list."

"What are you talking about?" Boone said. "Chase, the building is *gone*. It was either a cruise missile attack, or the Fire Bomber. No one else can unleash that kind of destruction."

"But why Balance? It's not even on the—"

Wen hit Chase again and gave him a glaring stare.

"What list?" Boone asked.

"We've been developing a list of potential targets that fit a pattern," Chase lied. "Balance has no connection to any of the others." Chase looked at Wen, his eyes seeking her approval for the covering of his slip, then changed his expression to one of questioning.

She shrugged, obviously trying to figure out what the motive was to hit Balance and some of the other companies that had nothing to do with horUS—the "second track", as the Astronaut called it.

"Wait," Boone said. "Two more companies were hit by the Fire Bomber. Boeing in Seattle, and WatchIT in Raleigh, North Carolina."

Wen turned on the television.

"Four in one night," Chase said, shocked, and then thought of the more obvious question. "How did the Fire Bomber get into Balance? That building was an armed camp."

After Chase ended the call with Boone, they linked up with the Astronaut via the Antimatter Machine. The news continued to pour in even as they spoke with him. More than a dozen Fire Bomber attacks had occurred within hours.

"You were right about Balance," Chase said as the Astronaut came on screen.

"And about Google," the Astronaut said.

"They hit *Google*, too?"

"Tried, but an engineer there figured it out."

"*What?*"

"He discovered how the Fire Bomber could bring down a whole building with only a suitcase full of explosives."

"Leave it to an engineer," Chase said.

"That statement is truer than you can imagine," the Astronaut said. "They have paired the most advanced military-grade pliable-demolition substance in the world—ARMA2020 Poly Explosive—with an artificial intelligence program."

"Don't tell me," Chase said, dreading the possibility that the Fire Bomber had used Rapid-Artificial-Intelligence, what he and Dez had invented.

"What else could it be?" the Astronaut asked, rhetorically. "The Fire Bomber figured out a way to mix the poly explosive with RAI."

"But how does that bring down a building?" Wen asked.

"They amplify it," Chase said, thinking out loud. "I can't believe I didn't figure it out before. The Bomber uses RAI to tap into the building's electrical system, or natural gas source . . . that's it, right?"

"Yes. Glad to see you're still as smart as they say you are," the Astronaut said, no trace of humor in his voice. "The compounding effect expands the power and explosive force of Doomsday by a multiple of thirty-one."

"A super-weapon," Wen said. "And whoever is doing it leap-frogged the capabilities of the world's most powerful militaries." She couldn't help but think about WOLF. *If the Cause had such a weapon . . .*

"That obvious and unpleasant reality must be why Tess enlisted our help. They have no idea who could pull off something like this—first acquiring the highly-classified Doomsday and then developing a technology that turned the radically advanced explosive into something so destructive. It's decades ahead of its time."

"That's why they went after Balance?" Wen asked. "Because of their connection to RAI?"

"More than that," the Astronaut began, "they were

declaring war on technology. The deployment of horUS may have dictated the timing of these strikes, but make no mistake, the people behind this are attempting to destroy the technological backbone of the future. That's the second track. They didn't care that Balance sold RAI, they knew Chase and Balance were on the leading edge of tech. That's what all the non-horUS companies have in common—creating the future . . . a future the Fire Bombers don't want."

Chapter Seventy-Four

As Chase and Wen rushed to leave the Mirage hotel, Wen linked into Heaven and sent CISS a zoomed photo she'd taken of Powder. Wen didn't have the time or easy access to search for his identity. She was about to sign off the ultra-classified intelligence network when she noticed an anomaly. A source line of numbers that the Astronaut had discovered pertained to horUS appeared in a large data dump.

"Hold on," Wen said, "I need another minute."

"Did you send Tess the Fire Bomber photo?" Chase asked, knowing that would essentially fulfill any obligation he had to her.

"Yes, but someone is doing something big on the horUS program right now. The Astronaut had me memorize these sequence strings so I could explore Heaven for horUS, and I just spotted one in a large—"

"Where'd he get the codes?" Chase asked as she typed.

"He wouldn't say. He may have created them himself."

"That would be an impressive trick."

Wen nodded. "Here it is, horUS-ARES."

"What's Ares?"

"Ares is the Greek god of war who endows savage, dangerous, and militarized qualities."

"Sounds like more than drone surveillance," Chase said. "But we need to go."

"I know, one more second. We know horUS is High Optics Reconnaissance of United States, so what does ARES stand for?" she wondered, navigating the endless streams of unassembled data.

"Wen, it's time to leave."

"Here it is! Adaptive Response Enhanced Surveillance. What does that mean?"

"We'll look on the plane," Chase said, stepping into the hallway.

Wen clicked a button and then closed the Antimatter Machine. "Okay." She stared into her phone as they walked briskly down the hall.

"Now what are you doing?"

"The Astronaut created an app so I can access the Antimatter Machine on my phone."

"Impressive to the second power, but is it secure?"

"Of course it is. It's the Astronaut."

A silver minivan carrying three of Flint's men, engine running, waited outside the Polynesian-themed entranceway of the Mirage. Wen noticed a fourth man standing by one of the square stone columns as she scanned the area. He followed Chase and her into their vehicle.

"Still going to the airport?" the driver asked.

"Yeah, but make sure we aren't followed," Chase said. He'd already briefed them about Ryker and Damon. As much as he wanted a shot at Ryker, Chase wasn't interested in a surprise visit from the man who'd killed his father.

As they departed the reception area in the predawn darkness and pulled around the circular drive in front of the resort, Wen remained vigilant. The driver began to turn left onto Las Vegas Boulevard when the vehicle suddenly rocked. A crunching metallic jolt came as a large SUV rammed the back corner of their van. Bullets blew out the side window. Glass crystals rained in as one of Flint's men took several shots to the head, instantly dead.

The driver attempted to maneuver the vehicle out, but they were pinned in between a large stone column supporting the MIRAGE sign and a picturesque lagoon. Wen brought up her weapon and began shooting out of the blown window. Chase got the sliding side door open. He and Wen tumbled out onto the sidewalk, weapons firing. They engaged the SUV behind them, but quickly realized they were out-gunned.

"It's an ambush!" one of Flint's men shouted.

Chase counted three vehicles with armed men pouring out before diving into the landscaped grounds bordering the lagoon. A palm tree took a string of bullets as he passed. Wen disappeared into a group of large shrubs topped with tropical flowers. Flint's three remaining men were returning fire, but they weren't going to last long. The Vegas strip at five AM wasn't the same as other places. Darkness in Sin City is but a myth among the neon.

"You think it's Ryker?" Chase yelled as they found their first area of concealment.

"I'm sure of it," Wen shouted back. "I saw him. Positive ID."

Chapter Seventy-Five

Travis looked at Tess. The woman he'd worked with for so many years suddenly appeared twice her age. "Are you okay?" he asked, having just heard about the attack on her home and Flint, but having no idea what the man meant to her.

"Not really, but there's no time to be what I really feel like being."

"Maybe you should go home." He regretted the suggestion as soon as the words escaped.

Her eyes questioned his sanity for a moment before she smiled. "There is progress."

"Fill me in," he said, happy to change the subject.

"We've arrested the Fire Bomber."

"Where?"

"Las Vegas. Chase Malone sent us his photo."

Travis nodded, absorbing the fact that apparently she'd been right about Chase.

"Do you know what the Bomber said when they caught him?" Tess asked. "'*It ain't gonna stop, it doesn't end with me.*'"

"What does that mean?"

"They didn't use the Bomber in at least sixteen of tonight's strikes. They had pre-planted explosives in the buildings. A Google engineer figured out they tied Doomsday into the electrical or gas connections. But how long have the bombs been there? How many more are out there? We have no idea."

"Will the Bomber talk?"

"He doesn't have to. We used horUS to track down his boss and captured him. Ironic, isn't it?"

"When did you get him?"

"Just now." Tess clicked a button and a giant screen filled with the live feed of Gunner being arrested. Recognize him?"

"No."

"Are you sure? Because you served in the army with him."

"What? Who is he?"

"Travis, I'm disappointed with you. Even before we discovered your old friend was the mastermind, I knew you were the source. What I don't know is why you committed treason."

"Because *you* committed treason," Travis said, narrowing his eyes.

"Me?" Tess said, shocked. "I live and breathe every moment to protect this country."

"The country maybe, but not her people," Travis said sharply. "You know what horUS is. It's the beginning of the end. The government will manage the program to control, not protect the people."

"Who are you to decide?"

"It is my duty to protect the public, the innocent populace, from people like you. It is my *duty*, damn it!"

"Your duty to aid terrorists. *They* are killing your 'innocent populace.'"

"Don't get hypocritical on me. You kill people every day Tess. Who are *you* to decide?"

"Our elected officials gave me that authority."

"Did they? You know they don't have any idea of everything CISS does? And what about horUS? Why do only *nine* people know about it? What would happen if we gave it to the people for a vote?"

"I admit I don't like it, but it is necessary. If we don't use technology to maintain order, than surely the technology will lead to our demise."

Travis nodded. "I know you believe that."

"I'm sorry, but you are in a terrible place," she said, looking genuinely sad. "With your knowledge of horUS and the fact that you were the source for Gunner's militia . . . "

"I knew the risks," Travis said. "Tell me which street corner to stand on and I'll take the bullet."

She smiled solemnly. "I'm afraid you'll never leave this building."

He nodded slowly and forced a smile.

Two men appeared at the door. She buzzed them in.

"Mr. Watts, please come with us," one of them said.

"Tess, think about what you're doing."

"You left me no choice, Travis."

"Not with me, with horUS. Ask yourself why Westfield targeted you. Dig a little, you'll discover there is more to horUS than even you know. Much more."

She stared at him.

"You know," he said, aghast. "Of course you do. You've known all along about ARES, haven't you?"

"Take him away," she said.

The two men stepped up and cuffed Travis. As they were leading him out, he turned around.

"You may think you have it all under control, that you know everything, but it's bigger than that! I assure you, it's beyond all of us!"

A few minutes later, another agent entered Mission Control.

"I want to be absolutely certain I understand this order," the agent said. "I am to deploy a CoD on Deputy Assistant Secretary of Defense Cain Westfield."

"Correct. It is to be done immediately," Tess said, sorry not to do it herself. A CoD, or CISS of Death, was an order to kill. In this case, it would be carried out as if Westfield had killed himself.

Tomorrow there would be another CoD for Westfield's boss, the Secretary of Defense, who would die of "natural causes," a heart attack due to the extreme stress.

She still hadn't decided if her boss, the director of the CIA, would be spared a CISS of Death. First she needed to have a chat with a very loose end—Chase Malone.

Chapter Seventy-Six

Chase scrambled up the rocks of a large, circular, cascading waterfall. The stone outcroppings formed a series of natural-looking steps that could have been along any jungle river in the tropics. The landscape provided plenty of cover, but he wasn't interested in hiding. Three objectives flashed in his mind: protect Wen (although that might be the other way around), stay alive, and kill Ryker.

The sun still hadn't risen. Regardless, floodlights reflecting off the building made the Mirage hotel like a giant full moon. Chase had already dodged several spotlights meant to accentuate the waterfall and palm trees of the 'oasis', and he noticed Wen had smashed out a few of the ones near her. He wedged himself in behind a large boulder and went to work on objective number three. He fired his submachine gun in the direction of the vehicles where three of Flint's men were engaging at least half a dozen of Ryker's men.

The bursting rattle of gunfire behind Chase alerted him to Wen's whereabouts. He turned and saw her. Somehow, from an impossible angle, she had managed to take down one of Ryker's people back at the van. But the ones still fighting weren't their problem. At least five others had now taken up positions in the small patch of jungle around the waterfall. One of them was almost certainly Ryker.

Chase knew that in less than a minute they'd have him surrounded. Taking a chance, while continuing to fire, he climbed to the top of the waterfall. Wider than expected, it was too far to leap across. He'd be safer on the other side, so he sloshed through the water. He lost his footing on the slippery rocks and almost went over, his leg still weak from the dam injury, nearly losing his gun. His silhouette drew fire from below just as he rolled over the stone border backing the falls.

Wen stopped firing and was able to work the blinking shadows as they transformed in size, shape, and shade based on the blinking neon and light filters. She moved behind one of the men shooting at Chase and silently snapped his spine.

At the top of the waterfall, as Chase reached the rock on the other side, a hand pulled him. One of Ryker's men, who'd lost his gun on the treacherous climb up, got Chase in a choke hold. Chase used his legs to push against the big rock he'd just climbed. The two men struggled while Wen, unable to get a safe shot off, moved in their direction.

The firefight at the van had ended badly. Flint's men were all down—dead or badly injured. The lone surviving person from Ryker's squad fired at Wen, forcing her to retreat into the palms. She counted bodies and calculated. Flint's team had taken out seven—an impressive feat—which might mean she and Chase had a chance to survive this. Sirens meant the police would be there any second and complicate matters more. Arrest was not an option for any of them.

Chase spun and flipped backwards into the top of the falls. The man gripping his neck went over the edge, but managed to hold on for a few seconds, trying to strangle Chase, who desperately fought to keep himself from being swept off. His hands clung to the jagged concrete edges of the pool. If he let go to free his neck from the man's grip, he'd go down the cascade with him.

Just when Chase didn't think he could breathe much longer, the man's fingers slipped. He careened backwards over the falls, his head smashing on the wet rocks below.

Chase took a moment to recover, trying to get air, and then scanned for Wen and Ryker.

In the lagoon, Wen, camouflaged, in water up to her eyes, fired a single shot and killed the man who'd been pursuing her. Another calculation. "It's Chase, me, and two others," she whispered to herself as she emerged from the water.

She searched the area through her scope and spotted a man up in the volcano. "Ryker." She lined up to take the shot, but he suddenly moved. *He's seen something, or someone.* She traced his line of vision, and then saw who.

Ryker has his sights on Chase!

She yelled for Chase. Apparently he couldn't hear her over the sirens and rushing water. Wen tried to get a clear shot, but didn't have it. She ran, hoping to reach him in time. Ryker had killed the father, and was now going after the son.

Chapter Seventy-Seven

Wen pushed the Astronaut's app button on her phone as she ran along the edge of the pool, trying to get a shot at Ryker. His shot at Chase went wide. As Wen had also discovered, shooting into the carnival of lights and shadows was not easy. The depth, angles, and rise were all off. Ryker, still positioned atop the volcano, seemed to have lost his prey for the moment. So had Wen.

"We're in Las Vegas at the Mirage," Wen said as the Astronaut answered.

"I can see that," he replied.

"Can you hack into the hotel's computer system? They have a volcano show every evening. I need you to make it erupt."

"Whatever for?" the Astronaut asked, his fingers blazing rapidly across the keyboard.

"There's a man inside."

"Must be a very bad man if you want me to turn on the volcano while he's in there?"

"He's the devil," Wen said, spitting the words. "He killed Chase's father."

"Okay. I'm almost there."

Wen could see Ryker only as the light moved and the blinks of nearby neon hit just right. He wasn't staying still. His training, like hers, had taught him to use the high ground for tactical advantage. He'd also, obviously, liked the vantage point to locate Chase.

"Where are you?" she muttered, searching the area for Chase as she moved closer to the volcano.

"I'm in," the Astronaut said, thinking she meant him.

Wen turned at the sound of gunfire behind her. Someone picked off two approaching police officers. That brought the evening's total of LVPD fatalities to five, as she'd already encountered three bodies.

"Can you do it now?"

"I am definitely not excited about killing someone, even the devil," the Astronaut said.

"Don't worry, it's not lava. Only water and lights come out the top."

"Of course. Las Vegas, all smoke and mirrors, the city of illusion."

"Yeah," Wen said, looking around at the spectacle of monuments and towers. "And once the show starts, I'll take care of the killing."

"I'm starting it now."

"Do it!"

Suddenly, she crashed into the lagoon. Wen had heard the shot at the same moment she felt the bullet rip into her. As she reeled in pain, Wen stayed under the shallow water. Whoever shot her would keep shooting. She moved away from the impact spot, avoiding two other bullets, which told her that the man was not firing a machine gun. Wen reached down to feel the gunshot wound; her right thigh was bleeding badly.

Finally, out of air, she surfaced only to stare into Damon's pistol. She swept a wide splash of water in his face and grabbed his legs. Wen twisted and kicked, her leg raging in agony. Still, the blow was enough to knock his gun loose. She grabbed for his arm. He recovered and jabbed back, punching her thigh. Wen collapsed to her knees. Damon shoved Wen hard, forcing her under water.

They splashed and slipped in a tugging match, wrestling with hellacious fury. Wen, outmatched by Damon's bulk and strength and her loss of blood, relied on pure instinct and muscle memory from years of training and actual fights. But he got her down, and held her. The air, she figured, was her only weapon. Wen had practiced since a child, and could hold her breath for up to four minutes in ideal situations. With the leg injury and exertion, she guessed she had two and a half minutes at most. She went still. It took what seemed an eternity, yet was actually just over a minute of him holding her under the black water before he released, stood, and turned to go find Chase.

Wen came up with fury and pulled him back. As he tried to turn, she elbowed his face between his eye socket and nose. He collapsed back into the water and she lunged. A few seconds later, Damon was no longer breathing. She had not made his mistake. Instead of wasting time, Wen finished him.

As she came out of the water, bloody and drenched, Wen grabbed Damon's dropped magnum just as she caught a glimpse of Chase scaling the far side of the volcano. Even if she still had her phone, which had vanished into the murkiness, it would be too late to stop the eruption. The beast had already begun to rumble. Flames lit up around the base—*real flames!* More fire ignited around the rim—*Real fire!* She tried not to panic as she raced across the lagoon toward the now active volcano.

The flames reflecting on the water were blinding. Just twenty feet from the churning fires, a man burst through the bushes, grabbed her around the waist, and flung her back into the water. The last thing she saw before going under was Chase going over the rim of the glowing volcano.

Chapter Seventy-Eight

Ryker, unknowingly standing right over one of the water jets, became alarmed as the glowing mist and rumble started all around. An eerie soundtrack of mystical chants and drums began.

Suddenly, the jets erupted under him, its force and thrust lifting him into the air several feet in a blast of water and light that shot thirty feet past him. When the spray disappeared, Ryker slammed back down to the ground in a disoriented daze amidst blinding orange lights and a drowning stream of returning water. He clawed for his machine gun, but it was lost in the dazzle. Another eruption shook him as the drumming beat in-time with dozens of flaming posts at the base of the lagoon. The third round of jets tossed him into a rock wall, bloodying his head. A brief pause allowed the now beaten and drenched Ryker to see Chase coming at him.

He reached for his holstered handgun. At the same moment, another jet burst into him. This one felt like getting hit in the stomach with a telephone pole fired from a rocket. He crashed down six feet away, closer to the edge, as the lights frantically blinked and mock lava flowed. The eruptions quickened along with the frenzied music.

Ryker, trying to find Chase again, realized he was backed up against the real flames on the edge of the caldera. Singed and steaming, he spun away, trying to avoid the next geyser.

"You killed my father!" Chase screamed, pointing a gun at the beleaguered agent. As Chase pulled the trigger, a thrust of water erupted and nearly tore his arm off. Unlike Ryker, he wasn't lifted off the ground, but he felt like his shoulder had been dislocated, and he, too, was now weaponless.

The man came down on top of Wen with a large knife. She fired the magnum at the last instant, destroying his face. He crashed into the water next to her. Dizzily, she stood and looked up at the volcano. All she could see were towering flames and 'lava' streaming into the sky, a dance of countless fires blasting out of the water surrounding the base.

Wen tried to run, but her leg was too injured, a mix of searing pain and numb nothingness. She somehow stumbled out of the lagoon, forced away from the volcano by the flames, which seemed to be building toward a finale.

Chase charged at the bigger man. Ryker readied for the attack, bending his knees slightly and flexing his arms out toward Chase. A ring of jets exploded all at once, knocking both men off their feet. A torrent of water rained down on them as the lights made everything appear to be on fire. Chase, focusing with every last ounce of energy, crawled toward the edge. Ryker, somewhat foggy, stood shakily, scouring the faux crater for his adversary. Before he saw him, Chase bulled in fast, like a lineman looking to bury a quarterback in the big game. Ryker, absorbing the blow, picked Chase up, about to throw him into the caldera wall.

Everything erupted in a spectacle of drumming music, orange, red, and yellow lights, pulsating geysers, and steam. The entire rim blazed real fire like a massive torch. Caught in the middle of it all, the two men took the blows one after another. Chase felt like a punch drunk prize fighter in the tenth round. He didn't even know the difference between up and down anymore as the water tossed him in a tortuous bashing.

He struggled to his feet only to be knocked down again, but on the third try he somehow managed to dodge the jets and stagger to the edge, where he found Ryker still down. Chase kicked his nemesis repeatedly. Ryker rolled over and pulled Chase back into the stew. The two slugged it out. Ryker connected several power blows to Chase's face and chest. The jets and lights continued to swirl around them. Drums building to a crazed climax made Chase feel as if he were in a jungle horror.

Ryker pressed his size and muscle advantage, but Chase hadn't been as punished by the eruptions. They locked together and flew into the flames at the rim. Ryker, smoking and smoldering, released Chase, who had also been burned.

Through blurry-eyed pain, as the drumming became intolerable, Chase went at Ryker's legs. He pushed and fought with all his remaining strength until suddenly there was no resistance.

Ryker went over the rim, screaming through the flames,

plunging thirty feet. Seconds later, the drumming stopped. The lights and water ceased. Flames were suddenly extinguished. Chase crawled to the edge and peered over. Ryker lay, still burning, impaled on a fire post at the base of the volcano.

Chapter Seventy-Nine

Chase and Wen were detained at the hospital, expecting to be charged, until a reluctant lieutenant released them. Chase didn't ask any questions. He knew only one person could have gotten that accomplished.

Not until they were safely in the air did Chase call her.

"Thanks for getting us out of that mess," Chase said, drinking a shot of whiskey instead of taking the pain medication he'd been given for his burns. "But this doesn't mean I owe you again."

"Speaking of owing," Tess said. "Why did Flint owe you?"

"I don't know what you're talking about."

"Why was Flint so loyal?"

"Because I pay him a fortune."

"No," she said, trying to understand how Chase couldn't know how Flint felt. "You can't *buy* loyalty like that. It's more than that."

"Wait, is Flint okay?"

"He's dead. I'm sorry." *Sorrier than I can say.*

"Oh . . . *no*."

"He died saving me."

"Who killed him!?"

"Someone trying to get to me. He's dead now."

"It was about horUS, wasn't it?"

"The program is critical to our survival. It's surprising that you don't understand that."

"Really? Aren't *you* all about keeping peace between the corporations? How does spying on citizens help that?"

"We need to make sure the people don't get swayed. Humans are emotional beings. That makes for an unpredictable future, and too much is at stake."

"Do you *hear* yourself?"

"You make my point. You're an idealistic young man. We're in a war, a complex war unlike anything we've ever faced. China, extremists, rich and powerful multinational corporations, loyal to no flag."

"You have a big job, don't you?" Chase said sarcastically as Wen showed him a report from the Astronaut on her screen.

"The Chinese will win. They have the numbers—they could lose the equivalent of the entire US population and wouldn't even miss them. AI, quantum computing, robotics, military, belt and road . . . they're leading the world. Their corporations are already fighting ours. It's a balancing act. I'm trying to save the world from their tyranny."

"Is your tyranny any better?" he asked, ignoring Wen's eye signal to not push further.

She took a deep breath. "For your own good, forget about horUS."

"No, because it's much worse than just mass surveillance. I know about ARES—Adaptive Response Enhanced Surveillance. You're going to use those drones to intercept everything, and with the NSA already recording every call, collecting every email, and mixing that with search, browsing, social media histories, and Alexa, you know us better than we know ourselves."

"You're being dramatic," she said, hiding her shock that he'd discovered ARES.

"Am I? Deny that the drones will be used for systematic specific elimination of problems through ordinance equipped units," he said, reading from the Astronaut's report. "And the spread of viruses for larger—"

"The program is for the good of the country," she interrupted.

"Who decides!?"

"Chase, you are *way* beyond your realm here."

"I'm going public."

"That won't be allowed."

"Why? Will it embarrass the president?"

"The president does not know about ARES."

"The *president* doesn't know? Then who authorized it?" He couldn't resist giving Wen a look that said, *See? It was right that I pushed*.

"The people the president works for."

"You mean the American people?"

"Are you joking? The president doesn't work for the people. That's an old fairy tale meant to keep everyone believing in democracy."

"Why hasn't the media uncovered this?"

"Because they're in on it! Who do you think owns them?"

"You're going down."

"It's never going to get to me. I'm completely insulated, and it won't get to the President either," she said, speaking to him as if he were a child. "Don't you think we planned these things, making a contingency for everything? We have contingencies for the contingencies."

"They won't be good enough. I have proof."

"Your proof is nothing." She laughed. "We are practiced at deception. The public buys it every single time. You'll recognize our work when you see it in the news headlines. A pentagon official has a heart attack. The CIA Director will take the fall for horUS/ARES, but he'll be caught in such a quagmire when he resigns, and there won't be enough information to prosecute. The public attention will move on very quickly. There'll be a headline, a little war somewhere, something else happens, diversions that *you* will notice when they occur, but the public's attention is so *easily* swayed."

"Particularly when *you* control the media."

"Yes, particularly."

"How do you sleep at night?"

"Grow up, Chase. Whoever has the gold, makes the rules. The ones with the biggest guns have all the fun."

"Catchy, but I'm confused," he said in a mocking tone. "Is it the Chinese, the extremists, the corporations, or the average American citizen who is the enemy?"

"Poor Chase . . . you want everything so simple. It's all of the above. We can't sustain tens of trillion of dollars in government debt and continue to spend this much money on weapons. The problem with China is their leaders think they can beat the multinationals, but the corporations won the invisible war—they robbed the treasury and enslaved the people through taxes and debt. *They* are in charge now."

"Not if I can help it."

Epilogue

Although Chase and Wen did get the information about horUS and ARES out to the world, Tess was right. Ultimately nothing happened, and it quickly faded. Instead, the mainstream news outlets hyped the capture of Gunner, Powder, and the other militia members now branded as terrorists. Twenty-six other buildings were found to have been pre-planted with AI-Enhanced-Doomsday. Gunner had been planning attacks on tech companies for years and had begun secretly installing the explosives eleven months before he even found out about horUS.

Facing life behind bars, Gunner allegedly hung himself in prison while awaiting trial. Powder never recovered from injuries sustained when he "resisted arrest", and also died before he could be tried. The US Senate convened hearings after public outrage concerned about Pentagon, CIA, and NSA overreach, but after Deputy Assistant Secretary of Defense Cane Westfield, considered the mastermind of horUS/ARES, killed himself, coupled with the death of the Secretary of Defense from an apparent heart attack, the committee reached too many dead ends. However, they promised stronger oversight in the future. The CIA Director resigned.

Allegations about the president's involvement were categorically denied, and after two successful terms, the public seemed more focused on who would be coming next. And, as predicted, a headline-grabbing situation occurred almost as if it were a planned diversion. Iran began test firing nuclear missiles toward Israel, and suddenly the world could only see the Middle East.

Chase's mother was expected to make a full recovery, and would be moving in with Boone for a while. Chase had a private memorial foundation created to honor his father, its single mission in arranging that in every US hospital that catered to minorities and low-income people, when a baby was born, the parents would receive a new photo album and a simple camera.

Dez and Chase had decided not to rebuild the Balance Engineering headquarters, but would continue to secretly develop SEER in an undisclosed location. Wen had suggested it to be somewhere far away from San Francisco.

"It's just like with Snowden," Chase said to Wen as they flew to Amsterdam to meet members of WOLF. "The public doesn't care. They're giving their masters a pass."

"It's all a big 1984 warning," Bull said. Lenny had died the day following the attack at the mall due to complications from the gunshot wound. It had hit her harder than expected. Bull decided to join The Cause after Wen persuaded her to use her brilliant hacking skills for the better good. "And everyone is missing it," Bull continued. "You always think when you see something terrible happen in books and movies—a dystopian society, a dictator's rise, whatever—how did no one see that coming? It's because we all choose to ignore the warning signs."

"I just heard from the Astronaut," Wen said, smiling. "He's agreed to help The Cause. He's heading to Amsterdam, too."

"We're going to need all the help we can get," Chase said. "Especially if . . . " He paused and looked out the window as a red and yellow sunset lit the clouds.

"If what?" Wen asked.

"If," he said, turning and staring into her dark eyes, "we're going to change the world."

Next in the Chase Malone Thriller series

vinci-books.com/chasing-wind

Control the weather, control the world. But first, survive the storm.

When a brilliant scientist disappears, leaving behind groundbreaking technology capable of controlling the weather, Chase Malone and Wen Zhou find themselves in a deadly race against time. With global superpowers—from the U.S. to China and Russia—scrambling for control, the stakes have never been higher.

Turn the page for a free preview…

Chasing Wind: Chapter One

Chase Malone stood near the center of one of the largest and oldest outdoor markets in South America, lost among thousands of locals and tourists. Hiding in plain sight, where no one would think to look, had become his life. Weeks away from his thirtieth birthday, the billionaire considered himself lucky to be alive.

He paid the old woman three US dollars, Ecuador's official currency, for a basket of fruit, and waved off the sixty cents of change. She smiled a toothless grin. "Gracias."

"De nada," Chase replied, turning to look for his partner, Wen Sung. The two of them had been in Otavalo, Ecuador for twelve days. They would leave tomorrow—always on the run. He spotted her haggling with a man over the price for a loaf of bread. Although Chinese, Wen spoke fluent Spanish, among other languages. The MSS, China's equivalent of the CIA, had trained her to be a lethal spy.

"I told you to pay their asking price," Chase said quietly, self-conscious about his billionaire status. He pulled off his jacket. Even though it was only fifty-three degrees, the sun, at 8,300 feet above sea level, was intense—a good excuse for sunglasses, as they always tried to remain incognito.

"And I told *you* they like to negotiate. Anyway, I always let them win," Wen said, paying the man only a few cents less than his original quote.

The merchant beamed, believing he'd bested the foreigner.

"I love it when clouds ring the top of Imbabura," she said, whirling around and pointing the bread toward the dominant feature shadowing the town, a 15,190 foot, snow-capped volcano. They'd hiked it on their second day in the country, back when they could still semi-relax. Each passing day meant it was more likely someone would find them.

Wen handed him a Morocho, a warm, spiced, corn pudding drink he'd come to love during their short stay.

"I'm going to learn how to make this when we get home," Chase said. They shared a long glance. *Where is home anymore, and when will we ever get there?*

Wen headed to another vendor for vegetables while he sat on a bench and enjoyed his beverage. He thought about the people who were after them. Wen had killed a number of adversaries since they'd gone on the run. Her knowledge of martial arts and weapons scared him sometimes, but those skills—and his smarts—were the only things keeping the two of them alive. They'd used his money and her specialized knowledge of Chinese espionage to vanish as well as anyone could in the modern world. Utilizing an array of sophisticated technological techniques to make sure they were regularly "spotted" in parts of the world where they were not also helped throw off the pursuers.

Wen glanced up and caught Chase looking at her, but could tell immediately that he wasn't thinking about her.

She paid for the vegetables, joined him, and they resumed their stroll.

"You're worrying again," she said, taking his hand.

"Sorry. Sometimes I like to pretend we're a couple of tourists on our honeymoon, but we're not, and we—"

"Is that your way of proposing?" Wen teased.

A woman coming out of a merchant's stall backed into Chase.

"Pardon," Chase said in Spanish.

"Excuse me," the woman said in English.

Chase immediately recognized the voice and turned to find an escape. Wen quickly did a visual search of the area and spotted several CIA agents dressed as locals.

"How'd you find us?" Chase asked, deciding not to run.

"Please, Chase, you're too smart for silly questions."

Tess Federgreen, the director of CISS—Corporate Intelligence Security Section—the CIA's most powerful and secretive division. The fast-growing agency within the agency—a joint operation of the CIA, NSA, and FBI—had almost unlimited power to pursue its mandate of preventing war between corporations and nations.

"Are you going to take me in?"

"Not today," Tess said, waving hello to Wen.

Wen just scowled.

"Then why are you here?"

"I don't often bring good news, do I?" Behind her sunglasses, Tess's green eyes flashed with confidence. Her strawberry blond hair glistened in the Ecuadorian sun, although Chase recalled it had been auburn last time he'd seen her. "I need you to do something for me."

He almost laughed. "Why would I help you, Tess? I don't even *like* you. And I sure don't trust you."

She laughed unpleasantly. "You should never let your personal feelings get in the way of what's good for you."

"What do you know about feelings?" Chase thought, for a quick instant, he detected a hint of pain in her eyes, but it didn't last. They strolled through the crowd, Wen a few steps behind.

"Does the name Curtis Lindbergh mean anything to you?"

Chase stared at her for a moment. "You must know it does."

"I'm afraid your old friend is mixed up in some trouble."

"Doesn't sound like him."

"Yes, well, like you, he is apparently not as smart as his brilliance would suggest."

"If you're done insulting me, I've got—"

"He needs your help." She scraped her gray snakeskin cowboy boots against the curb.

"Lindy can take care of himself," Chase said, thinking of the only person he'd ever known who was miles ahead of him in IQ points.

"I've just given the order to terminate Lindbergh."

"*What?*" Chase said, a little too loudly, knowing Tess was serious. Even if they hadn't been friends, he believed the world needed all the Lindys it could get. "Why?" He fidgeted with the multitool in his pocket. Wen caught up and held his hand, not wanting others to notice his agitation.

"He's made a breakthrough in geoengineering—weather manipulation—and he's planning to sell it to the Chinese and Russians. We obviously can't allow that to happen."

Chase immediately thought of their time together at

MIT and the years since. Lindy was always focused completely on his work. Chase couldn't imagine him blatantly going against the US government. "There must be a mistake."

Tess glared at him. "Yes, the one Lindbergh is making."

"What am *I* supposed to do?"

"Find him. Change his mind."

"You don't know where he is?" Chase scoffed. "Then how are you going to kill him?"

"He'll be found shortly. You have thirty-six hours to work your magic."

"Or?"

"CISS of Death."

Chasing Wind: Chapter Two

The bustle of the Otavalo market blurred as Chase squeezed Wen's hand, catching his partners look, knowing it meant they could run.

"CISS of Death?" Chase repeated her words, facing the forty-something, fit, youthful looking, master of espionage. "Do you think that's cute? How do you sleep at night?"

"Absolutely horribly," Tess admitted.

"How come you can find me, but you can't find Lindy?"

"Lindbergh disappeared before we knew we wanted to keep track of him," she replied. "But we're getting closer. We may get him before you do."

"Then what?"

"Then you can go back to eating fruit and bread, or whatever it is you fill your time with these days."

"How long have you been looking for him?"

"Ten days."

"But I can find him in thirty-six hours?"

"I have complete faith in you, Chase."

"I'm flattered," he said sarcastically.

"You should be." Removing her sunglasses, Tess gave him a long, almost maternal, stare. "I want updates every step of the way. Let me give you my private number?"

"I've still got it."

She smiled. "It's been changed." She handed him a card. "Then I can count on you?"

"I'll have to think about it."

"Clock's ticking," Tess said, signaling to her agents that they were leaving. "Here's everything we have on Lindbergh." She handed him a flash drive. "Don't forget, I'll need regular reports of your progress."

"Why, so you can kill him?"

"I don't want to kill Lindbergh." She looked at him warmly. "You're just going to have to trust me on that."

Wen closed her eyes.

"Forgive me," Chase said incredulously, "but that's impossible."

She looked sad for a moment. "I've come here and enlisted your help because I want the same thing you do—to save him."

Chase searched her eyes. "I've got thirty-six hours?"

"Maybe less, depending if things change."

Chase moaned, exasperated.

A small, red, beat up ball rolled and hit Chase's feet. He looked down, and then up. A young girl with big brown eyes caught his. She smiled sweetly, he choked up for a second, then picked up the ball and tossed it gently to her.

"*Gracias, hermano*," she exclaimed and ran off.

Tess's expression softened at the little Ecuadorian girl, and then hardened as she turned back to Chase. "If your friend 'Lindy' suddenly turns up in Beijing or Moscow, the timetable will change. That's why you must stay in touch with me, or you may end up just finding a corpse."

Putting on her sunglasses, Tess disappeared into the crowd as easily as she had arrived mere minutes ago

---

Sitting in her private jet, Tess gave final instructions to a CIA agent who would remain in Ecuador. "Make sure we get his plane. I want to know everywhere he goes. If he stops to take a leak, you let me know immediately."

She worried about trusting something so important to a man known as the Buddhist Billionaire and his "killer" girlfriend, but desperate times . . .

Tess also knew that the unlikely duo had defied the odds many times. The fact that Wen had escaped Communist China's Ministry of State Security and remained alive and free was, in itself, an extraordinary accomplishment.

And Chase is a whole other side of extraordinary.

She remembered a promise she'd made long ago, to a man she loved, to help protect the rogue tech genius. It bothered her that Chase despised her, especially since she'd saved his life more than once.

Tess called Dr. J. W. Skyenor, the Director of Defense Advanced Research Projects Agency. DARPA, the Pentagon's emerging technology agency, had been formed in 1958 by President Eisenhower after the Soviet Union's surprise success with launching Sputnik, the first manmade object into space, in 1957. One of the agency's earliest accomplishments was helping to launch the world's first weather satellite.

"Have you found Lindbergh yet?" he said without bothering with a hello.

"Jay, are you okay?" she asked.

"We're being challenged by China every minute of

every day on almost everything we do, and as soon as we get ahead, they steal it."

"I know." That issue was at the heart of the mission of CISS.

"The best chance we have right now is the weather, but I've never seen them so aggressive."

Tess bit into a green apple she'd picked up at the market. "It's the top priority of the MSS right now."

"So, I'll ask again . . ."

"Lindbergh is our biggest priority. We're closing in on him and his stations. Things will look a lot different this time tomorrow."

"I hope so," Skyenor said.

Grab your copy…
vinci-books.com/chasing-wind

About the Author

USA TODAY Bestselling Author Brandt Legg uses his unusual real life experiences to create page-turning novels. He's traveled with CIA agents, dined with senators and congressmen, mingled with astronauts, chatted with governors and presidential candidates, had a private conversation with a Secretary of Defense he still doesn't like to talk about, hung out with Oscar and Grammy winners, had drinks at the State Department, been pursued by tabloid reporters, and spent a birthday at the White House by invitation from the President of the United States.

At age eight, Legg's father died suddenly, plunging his family into poverty. Two years later, while suffering from crippling migraines, he started in business, and turned a hobby into a multi-million-dollar empire. National media dubbed him the "Teen Tycoon," and by the mid-eighties, Legg was one of the top young entrepreneurs in America, appearing as high as number twenty-four on the list (when Steve Jobs was #1, Bill Gates #4, and Michael Dell #6). Legg still jokes that he should have gone into computers.

By his twenties, after years of buying and selling businesses, leveraging, and risk-taking, the high-flying Legg became ensnarled in the financial whirlwind of the junk bond eighties. The stock market crashed and a firestorm of trouble came down. The Teen Tycoon racked up more than a million dollars in legal fees, was betrayed by those closest to him, lost his entire fortune, and ended up serving time for financial improprieties.

After a year, Legg emerged from federal prison, chastened and wiser, and began anew. More than twenty-five years later, he's now using all that hard-earned firsthand knowledge of conspiracies, corruption and high finance to weave his tales. Legg's books pulse with authenticity.

His series have excited nearly a million readers around the world. Although he refused an offer to make a television movie about his life as a teenage millionaire, his autobiography is in the works. There has also been interest from Hollywood to turn his thrillers into films. With any luck, one day you'll see your favorite characters on screen.

He lives in the Pacific Northwest, with his wife and son, writing full time, in several genres, containing the common themes of adventure, conspiracy, and thrillers. Of all his pursuits, being an author and crafting plots for novels is his favorite.

Acknowledgments

A substantial part of *Chasing Fire* was written in Mexico, specifically, Yelapa, which then became one of the main settings for *Chasing Wind*. *Chasing Fire* was a hard book to write at times. I'm not sure why, but certain books are easier than others. Often the more difficult ones become my favorites.

To my wife, Ro, I run out of adjectives . . . but this word sums it up . . . everything.

I also want to acknowledge all my friends and family who put up with my disappearances during my self-imposed exiles while I created these books. It means a lot that you are still there when I emerge from the woods.

Special thanks to my mother, Barbara Blair, for the countless hours she spent going back into the tunnels, and into the fire.

I always appreciate Jack Llartin, my copy editor, for the final sweep.

And, finally, to Teakki, who patiently waited to tell me all about Godzilla until I finished writing each day, although he didn't wait to hum the soundtrack—that was constant.

Mostly, thank you, and all the readers, who make it possible for me to support my family by writing books. These stories are for you, and I owe you more than I can say. I appreciate you spending your time and money to go on these journeys with my characters and me. I look forward to going on many, many more adventures with you.